THE MORNING OF

S.B. CODY

BLOODHOUND
— BOOKS —

www.bloodhoundbooks.com

Print ISBN 978-1-914614-31-6

For Nicole & Taryn

PART I
LOCKDOWN

1

It could never actually happen here. Everyone in town held this general belief. Of course, they would never say so out loud; most weren't even aware that they held it. Common sense dictated that, of course, it could happen here. What was stopping it? You heard stories all the time about it happening in places just like this. So while basic logic insisted that it was entirely possible, everyone went about their day-to-day lives confident that they were safe from what had become an all-too-common occurrence. We shouldn't judge too harshly for their naiveté though. Doesn't everyone share this belief? That they are somehow immune from the worst that life has to offer. Other people had to deal with the debilitating illness, the awful crimes that made the front page. If we actually believed we were susceptible to the awfulness of the world, would we ever actually head outside our doors? Would we ever walk down a dark street if we believed a heinous killer laid in wait for us? Would we ever get on a plane if we believed that it would end in a fiery mess of twisted steel? Would those 1,067 people have walked into Stanford West High School if they believed that twenty-eight of them were never going to leave alive?

The town of Stanford sat in the center of Missouri with a nice, manageable population of about 120,000. It avoided the small-town atmosphere, so you were never under any obligation to say hello to every person who crossed your path. At the same time it wasn't so large that you had to take three different buses and a subway just to get to where you were going. What constituted downtown was really just about ten blocks all situated around one street, appropriately titled Main. If someone wanted to walk it, they could do it no problem, and with no real fear of getting mugged. Of course, that's not to say that there weren't some bad parts of town. The southern and eastern parts were where you'd find some of the more low-income areas. West Stanford High, however, had the good fortune of being situated in the middle-class part of town, making it the more desirable of the two high schools in the district.

The school was situated at the bottom of a small hill that would be filled with cars every morning at arrival time. The red-brick facade of the school stood tall against the sky. A line of glass doors stood at the end of a concrete patio. These doors led into the lobby where a security desk sat front and center. At this desk, Zach Levinson lounged, watching the seconds tick by. He fought to keep his eyes open, willing the school day to come to an end. But it was only 8:30, and the kids were just now settling down for their second period. All day, he buzzed in person after person; hardly stimulating work. But it was only something to hold him over until he got accepted to film school. One day, the theaters would flock with people to see the new blockbuster from the next Spielberg. At least that was his plan, but the best-laid plans of mice and men...

Zach forced his eyes open just in enough time to see someone walking towards the front doors. Normally, he would think nothing of it, but this person was dressed all in black, standing out sharply from the bright sun pouring in. He had on black cargo pants, a worn-out black hoodie, a book bag strapped to his back, and most concerning of all: a Michael Myers mask covering his face. Zach didn't need to force his eyes open any longer. They shot open in shock. Given a bit more time, he may have been able to sort the whole situation out, but after just a few steps inside, Michael Myers drew something shiny and metallic from one of his pockets. Zach only had time to get a brief glance at it before it became level with him and screamed out a bullet which hit Zach square in the forehead, sending him sliding back in his chair and to the ground. Blood spat from the back of his head. Michael then quickened his pace. He hurried to the desk, reached over, and pressed a small button. To his right, the front office door clicked and unlocked. Not wasting any time, he hustled inside.

At the main desk a group of women, most of them older and graying, stood to await the school's new guest. Michael raised his gun again and fired off two more shots, not really aiming. Still, he managed to nail the attendance secretary, Dolores Lewiston, in the side which sent her tumbling and all others ducking down. Michael now turned to the right so he could head behind the desks. Just as he did so, Sergeant Blake, the school resource officer, rushed out, his hand on his own gun. He got it about halfway up before Michael fired off one more round, landing a shot in Blake's eye. Blake hadn't even hit the ground before Michael pounced and began going through his belt. From it, he withdrew a set of keys including one allowing access to any room. He grabbed the gun, stood, and rushed out of the office.

Behind the desk, one of the secretaries had pulled herself out of shock and gone to the intercom. Pressing the button to broadcast to the entire building, she screamed out, "Lockdown! Lockdown! We have an active shooter! This is not a drill! Shooter is in the main hallway!"

That message rang out in every corner of the school. Michael Myers ran down towards the library which lay at the end of the hall. At the doors, the librarian struggled to get the doors closed and locked. But the doors were heavy and Michael rang out another shot that sent her sprawling onto the blue carpet. A stream of blood pooled beneath her gut. Michael burst inside. The students ducked beneath tables and behind shelves, desperate to do anything to shield themselves. Michael, quick around the shelves, staked out anyone who thought they'd hid in time. One girl huddled in a corner, her hands held high in defense. "Please. Please. Please!" she cried out. Michael didn't spare her a glance. He simply sped by her while lowering his gun, and fired; sending a bullet into her head. He ran over to a table where a boy and a girl crouched underneath, arms clutched to the legs as though they thought they'd be carried away. Michael stopped by the table, reached under with his gun and shot off two more rounds. The boy caught one right at the bridge of his nose. A hole opened up in the girl's shoulder. A few more students and another librarian laid in wait. Michael just ignored them and headed back into the hall, knowing he had to keep moving.

He sprinted, his footsteps pounding against the tile and echoing off the walls. One student dashed across at that moment, desperate to duck inside a bathroom. Michael fired off a couple rounds, hitting the student in the leg, sending him crumpling to the ground. Right as Michael walked by the bathroom, the door creaked open a sliver and one more shot was fired into the door, but he didn't bother to check to see if anyone had been hit. There were a lot of rooms to peek into. As he continued, he stashed away his gun into his book bag and withdrew another. And so down the hall he went, rocking the handles of each door that he passed, seeing if any prey laid in wait.

Back before the first shot had been fired, and Michael Myers was still heading towards the school, someone else stood in a bathroom on the bottom floor. They went right to the trash can to find a bag just where they were told it would be. This new figure found an Uzi, another dark hoodie, a pair of cargo pants, and a hockey mask. With all of that on, the two figures were indistinguishable, except that this new one now resembled Jason Voorhees. Decked out, Jason took the gun and stood by the door. Quick muffled breaths came from behind the mask. Beneath it, Jason poured sweat. He just couldn't believe that this was happening. Before it had all seemed hypothetical, but now it was all too real.

And then there it was. The call for a lockdown. Just what he had been waiting for. He knew what he was supposed to do, but now found that his feet wouldn't move. Couldn't move.

Upstairs, Michael Myers unlocked a classroom door where over a dozen people waited. He yanked on the handle only for it to come to a halt after only opening a crack. Tied to the inside handle was a cord that snaked up and wrapped around a flagpole. From inside came a sea of gasps and whimpers for help. Michael reached inside and fumbled for the knot around the handle. Someone pounded against his hand, trying to get Michael to back off. He couldn't get a good enough grip on the cord to untie it. He retreated only to stick his hand back in with the gun this time. He fired off a few blind shots. A couple hit the back wall. A shrill cry made it clear that at least one made contact with someone. Michael immediately went back to the cord and got it untied in no time. The door swung open wide now. A small cabinet sat in the doorway, but a quick kick got rid of that. Michael stepped inside. Right beside the door, the teacher lay on the ground clutching his gut where the bullet had landed. Michael fired a single shot down, hitting the teacher in the head. Students huddled against the wall closest to the door. A few took off running, managing to squeeze by and escaped into the hall. Others stood and shuffled their feet, not sure what to do or where to go. Most of them just sat on the floor looking at the figure above them. Mouths open. Tremors traveling throughout their bodies. This situation had been practiced, and in their heads, they all had an idea of what to do. They could run like a few had. They could rush the shooter, throwing things at him, wrestling the gun away. So many of them imagined themselves doing just that. Charging forth into danger and saving the day. Being the hero of the school. That didn't happen though. Instead, they froze. A few cried out realizing that this was it. All the plans for their life wouldn't come to pass as Michael raised the gun and began popping off shots, firing into the huddled crowd.

2

————

Two hours before Michael and Jason would lay siege to the school, Connor Sullivan pulled his car into a spot right up front, the perfect place to park. Front entrance was within spitting distance and a back road out of campus wasn't much further. Made getting out of here at the end of the day really easy. And as he prepared for the day, getting out of here was the only thing on his mind. It was only October, but Connor had already begun counting down the days until summer. He looked up at the building, feeling like there might as well be bars on the windows.

Connor looked down at his watch. There was still an hour until the day officially began. He typically didn't get to school this early, but he had been desperate to get out of the house without a fight with his wife, Brandy. He began to relive the whole thing, feeling the simmering tension of the morning heating up once again; he pushed it away and forced himself out of the car.

As soon as he was inside he headed right to the teachers' lounge where he knew there had to be a fresh pot of coffee waiting for him. Once he opened the door to the lounge the scent wafted right up into his nostrils, and he made a beeline for the pot that still had steam rising up from it. Off to the side sat one of Connor's fellow English teachers, Lance Milton, sipping on his own cup. He had a pair of glasses with huge lenses. Students constantly debated whether he wore them ironically or not. His gut had just begun to spill over his belt which he seemed to own with pride.

"Sully, what's happening, man?" Lance called out.

Connor offered a groan, just barely audible, in reply.

"Well. Aren't you in a good mood this morning? Seems like you..."

"If you even say that I have a case of the Mondays, I will kick your ass," Connor muttered, taking a seat across from Lance. That had often been a favorite saying of Lance's that had soon worn out what little welcome it had.

"Damn. Something crawled up deep in there, didn't it?"

"Having a bad morning," Connor said, wincing through the hot, bitter taste of the coffee. "Goddamn," he spat out.

"Put some sugar in there, dammit. I will never understand how you drink this black."

"I drink it for the caffeine. Not the taste."

"You should advertise for Starbucks. So who died that put you in the funk? Haven't even seen a student yet."

"Brandy and I almost got into a fight this morning."

"Almost?! How will your marriage ever survive?" Lance shouted in a high-pitched voice and threw his hand over his chest.

"Shut up. I say almost because I got my ass out of there before it could get going."

"Avoidance. The key to any healthy relationship," he said with a smile and tilt of his cup. "So what'd you do?"

"Who says it was me?"

"Come on..."

Connor sighed, wondering how he got roped into actually having this conversation. He had been hoping for some peace and quiet. "She found out that a friend of hers from college just got pregnant."

"And how does that make you feel?" Lance asked in his best impression of a shrink.

"Will you knock it off with that shit?" Connor knew that Lance's insistence on always being a smart-ass endeared him to his students, but it wasn't working on him.

"Sorry," Lance said, hiding his eyes, realizing that he'd taken his shtick a bit too far.

"It's just that lately she's been dropping some none too subtle hints that she wants to have one."

"How long you been together?"

"Twelve years. Married for five."

"Well, what are you waiting for?"

"Why would I want to have kids? All the bitching and moaning and complaining that we have to deal with here every day... I'm going to go home and deal with it all over again?"

"Is that mug half full there, Sully?"

"Helpful."

"What are you still doing here?"

"You think I don't ask myself that?"

"You need to shit or get off the pot."

"They should put that in a fortune cookie."

"I think I missed my true calling."

Right as he finished talking, the door swung open again, and in walked someone who could easily have been mistaken for an FBI agent. He wore a firmly pressed black suit, and blond hair cut into a flattop that wouldn't even shake in an earthquake. This was Dr. Leland, the Associate Principal. He didn't even spare Connor or Lance a look. In fact, his face didn't so much as quiver. He went over to the coffee pot and poured himself a small cup. "Mr. Sullivan. Mr. Milton," he whispered in way of a greeting.

"Dr. Leland," Lance blurted out in a voice that came off much more mocking than he intended. Connor shot him a quick look as a way to tell him to shut up. Lance's eyes went wide, realizing that he might have crossed a line. But if Leland noticed, he didn't let on. He simply turned on his heels and headed back out.

"Do you think he realizes that he's a douche?" Lance asked the moment the door was shut.

"Not a chance," Connor replied.

"That son of a bitch chews me out yesterday because when I let kids go to the bathroom, I don't have them sign out."

"Well, rules are rules," Connor said in an authoritarian voice, suppressing a chuckle.

"Please. I teach Senior AP. I don't exactly have a lot of kids cutting class."

"I hate you."

"Hey, you're the one who volunteers to teach sophomores every year."

"Well, I guess I'm a glutton for punishment." The two sat in silence for a few more minutes, each sip of coffee making Connor more and more awake. He was getting up to grab himself a second cup when the door burst open yet again.

"I am nailing that thing shut," Lance barked out.

A small, round face crowned with curly blond hair poked its way inside.

"Debbie Tomlin, ladies and gentlemen," Lance said with a nod.

"Hi, Lance," Debbie replied with a smile in a soft, mousy voice.

"Connor, I'm glad you're here. I think your protégé is about to snap."

"Kristin?"

"Yeah. I could hear her crying down the hall, and I just don't really know her so..."

"Always passing the buck, the Debbie Tomlin way," Lance said through a laugh.

"Will you shut up already?" Connor shot back while slinging a packet of Sweet'n Low at him. "All right," Connor said with a deep sigh, turning back to Debbie. "I'll go check on her."

Connor set down his mug and made his way out of the lounge. He headed for the main stairs and lumbered down them. Right as he came into the lower hallway, Connor was greeted with a plaque on the wall with a picture of a student and some writing underneath. He avoided looking at it though. He always avoided looking at it. He just kept going along at a half jog, the entire time wondering what the hell the matter with him was. Wondering why he ever agreed to be a mentor for a new teacher. It just created a number of headaches that he didn't need. Girl came to him every day with some inane question. He guessed that stipend they waved in his face was just too appealing.

Connor passed the bathroom door where Jason would soon lay in wait. Right across the bathroom was Kristin's room, and down from both was the door leading out to the fields. Connor swung himself into Kristin's room where he was greeted with the sight of a twenty-three-year-old girl with a mop of brown hair hanging in front of her face, hiding the black-rimmed glasses underneath. She had a tight grip on her hair as though she was getting ready to yank it out. A steady sound of sobbing came from within the whole mess. Kristin sat right across from the door at her desk which couldn't even be seen underneath the tidal wave of papers that had hit it. What a far cry this image was from the girl he first met back in August. She would always come in cheery, grinning from ear to ear. Always spouting off about the wonderful ideas she had for her classroom; talking about her dreams of inspiring students.

"Hi, Mr. Sullivan," a choked voice said.

"Connor," he corrected her. "What's going on, Kristin?" he asked with some hesitation, knowing that this would be a long day.

"I can't do this."

"What do you mean?"

"There's too much."

"You're putting too much on yourself. Let's see what we have here." Connor walked up to Kristin's desk and picked up a stack of half sheets held together with a paperclip. "What is this?"

Kristin finally peeked her head out from behind the brown curtain. "It's a warm-up that they did last week."

Connor dropped it into the trash can that stood beneath him. "Well, that we can forget about. What else?"

"But..."

"You don't need to grade everything. Give yourself a break."

"But I said that it was going in the gradebook."

"Yeah and most of them won't even remember. Tests, projects, most homework assignments. Little crap like this gets recycled. Okay?"

"Okay. And then there was my evaluation from last week. Dr. Leland didn't have anything nice to say to me."

"That guy wouldn't have anything nice to say to a nun."

"But just look at what he wrote," Kristin cried, waving a piece of paper in her face.

Connor grabbed the paper and took a look at it, noticing a few notes on there about the learning objective not being posted clearly enough. There were five unstructured minutes at the end of class. Same crap that Connor had been seeing for a while now. He laid the sheet down. "We'll go through all of it later today, okay? Just clear away what you can and then get ready for today. And I have to do the same. Sound good?"

"I guess," she uttered with more than a hint of disappointment in her voice.

"Hang in there, kid," Connor said, slapping her on the shoulder before heading out of the room and finally making his way to his own classroom that sat just a bit further down the hall. Right outside his door was a bench currently occupied by a sleeping student with caramel skin and a slender build that Connor recognized. It was Terrance Lipton. He'd had him last year in Sophomore English. Nice enough kid. His mom was a cop so he didn't dare to mess around at school. "Terry!" Connor yelled, waking him up.

Terry sprung up as if out of a dream. He rubbed his eyes and ran his hands across his nearly bald scalp. "Wha..." he groaned.

"Terry," Connor said again, in a much softer voice. This snapped the kid back to reality as he trained his gaze at the teacher ahead of him.

"Hey, Mr. Sullivan," he said in the raspy voice of the recently woken.

"What the hell are you doing here? Bell isn't for like another forty-five minutes."

"My mom had to drop me off early today. That... that... protest thing is happening on the East side of town."

"Black Lives Matter protest?" Connor asked. A couple weeks ago, a black teenager had been shot by the police. Some small protests had been happening here and there, but the news had said this one would be significantly larger. Other groups from around the country were coming in this time.

"Well, most of the force is down there today. And everyone is working overtime for it. Want to make sure things don't get out of hand."

"Well, why are you sleeping outside my room?" Connor asked.

"I like this bench. It's comfy."

"Well, don't let me keep you. Please, get your beauty sleep."

Terry gave a small smirk and collapsed down to the bench, back asleep before his head was on his makeshift pillow that appeared to be some torn-up hoodie. Connor unlocked his door, forced his way across the threshold into his room, and flipped on the lights. Right as he stepped inside, he heard a voice call from down the hall.

"Lipton! Wake the fuck up!" the voice cried out. Connor glanced back to see the source, Johnny Lemming, strutting down the halls. Connor rolled his eyes, wondering why Terry would spend any time with that kid. He'd never had him in class, but all the teachers knew of him. He'd get back from one suspension and then promptly start another.

Connor just shook his head and went into the classroom. One-piece, tan-colored desks that no average-sized person should be able to fit into were arranged in a horseshoe pattern. All around the room were posters depicting famous books. Others gave your faux inspirational quotes. Same bullshit about hard work and dreams. Connor never really understood putting them up. He couldn't think of a single instance where those posters made a significant difference for anyone. But he needed to fill up some black space on the walls, so up they went.

Tucked in the corner across from the door was Connor's desk, practically bare, except for a couple pictures, paper tray, and jar of pens. Connor walked over to his desk and sank into his chair. Large, black, leather, and oh so very comfortable. He loved this chair. Felt like he could fall asleep right here and now. Of course, that wasn't an option. There was work to be done. Beside the desk was his black computer bag. He'd left it behind last night, determined not to bring his work home with him.

Connor fished the laptop out and started it up. He had to make sure his PowerPoint was ready to go.

His class was reading *The Chocolate War* and the lesson they were getting today was one that he always enjoyed teaching. The book told the story of an all-boys' school crumbling into chaos after a student's refusal to sell chocolate. In the school was a not-so-secret society, The Vigils, which manipulated everything and punished any who got in their way. Leading it all was a kid named Archie. Getting kids to read nowadays was worse than pulling teeth, but this book usually caught their interest. Some even began searching out other books by the author.

Today's lesson was about the nature of evil and whether any characters in the book qualified. It typically got some good discussions going. Connor was just pulling up a clip from a TV movie about the Nuremberg trials. In it, two people are having a discussion and end up defining evil as the absence of empathy. That definition always stuck with Connor.

Next half hour was spent getting everything together, the only sound being the music coming from the iTunes open on his computer. This was his favorite time of day, usually being a time for him to relax, but that was hard to come by today. His mind kept drifting back to this morning with Brandy. He had been getting dressed, and she was sitting up in bed, just getting up herself. The only light in the room came from the glow of her phone.

"Huh," she said in her hoarse, morning voice.

"What's that?" Connor asked as he slipped on his shoes.

"Laura just found out she's pregnant."

"Who's Laura again?"

"Freshman roommate."

"Oh that's right. Good for her," he replied as he gathered his wallet, watch, and keys from his dresser.

"Yeah. Good for her," Brandy said in monotone.

Connor wasn't much awake at this point, so it didn't even occur to him what could be bothering her, so it seemed odd that she'd seem so indifferent towards the whole thing. "What's going on with you?" he asked, turning towards her. Once it escaped his mouth, he wished that it hadn't; realizing that he had just opened up a can of worms.

"They've only been married a year," she replied, only looking up once to meet his eyes.

"I have to go," Connor said, desperate to remove himself, knowing what was coming.

"We can't talk about this?" Her voice was finally above a murmur.

"I need to get to work. We can talk later."

"You don't leave for another half hour."

"Need to get there early today," he lied. He didn't even wait for a response this time. He simply turned and was out the door. "Love you. Bye!" he yelled as he walked towards the door. He felt bad about ducking out that way, but he knew there was no good end to that conversation, and that is not how he wanted to start his day. And what he had told Lance was only half true. Yes, he didn't want to deal with more kids after doing it here all day, but it was more than that. More than anything, he just didn't trust himself to be decent at it.

All of this swam through his head again and again as the bell rang and students started to pile in. The vast majority of them plopped into their seats and played on their phones, all the while the world kept at a safe distance by means of the headphones that seemed to be glued to their ears, but there was one kid who never showed a phone at all. This was Dennis Clements. Kid was decked out all in black. Dark hair swept over his eyes. Typical emo kid, even though Connor had thought that fad had died out around 2007. Every day, Dennis came in, sat in the back, and hunched over a pad of paper where he began to draw, never once looking up. Kid hardly ever spoke up in class, but Connor knew he was bright. Reading over his homework, he seemed to have a better understanding of the material than about ninety percent of the class. Seemed like a good kid too. Always saw him opening the door for people, giving directions to lost freshmen. It didn't do much to endear him to people unfortunately. Connor had, on a few occasions, heard kids cracking jokes about him having bodies buried in his backyard. Today, Dennis didn't go right to his desk. Instead, he walked right up to Connor.

"Hey, Mr. Sullivan," he said with his head hung low. "Wondering if you could take a look at this for me?" he asked as he handed forward a thick sheet of papers.

"What is this?" Connor asked as he leaned forward and grabbed it.

"It's a story I wrote. I was hoping you'd look at it and tell me what you think."

"You wrote a story? Impressive."

"Yeah." He laughed.

"I'd be happy to. Any particular time you need it back by?"

"No. Not really."

"All right. I'll try to get to it this weekend."

"Awesome. Thanks." Dennis turned and trudged to his typical seat in the back. Coming right on his heels was another student that Connor recognized all too well, Richard Lowe. Polo shirt tucked into a pair of designer jeans. Much better dressed than any other kid who walked in. Head of dark hair without a single strand out of place, parted perfectly on the left side. Richard was a senior, so Connor didn't have him in class anymore, but had had him in a couple different classes over the past four years. Richard had shown himself to be one of his best students and had really connected to Connor, so they kept in touch.

"Oh God. What do you want?" Connor joked once he saw him.

"Hey Mr. S. Got your book back," he said, pulling a copy of *The Origin of Species* from his book bag.

"Please. I said you can keep it," Connor said. Richard had been talking about having wanted to read it, and Connor happened to have a copy from his college days that he offered to give him. "Do you think I'm actually going to read it again? That had to have been the most boring thing I've ever read."

"I thought it was great," Richard said with a big smile.

"Nobody reads this kind of thing for fun. I don't even know who you are."

"Hey. I'm reading some Nietzsche next."

"You are a very strange young man."

"Richie," a voice called from the hall. Connor and Richard both looked out to see a very pretty girl standing at the door. Perfectly straight brown hair down right to her shoulder. Bright green eyes. Round cheeks. "I need to talk to you," she said in a soft voice that just barely carried itself across the room.

"Not too strange for her," Richard said, laughing, turning back to Connor.

"Are you saying that's your girlfriend?"

"Oh yeah."

"How the hell did you end up with her? Are you blackmailing her?"

"Yeah, but don't tell anyone," Richard replied with a whisper and knowing smile. Just then a warning bell rang. "Oh crap. Got to get to Mr. Milton's class. See ya, Mr. S!" he yelled as he took off out of the room. Around the class, all the kids took their places as the tardy bell rang. And the day had begun.

"Good morning. How's everyone doing this morning?" Connor said as the class got settled.

He was met with "fine" from a few kids and non-committal mumbles from the rest.

"Awesome," he said in a phony, excited tone. "Everyone caught up on *The Chocolate War*?"

"This book sucks. Boring as hell," one kid up front yelled out.

"Jamie, your astute analysis, as always, is welcomed."

"That's what I'm here for," he said, very pleased with himself. Snickers had popped up in different parts of the classroom.

"Any other literary critics want to comment?" Nothing but shrugs were given in return. "Okay, well I did want to turn your attention to one part of it. We're looking at Archie and The Vigils. So we're going to watch this quick video, and then we're going to do a quick write of it. So get out your journals and pen or pencil."

"Can I borrow one?" a voice yelled out just as Connor knew it would. There was always one. He walked over to the jar on his desk, grabbed a pen, and tossed it over to the student. From there he went and switched off all but one of the lights.

"Can't you switch off all of the lights?" someone asked.

"Nope," Connor said back. He ran over to his desk, flipped on the projector with a remote, clicked play on the video, and let it roll. He stepped back and looked on at the class. Half of them were watching. Other half were either on their phones or off in la-la land. *Dead Poets Society* hadn't shown him this side of teaching.

The video came to an end, and the lights came back on. "All right. In that clip evil was defined as the absence of empathy. Now who knows what empathy is?"

A hand went up. "Isn't it like feeling sorry for someone?"

"Close, but not quite. That's sympathy. Empathy goes even further. Instead of just feeling sorry for someone, you actually feel what they feel. So what they're saying in this video is that evil is the inability to do that. So what I want you to do on your sheet is to answer these two questions. First, do you agree with this definition of evil? How do you define it? Second, do you consider Archie and the Vigils evil?"

"Wait, but…" someone blurted.

"Hold up. Put it on your paper. We'll talk later." And they were off. Some got full pages' worth. The overachievers. Some did a few sentences. Those who did just enough to get by. Others put down some random collection of words. Those who just went through the paces. He gave them a few minutes and then proceeded. "All right. I want to hear what you have to say."

"I don't see how you can call them evil," a girl named Jessica spoke up from the back.

"Why not?" Connor asked.

"Because we're just talking about chocolate. Can't really be evil when it comes to that."

"Well, it's chocolate now. What comes after that?"

"But they're only kids," Jessica shot back.

"And Hitler was just an art school dropout," someone called from the back. Connor looked to see that it was Dennis speaking up for maybe the third time all year.

"Yeah! Let's hear from the psycho! He knows all about being evil!" Jamie called out. There was some restrained laughter throughout the room. Dennis didn't say anything in response, but a small frown found its way onto his face.

"Knock it off, everybody. Jamie, talk to me after class," Connor told him, feeling his blood boiling. He didn't have any patience for that kind of shit. He took a breath to compose himself. "Anyway," he continued. "Point is, that Archie and the Vigils view themselves as better. They never feel bad about the things they do because they think they're entitled. Those people can be the most evil of all."

The lesson proceeded and Connor was pleased to find that it

went better than he anticipated. Kids caught on much faster than he thought, and they ended up having ten minutes before the bell rang. He just told them all to continue reading in the book. Once they got going, Connor called Jamie up to his desk to discuss his little comment from before. He stood there, wavering from side to side, eyes up toward the ceiling.

"Jamie, why are you making fun of people? What did Dennis ever do to you?" Connor asked.

"What? It was just a joke," Jamie replied as though he was offended.

"Maybe for you. But I didn't see him laughing." The only reply to that was a shrug of the shoulders. "Nothing?" Connor asked. Another shrug. "Well, if you decide to make another joke, you're going to be laughing by yourself in detention. Go sit down." Jamie headed back to his desk with a scoff. That one Connor ignored. He would have checked in with Dennis next to make sure he was okay, but he'd asked to go to the bathroom a few minutes before that, and wasn't even back before the bell rang, signaling the end of first period.

And now it was time to do it all over again. To Connor this job often felt like *Groundhog Day*. The kids had shuffled in blabbering about some nonsense. After a while it all started to sound the same anyway. The tardy bell rang and everyone sank into their seats.

Connor hoisted himself out of his seat, ready to recite his script again. But before a single syllable had been produced, it came over the intercom: "Lockdown! Lockdown! We have an active shooter! This is not a drill! Shooter is in the main hallway!" With that, Connor's stomach dropped. He and the rest of the class just looked around as if something in a foreign language had been shouted at them. No one really seemed sure of what to do. They all just waited. Waited for someone to come on and say it was all a joke, but with every passing second it became more and more clear that this wouldn't happen. The silence was broken with a whimpering that came from a girl sitting in the back. This broke Connor out of his stupor and he sailed across the room towards the door. He didn't even realize what he was doing until he had already gotten there. He opened the door and swung his way into the hall while fumbling his key out of his pocket. It slid in and twisted, locking the door. Connor slammed it shut, trapping him and all the students inside the room. And hopefully keeping anyone else out.

"Everybody get against the wall," Connor said in a rushed whisper, pointing to the wall closest to the door. They all moved over in a mad rush. Meanwhile, Connor went about throwing his weight against the cabinet that stood beside the door. It slid in place, hopefully serving as one more barrier against anyone getting in. With that done, Connor killed the lights and huddled next to the barricade, knowing that if someone got through all of this, he may need to act. The whole time he shook as though he was having a seizure. His stomach threatened to come rocketing up any second, but he still felt a certain amount of relief. Relief that he actually managed to remember the procedures. Except for one thing. He felt his phone shift in his pocket which reminded him. He fished it out and dialed in 911.

"911. What is your emergency?" the operator said, coming on after a single ring.

"Yes. I'm at Stanford West High School..." Connor started in a hurried voice.

"Yes, sir," the operator said, interrupting him. "We have gotten multiple calls. Units are responding. Have you been able to secure yourself someplace safe?"

"I've locked up and blocked the door."

"Very good, sir. Can you hear anything from in the halls? Do you have an idea of where the shooter is?"

Connor took the phone away from his ear for a moment and

listened. The distant cracks of gunfire could be heard, but he had no idea of the origin. "No. I have no idea," Connor said back into the phone.

"That's fine, sir. If you remain where you are, you should be fine. Just make sure that you do not open the door for anyone. Repeat, DO NOT open the door for anyone. Once the building has been secured, someone will come by to let you out. Do you have any questions?"

"No."

"Okay. Stay put. Do not make any noise. And do not open the door."

"Thank you." With that the line went dead. And now there was nothing left to do but wait. And hope.

3
_____

As Kristin waited for her second hour to begin, she struggled to hold back her tears. Her first class had been a train wreck. She'd had this great lesson planned that she had been excited about. It was just the kind of lesson she wished someone would come in and observe, so that they could finally see what a good teacher she could be. But it wasn't meant to be. From the moment class began, things began to fall apart. It started when some little cocksure punk named Danny came in telling her how good she looked while eyeballing her up and down. Just being near him made her squirm. Nevertheless, she persisted and tried carrying on with the lesson. It soon crumbled as the kids took things into their own hands and started yelling across the room. Kristin wasn't sure what happened in that moment, but she flipped; and soon found herself yelling louder than she knew possible. From there she printed off some random worksheet to keep everyone busy and let them know that a single peep would result in detention. The entire time, she just sat at her desk and tried to get herself back under control.

As first period came to an end and the second began, Kristin wondered if she dared tried to do it all again, but it soon didn't matter as the message screamed out over the intercom: "Lockdown! Lockdown! We have an active shooter! This is not a drill! Shooter is in the main hallway!" Kristin's head snapped up, her eyes scanning the room assuming that one of the kids must have shouted this out, that being the only rational explanation. But every student sat there with their mouths open like caverns. Kristin's mind whirled. She continued to look out, waiting for one of them to tell her what to do. But that was up to her. She ran her mind through all the steps they'd been taught. She needed to lock up! She needed to barricade the door! She needed... Wait... They said the shooter was in the main hallway... And they were right by the back door. They could get out of here!

"Everybody get up. We are heading right outside," Kristin said in a quivering voice, scrambling out of her seat and heading towards the door, practically tripping over her feet. The students started to rush toward the door. "Okay," Kristin began again through deep breaths. "Head right towards the door and go outside. Stay together. Head for the nearest road. I'll be behind you." Kristin poked her head outside the door. There was nothing. No one. No sound. You'd never think that someone was upstairs with a gun. She stepped out and began to usher the students out the door and towards the exit. They all hurried out at a quick pace.

Kristin watched each of them pass by her. She couldn't help but let a small grin creep onto her face. It was going to be okay. She and all her students would be safe in no time.

But, of course, Kristin had no way of knowing about the second shooter waiting just inside the bathroom door across the hall, who was just now getting ready to emerge.

The bathroom door burst open. Kristin collided with the sight of someone decked out in a dark hoodie and hockey mask, and a gun in their hand; far away from the main hallway. The shooter recoiled a bit, not expecting a line of kids. Kristin let out a scream. The line of students all turned at once. Upon seeing the shooter they took off at a sprint. The gun jumped up and began to spit out bullet after bullet. Kristin looked on in horror as two of those bullets found a mark. The heads of two of the students opened up, spraying blood on the walls and on Kristin. The rest of the students flew out the door. The shooter took off, running the other way. Kristin stood there, blood all over her face, jaw hanging down, not moving an inch.

Connor and his class had been hunched down for ten minutes. The whole time, Connor forced out a series of uneven breaths. Every few seconds, he would glance back at the crowd of kids huddled up behind him. Every so often, there'd be a soft cry, but for the most part the room was dead silent. Connor kept glancing down at his watch, wondering when this would all pass. Wondering when they would be safe. The entire time a cacophony of gunshots, screams, and pounding footsteps echoed in his ears. He tried to figure out where it was coming from; needing to know if they would be next. But it was everywhere, and it was nowhere.

Until... A sound stood out from all the rest. No gunshots, but footsteps going back and forth. Unless someone had been stupid enough to venture out into the hall in the midst of all this, it meant that the shooter was closing in on them.

"Mr. Sullivan," a half whisper cried out from behind him. Connor turned to see a boy practically in tears. "They're right..."

Connor put an angry finger up to his mouth not wanting a peep to be heard. A fumbling came at the lock. A shaking of the handle. A key slipping in place. From behind him, Connor could hear a choked cry from one of the kids. But this time he didn't even shush them. The lock to the door had slid back and the light from the hall crept in from behind the cabinet. The hinges squeaked, sounding like the howl of a hyena. A hollow thud echoed from the cabinet as it started to scrape across the floor. Connor knew that he needed to act. Knew that he needed to jump up and fight them off. From behind him, the whole crowd of kids was a screaming pile. Desks even began to topple as some of them tried to find cover. Connor strained against himself, willing himself to move. Not until the tip of the gun began to peek around the corner of the cabinet did he bust loose of his shackles. Now he was up on his feet and falling forward. His shoulder drove against the cabinet, forcing it back, hitting the shooter in the arm. The gun flew back, a series of bullets rocking out and sailing across the room. Connor spun around and came face to face with the shooter. He froze for a second, absorbed in the hockey mask, but that didn't last long as the gun started to swing back into view. He reached forward and grabbed the shooter by his arms. The two pistoned back and forth, Connor desperate to keep clear of the gun. Their arms became twisted up like a pretzel. Connor's hands slipped up Jason's sleeves and felt smooth flesh interrupted every couple of inches with rough patches, like lines of rocks in the middle of a grassy field.

He gave a push and threw out his arm, throwing the shooter back. The shooter tumbled, tripping over his legs and sprawling out into the hall. Connor stared down, wondering if all of this had actually happened. He didn't have long to wonder, though, as he soon saw the gun begin to raise and point its way towards him. Connor ducked back behind the cabinet and shoved it against the door. A few shots rang off of it, sounding like a series of explosions inside Connor's head. Out in the hall came more footsteps. Fast this time and heading down the hall. Connor looked back out on his room. There were a few holes in the back wall and a crowd of kids in tears. But they were all there. And they were alive. Connor had been so shaken that he'd forgotten to breath. Once he got his lungs cooperating again he looked back down at his watch and saw the time. 8:50. Would this ever end?

Being thrown back by Connor, Jason tumbled out into the hall. He scrambled to his feet and found Michael staring right at him. Even with the faceless mask, he could tell that Michael was not pleased. Michael said nothing and just threw his arm behind him and pointed. Jason followed along like a shamed puppy. They headed down the hall and then up one flight of stairs before stopping in front of a classroom. Michael retrieved the keys from Jason and unlocked the door. He and Jason charged forth, heading into a pile of desks that had been stacked and served as a barrier. They both kicked and pushed at it, sending them clattering down onto the ground. From off to the right a student rammed into Jason, sending him crashing into the opposite wall. Michael turned and fired, sending the student to the ground. From the corner, a stapler shot forth, just missing Michael's head. He whipped around and let off another shot, this time hitting the teacher and laying her out on the desk. From there Michael and Jason gathered themselves and turned to look out at the rest of the class. There were only a handful of kids here, but they all sat, pinned against the wall. Nowhere to go.

Out in the hall, the gunshots sounded like a series of

fireworks going off, intermingled with grunts, groans, and shrieks. And then without warning, it all came to an end. Michael sauntered into the hall, looked up at the security camera on the ceiling, and gave a small wave of his fingers before disappearing back into the classroom, neither him nor Jason to be seen again.

4

The Stanford Police Department took pride in their measured response time to an active shooter within a school, at just under four minutes, coming in below the national average. Of course, the only experience they'd ever had with responding was during drills, under ideal circumstances. With the police force otherwise occupied, as they were this morning, that response time increased quite a bit.

On the other side of town sat the Evergreen Housing Development. In reality it was simply a set of tightly-packed, cramped apartments. The name wasn't meant to be ironic, but it certainly seemed that way to people since hardly any trees stood in the whole area. When the place had been built five years ago, the name had been chosen to invoke a sense of beauty and splendor. It didn't last long as it quickly fell into disrepair. The city council had pushed through the development as a means to service the low-income families of the area. Once it was built they largely turned a blind eye to it. Building it made them look good to constituents. Maintaining it meant raising taxes which was the death knell come election time.

Two weeks ago there had been a call to the police, just as

there often were in the area. Reports came in of someone walking around carrying a gun. Responding to the calls were Officers Clayton and Lewis. Once they arrived, they were out the door, Clayton already with his gun drawn; eager to save the day. First thing either men saw was a dark figure walking between buildings. In his right hand he held an object that in the dark of night, Clayton couldn't make out, and he wasn't taking any chances. Aiming and steadying his gun, he fired three quick rounds at the figure in front of him who sank to the ground before Clayton's and Lewis's eyes. When they stepped closer, it became clear what had just happened. What Clayton assumed to be a gun had been nothing more than a phone. And who Clayton assumed to be some deadly killer had instead been some kid, who couldn't be older than fifteen.

"Holy Christ," Clayton said upon realizing what he had done.

Lewis trained his eyes on him and simply muttered, "We're fucked." And fucked they were. It came out that the kid who Officer Clayton shot had been fifteen-year-old Noah Spaulding. That night he had simply been on his way home from visiting a friend who lived in the same complex. And far from being a criminal, he was on the honor roll at East Stanford High. All his teachers responded that he couldn't be more polite and friendly. It soon became clear that Noah's only crime was being black.

The very next day calls came for Clayton's arrest. Two days later a small protest formed right outside the police station. Captain Barron graced them with his presence for a brief moment to announce that Clayton had been put on paid leave and that there would be a thorough investigation. But that wasn't good enough for the crowds. Protests continued like that for the next two weeks, many of them gaining national coverage.

Today was the culmination of all of that. From around the country other groups bussed in, bringing what had at most been fifty people at any given time to over 200. And they had all gathered at Evergreen, only about 150 feet from where Noah had taken his last breath.

Included in this group were a swarm of police, posted on the outskirts. With them was Officer Julie Lipton. Julie had been on the force for the past twenty years. She had been in her share of tense situations over that time. This definitely placed near the top of the list. Felt like enough of a powder keg that she could practically feel the flames on the side of her face.

She looked out on the sea of people, the vast majority of them black, but some white people thrown in there as well. About half of them were holding up signs with sayings such as "Black Lives Matters" and "Who Polices the Police?". She had seen these kinds of things on the news from across the country. They seemed to be happening more and more as of late. And frankly, Julie wasn't even sure how to feel about it. As a black woman she could testify to the kind of crap that you could get because of your race. And if some high-school kid could get shot for doing nothing more than walking home, why shouldn't people feel pissed? She had a sixteen-year-old herself, and if something happened to Terry... she couldn't even imagine what she would do. At the same time, she couldn't help but be a little hurt by what people were saying about her and her friends. Long hours spent away from their families. Her husband sitting awake at night wondering if she would come home again. Her, petrified that she wouldn't see her son again. It also didn't help matters that she'd had a few sideway glances from the protesters and some mumbles of "Uncle Tom;" all of them upset that she would "fraternize with the enemy."

Fucking Clayton! she thought to herself. All of this was his fault. She'd been working with him for a couple years now, and she could say with confidence that he didn't have a racist bone in his body, but that didn't mean the guy wasn't a fucking idiot.

Trigger-happy son of a bitch. Seen one too many cop movies. And because of him, most of the force was here now, all in the name of keeping order. She felt more than a little worried that they'd only make the situation worse. They weren't exactly popular with this crowd.

She stood her post, looking on at the scene unfolding. It was a cool fifty degrees today, but that didn't stop beads of nervous sweat from rolling down her cheek. She took a few deep breaths and remained focused, keeping her mind on the situation at hand. She scanned the whole crowd, taking into account everything that crossed her field of vision. If she saw a bump in someone's pocket, she would examine it, determining if a gun laid in wait. If some errant noise popped up, she would divert her attention to it in order to find the source. It was her goal to make sure that everyone here, cop and protester alike, made it home at the end of the day.

At the head of the group, a small stage had been constructed with a lone microphone upon it. Speakers took turns getting up and addressing the crowd. It had started off with a prayer. After that came a list of the various unarmed black men, women, and children who had been shot dead by the police. As the names were listed off, Julie could feel her stomach drop. Next up, came someone listing off all the ways that those assembled could take action outside of this protest: writing to the district attorney, donating money to the family...

Julie glanced behind her. There were some of the other officers, hands already on their guns, seemingly oblivious that that was the kind of behavior that had gotten them into this trouble in the first place. Further behind them some other citizens stood, looking on out of mere curiosity. At least she hoped that's all it was. There was always the chance it was someone who felt the need to point out that "All Lives Matter." If so, no good could come of it.

One such person was Toby Henlon. The most that could be said about Toby was that he managed. At the age of thirty-one, he still lived with his parents as his job slinging a register at McDonald's didn't fill his wallet enough to afford a place of his own. Toby had always dreamed of joining the police force. However, his personality screening suggested that he had an undiagnosed form of bipolar disorder and was prone to bouts of rage. That same rage bubbled up in him now. While some saw a protest, all he saw were a bunch of uppity niggers. His only regret is that Clayton and Lewis didn't burn this whole place to the ground. And now he saw a bunch of cops protecting these bastards. If they wouldn't put them all back in their place, then he would need to think of a way.

Another speaker came to the microphone. She was introduced as Denise Liman, the head of the newly formed Stanford Society for Police Accountability. They had only been around for about six months, but the department had been briefed on them when it became clear that a number of the members were people who had made threats on police in the past. So far, they'd only been relegated to small meetings and some fliers around town.

Liman's lips were set in a firm, thin line. Eyes narrowed. She stepped up and surveyed the crowd, seemingly giving every person the death stare. The entire time, not a single word spoken. Julie began to wonder if she intended to say anything at all. Maybe her whole job was to simply stand there and scare the piss out of everyone. If so, it worked.

"Look around. We are standing mere feet away from where a life was ended. A fifteen-year-old boy who never hurt a person in his life. That doesn't mean anything nowadays, though, if you're black. Walking alone at night and carrying a phone is now worthy of a death sentence. And it is no coincidence that this occurred here. Here, where they send the black families of the community to live, so that the privileged are able to remain blissfully ignorant of the kind of hardships that we face day in and day out. When one of us is killed, they are able to remain on the high hills and turn a blind eye. It is not until their children are the ones left alone in a pool of their own blood that they will ever know our pain!"

Julie took a step back at that. Hand instinctively went towards her gun. Was she serious? Was that an actual threat? A few members of the crowd certainly seemed to think so; there were a few yells of "Yeah!" and "Amen!" Most everyone else began to look around in panic, apparently wondering the exact same thing as Julie. A quick glance behind her made it clear that some of the other officers were ready to draw and fire. The entire time, Liman had become silent once again, drinking it all in. Her thin lips curved into something resembling a smile. They then opened, ready to begin again, but before she could continue one of the other speakers ushered her off, making sure she didn't make it worse.

"I understand how angry we all are," the new speaker said taking the microphone, "but we all know that there is a right and wrong way to proceed," she continued, entering damage control mode. But Julie knew the damage was done. That one comment was going to be the whole story of this protest now.

The rally continued, a new kind of palpable tension in the air. The speeches had started to wind down, but next came the march five blocks down to City Hall. About half of the officers there were taking off in preparation of closing off the streets of the marching route. Julie had fallen back to the entrance to Evergreen. Once it was all clear, she would head down to City

Hall and help set up a perimeter. At the moment, she felt relieved that things hadn't gotten fucked up beyond all recognition, especially after Liman started shooting off at the mouth. That feeling would fall away soon because right as the crowd started breaking up, the call came over her radio: "ATTENTION ALL UNITS! WE HAVE REPORTS OF AN ACTIVE SHOOTER AT STANFORD WEST HIGH SCHOOL. REPEAT... THERE IS AN ACTIVE SHOOTER AT STANFORD WEST HIGH SCHOOL. ALL THOSE UNITS NOT BLOCKING OFF STREETS ARE TO RESPOND IMMEDIATELY!" Julie froze in place as though she had just looked in Medusa's eyes. Every syllable squawked out in perfect clarity. Her throat went as dry as the Sahara. All breath left her lungs. She couldn't see anything in front of her. Not the apartments. Not the crumbling gravel or unkempt lawn. Not even the crowd of people shambling towards her. All she could see was the image of Terry lying dead, full of bullet holes, a pool of blood beneath him.

"Shit! Lipton! We need to get moving!" a voice cried out from miles away. "Lipton!" it came again, this time much louder. Now the voice reached out and yanked her from her daze. Julie looked over to see Hicks, another officer stationed at the entrance with her. "Come on! Let's go!" he yelled again. Julie did nothing but nod at him, and after she snapped back, she moved towards her car.

She jumped in behind the wheel and started her up. She was ready to gun it, but the crowd now in full force, blocked her exit. The siren flipped on, but that didn't do much to part the sea of people. "Jesus! Fucking move!" Julie screamed from inside the car. Over to the left she saw that there was a small, open patch of grass. She swung the car over and plowed through it, ignoring the bump and scraping that her car took. Once she was over it, a quick turn to the right brought her back on the main road and ahead of the crowd. The car barreled down the street, the siren announcing its way. At this point, it was 8:40. The shooting had been going for ten minutes.

~

A line of five cop cars charged into the parking lot of Stanford West. They all stopped upfront forming a semicircle. Julie, staying in front, threw open the door and charged at full speed up the steps and into the school. Behind her the heavy footsteps of the other officers were close behind. The first thing that she faced was the body of Zach Levinson with a single bullet hole in his head. Off to the right more bodies had been strewn across the main office.

Julie and the other officers sailed through the doors into the main hallway, guns drawn. At the intersection they all slowed down. There were five of them; Julie and Hicks took off to the right. Two others went to the left and one other headed into the library. Along the way, they checked each door so that any unlocked room didn't go uninspected.

"Everyone! This is the police! Please remain calm and stay where you are! We will let you know when the building is secured!" Hicks belted out.

Julie marched down the hall, her hair drenched in sweat and her breath coming hard and fast. The only thing that could be heard were their footsteps echoing off the wall. She kept waiting for the thunder of gunfire to burst out at any second, but it never came. Along the way they faced smears of blood covering the hall. Bloody footprints. Long swipes from victims having clawed their way across the floor. Off to the right was an open classroom. Julie looked around to see a row of computers, but nothing else. Over to the left, Hicks investigated another and found the same.

Down the hall they went, continuing to check every door.

Hicks announced their presence again. "Please let us out!" a voice cried out from one of the rooms.

They continued, and a look into a classroom on the left displayed a room caked in blood. Glancing in further, Julie saw a scene that resembled a slaughterhouse for cattle. Eleven bodies lay on the ground, filled with bullets, some to the point that their intestines could be seen. Not a single person in the room had been left alive. The smell of metal filled the air to the point that Julie could taste it. From an open window, the cool October air filtered in.

"Dear Jesus," she whispered to herself. She stepped out of the room before she became overcome with tears from the sight. From there she continued her search.

The five officers that comprised of the first responders, now joined by another dozen, conducted another search of the building. But nothing else was found. Only a slew of victims and horrified students and teachers. The shooter, nowhere to be seen. When everyone was accounted for it was found that twenty-eight people had been killed. Another fifteen injured.

5

An army of police cars and ambulances descended upon Stanford West, along with reporters and other townspeople who came to see. Some of them family members of those who had been inside. Others, people who just needed to see the whole circus firsthand. Connor was ushered out of the building and looked upon the scene. Individual faces couldn't even be made out, all of it an ocean of flesh and hair. Flashes went off from all the cameras. He reacted to none of it. Simply observed. Able to do nothing more. At this moment, he couldn't feel the steps that he took. He wouldn't even have been sure of where he was going, but for the long line of people who were led out of the school and into the makeshift hospital that had been constructed in the parking lot. Someone took him by the arm and escorted him under a tent and into a chair.

"Hi. I'm Doctor Benning. What's your name?" a voice asked. To Connor it was all muffled half-speak. "Hello?" the voice continued.

"Wha...?" Connor said, staring blankly ahead.

"What's your name, pal?" The words had begun to make sense.

"Connor."

"Were you hit at all?"

"No." Now a light scorched his pupils. He winced and shut his eyes.

"Okay. You seem to be having normal pupil dilation." After that Doctor Benning pulled out a blood pressure cuff and wrapped it around Connor's arm. A few pumps and then he tore it off. "Blood pressure seems a bit high, but that's to be expected. Nothing to worry about. Okay, you can head over there," he said, pointing towards a larger tent. "Paramedics will be available if you need anything. From what I can tell you don't need emergency services. Let someone know if you need to go to the hospital." Connor stood up and shuffled off towards a seat under the tent. It was already filled to the brim with others being filtered out from those who needed immediate attention. Connor sank into a seat and stared straight ahead. Around him others threw up, wailed into the sky. Along with the countless voices, rumbles of engines, and snapping of cameras, it all coalesced into a general hum that now filled his ears. Through all of it, Connor felt like he should cry. Should pound his hands into the pavement. But he couldn't. So far he couldn't feel a thing. He looked around at it all, taking all of it and none of it in. That is until his eyes fell on a young girl who sat in the back of an ambulance. It was Kristin, who stared blankly and shivered all over. Her lip kept quivering. Connor stood up and shuffled over towards her.

"Kristin?" he said as he walked up to her, not recognizing the sound of his own voice.

She didn't respond. She didn't even look over at him. Bits of blood covered her face. All that came from her was some small utterance that he couldn't even make out.

"Kristin? What are you saying?" Connor asked as he leaned in closer. The utterances now became clear.

"I'll be behind you. I'll be behind you. I'll be behind you. I'll be behind you. I'll be behind you..." she repeated over and over again.

"Kristin? What the..."

"She's in shock," a voice interrupted. Connor turned to see a paramedic coming forward.

"Did she get shot?"

"No."

"What happened to her?"

"No idea. We can't get anything out of her." The paramedic produced a wipe and attempted to get off the blood on her face, but every time his hand came towards her she would throw her head back. "Shit. Okay, we'll have to worry about that later. Are you a family member?" the paramedic asked, turning back to Connor.

"No. We work together."

"All right. I'm sorry, but I'm going to have to ask you to step back. We need to get her moving." The paramedic climbed into the ambulance and guided Kristin back in with him. From there the doors closed and they took off.

Connor stood alone looking at the chaos around him. The building and parking lot were all the same, but it appeared alien now, as if he had just been dropped here. In the midst of it all, he heard an ungodly shriek come from the side of the building. Connor turned to see Richard run around the corner. He had to have been about 100 feet away, but Connor could see that his eyes had gone beet red.

"Natalie! Natalie!" he screamed. He rushed right up to Connor. "Mr. Sullivan, have you seen Natalie?"

"Who?" Connor asked, barely able to make out a word he said.

"My girlfriend. You saw her earlier today. I don't see her anywhere! I don't see her class! Where is she?!"

"I'm sorry, Rich. I don't know."

"Oh God," Richard breathed as he ripped at his hair. He staggered off and mingled back into the crowd, continuing his search. Connor watched him off, another stranger in a strange land.

He wandered back to his seat when a voice cried out to him, "Connor!" He turned around to see Brandy standing over at the police barrier that had been set up. When his eyes fell upon her, he broke into a smile and took off, running towards her. They embraced over the barrier. Brandy buried her face in his shoulder and let forth a waterfall of tears. "Oh thank God! I was so scared! I love you so much!"

"I love you too," Connor whispered into her shoulder.

Julie stood at the perimeter, meant to keep a check on the throng of spectators and reporters, but her attention was only half there. She continued to search the line of people filing out of the school, waiting, desperate to see Terry among them. She examined each person who came down the steps, looking for him.

She stood, shifting from one foot to another for twenty minutes before she saw him. He came around the corner, a blank expression on his face. She took off at a run, pushing through anyone and everyone that stood between her and her son. "Terry!" she screamed. His head snapped up and mouth dropped open in joyful shock. He lumbered to her like a zombie. They met in the middle where Julie wrapped her arms around her son.

"Jesus Christ, Terry. I was so scared." Julie shot out her arms and held Terry at arm's length. Her eyes darted around, looking Terry from head to toe.

"What the hell?" he said, taken aback by the sudden change in demeanor.

"Are you okay? Are you hurt?" she inquired. Julie whipped her son around and started running her hands along his back, desperate to make sure he didn't have a single injury anywhere on his body.

"Jesus, Mom! I'm fine," he insisted, pleading with her to stop. With that, Julie wrapped him back in a hug.

"I was so scared. I thought I..." Julie said.

"I know, but I was lucky enough to get out of there early on."

"What do you mean?"

"I was in the bathroom when it happened. When I heard the announcement I ran out of the building."

"Well it's over now. All that matters is that you're okay." She held on to him for another five minutes. From there she led him over to a doctor who gave him the all-clear. "Do you need to go to the hospital at all?" Julie asked as she led him out of the tent.

"No. I'm fine. I just want to go home," Terry responded.

"All right. Let's go." Julie got the okay to head out from her lieutenant. They drove home in silence. Every so often she'd glance over to see Terry staring down at his feet. After the short drive, they headed inside where Julie's husband, Brian, was waiting right by the door for them. She'd called on the way home to let him know that they were all safe. The moment they crossed the threshold, he pulled them both towards him, squeezing them as if he thought they'd fly away otherwise.

"Thank God," Brian said. "I've never been more worried in my life."

"We're okay," Julie replied.

"Neither of you are ever leaving the house again." They all released their hold on each other. "Do you need anything to eat?"

"I just want to go to bed," Terry replied.

"I think that's a good idea," Julie said, petting his head. Terry pushed forward and shambled up the steps, Julie and Brian close behind. Terry walked right into his room, pushing the door open with his whole body. He didn't stop or slow down at all until he got to his bed and tumbled onto it. He was asleep the moment that he hit the mattress. Julie and Brian both just stood, looking down at their sleeping son.

"What the hell happened?" Brian asked.

"I don't know," Julie said.

"Who was it? A student?"

"I don..." Julie paused. It hadn't been announced yet, so it wasn't something she should go around proclaiming.

"What do you mean you don't know? You said you cleared the building? Didn't you catch him?"

It was too late now. "No, we didn't."

"They got away?"

"Looks like it."

"But I don't understand... I... How?"

"I don't know." Julie turned and sat down on the top step. She buried her face in her hands. Brian joined her, throwing his arm around her. "How could this happen? Here? It's..." She couldn't even find the words anymore. Nothing so horrendous had ever occurred in Stanford prior to this. Crime happened. Bad people came through. But you never felt unsafe. That was part of what made this place perfect for Julie to be a cop. She still got to serve the public but avoided the truly horrible. Now she wondered if she had made a mistake, except this life was all she'd known for years. Longer than she even knew being a wife or a mother.

A lot of the people on the force got into it because they'd grown up around it. Not Julie. In fact, it had been just the opposite. Her father had been in and out of jail for most of her life. Began with some relatively harmless possession charges, but he soon graduated to armed robbery as a means to support the habit, but he was hardly John Dillinger. Ended up getting caught because he dropped his wallet at the bank he'd chosen to rob. When the cops came around for him, he went running. He proved to be no Jesse Owens either because after making it about thirty yards he tripped over his own feet.

She could never forget the shame that she saw on her mother's face when this happened. For years it had been hard to shake off the image around town as being the daughter of a criminal. Her goal in life was to make sure that she never had to feel such a thing again. Instead, she would be the one who put criminals away. From then on out, becoming a cop had been her sole focus. Even when she had achieved it, she kept a one-track mind on it. This, of course, meant that other things fell by the wayside, which is why she was the last of her friends to get married. Her mother had been kind enough not to badger her about it, but was not above dropping sly hints, such as constant updates about the girls around town.

That came to an end one night when she'd gone out for happy hour after she got off duty. There she had run into Brian, a guy she'd gone to school with. She had always suspected that he had a thing for her, and she had thought he was pretty cute himself. He got so flustered anytime he was around her and tried to act really cool. She found it funny. Meeting him at the bar, they recounted the time she'd seen him playing football and he insisted on running the ball the entire way just to impress her. It ended up with him on the ground having had the wind knocked out of him, of course. They'd decided to make a date to see each other again. And it became clear that this guy was just as cute and awkward as he had always been. A year later they were engaged. A year after that, married. Two years after that, they'd had Terry. None of this had ever been a part of the plan, but now everything else was secondary to it. And today she had been convinced that it was all about to be taken from her. Just about enough to drive her mad. And the worst part... this was just the beginning.

~

Connor and Brandy stuck around at West for about another twenty minutes. Connor insisted that he was ready to go right away, but Brandy insisted that he rest first. She worried that if he rushed home he'd end up hurting himself. The two of them walked into the house, and Connor went right to the couch and dropped onto it. Brandy sat down next to him, threw both of her arms around him, and nuzzled her face into his shoulder.

"Talk to me," she said. "Tell me what you're thinking. How you're feeling."

Connor simply stared straight ahead. He didn't know how to respond to that. Didn't know how to tell her that he wasn't feeling a thing. After all, how would she react? What would she think? He didn't even know what to think.

"Honey?" Brandy said, lifting up her head. Connor glanced down at her. His mouth fell open, but nothing came out.

"It's okay. You don't have to say anything. We'll just sit here."

Connor could only imagine what she was thinking right now. He was sure that she must feel disappointed in him. It seemed like he did a lot of that anyway.

They'd gotten together their second year of college. Part of the teaching program that he did required students to do some hours, assisting in one of the area schools. This year he'd been assigned at West, no less. Each day, he would need to go up to the front desk to sign in. And each day, signing in with him would be Brandy. Each time he was near her, he'd find himself feeling nervous, which sadly was the way he usually felt around girls. At least that's how he felt the few times he'd been talked into going to a party. He avoided them as much as possible because he tended to get way too anxious during them. So when he was at one, he would usually find a quiet spot in a corner where he'd observe the party rather than participate. People playing beer pong. Guys hitting on girls, desperate to bring them back to their dorm. And then Connor, looking on at them with a mixture of amusement and envy. He liked to imagine that he would go up to a girl and deliver those magical words in exactly the right order to make them swoon over him. In high school, he'd gone out on a few dates, but it never became anything. He just didn't know how someone did that. To him it felt like speaking a foreign language. Besides, he was convinced that once they got a whiff of the real him, they'd be repulsed. Especially when he started going to the student clinic for therapy and had been put on antidepressants. God knows what they'd think of him then. Probably that he was a basket case or something. And to be honest, that's how he ended up feeling most days.

As far back as he could remember, one thing he'd always been really good at was finding flaws in himself. His gut was just a little too pronounced. That blackhead just wouldn't go away. If someone passed by him and laughed, he naturally assumed they must have been laughing at him. And while his friends all found their niche, whether it be baseball, or writing, or public speaking, Connor always found himself to be painfully mediocre at everything. Sometimes he wondered if that was why he became a teacher. After all, those who can, do...

And when he'd look over at Brandy, he assumed that she would find something wrong with him. As nervous as he'd get, he still looked forward to seeing her. Her brown hair always tied back in a ponytail. Round face that just came to a small point at her chin. Each time he saw her, she carried a nervous smile. That nervous smile seemed to break into a real one when he'd walk in, and she'd greet him. But that was as far as their relationship went until one day as he walked to his car and he found Brandy softly banging her head on the roof of hers.

"You okay?" Connor heard himself saying.

"My car won't start," she said while continuing to bang her head.

"Why not?"

"No idea."

"Gonna call a tow?"

"I guess so. But I have a test in half an hour. I really need to get to campus."

"I could give you a lift," Connor said.

"Really?" she said, turning around with her nervous smile.

"Sure. Why not."

"That's so nice," she responded, her real smile emerging now. And so as he drove her, they had their first real conversation. Connor found that he wished the conversation would keep going when it was time to drop her off. And thankfully, she made sure that it would.

"Thank you so much!" She beamed. "I guess I'll have to pay you back somehow."

"Oh no. You're fine," Connor said.

"No. Let me buy you lunch. Or at least swipe you at the dining hall."

"Why not."

"Great," she said as she opened her backpack and took out a piece of loose-leaf and a pen and began scribbling on it. "Here's my number. Give me a call." And he actually did. And then seven years later they were married. And now here they were. Brandy hadn't hung around teaching for very long. Her dream had always been to be a writer. First novel got published their last year of college. Her second, two years after that. From there, she was rolling and was able to write full time. Connor struggled a bit more. First year out of school he couldn't find a job for the life of him. He'd gotten by subbing in the meantime before deciding to go back to school full time to get his Master's. Then he'd gotten his job at West where he'd been the last five years. The first two went pretty well, but then…

He'd like to be able to say their disagreement about children was their first big problem, but they'd been struggling together for a while now. As much as Connor hated to admit it, he'd kind of just been going through the motions the last few years. She always said she loved how passionate he was about things, especially teaching, but that passion no longer existed. And he just didn't know what kind of teacher or husband he was anymore. He often wondered why she put up with him. He'd often been amazed at her patience, and it seemed like it was in full effect right now. She seemed perfectly content to wait here until he felt ready to talk. No matter how long that took.

Connor tilted his head and stared down at his wife, her head buried in his shoulder. At last his mouth produced words, and he spent the rest of the night telling it all to her.

PART II
THE INVESTIGATION

6

Detective Kara Smalls woke up at 7:00am on the morning of the shooting. She hadn't planned on it. There was nothing that she needed to be up for today, but at this point it had been hardwired into her. On any typical day, she would be getting ready to arrive at the police station by 8:00, so she could begin work. But not today. Today, they didn't want her.

Yesterday, Kara had had to face the firing squad. She'd been ushered into the back conference room where she was sandwiched between two union lawyers who were constantly leaning over and whispering in her ear. While grateful to have support, she could really have done without their warm breath all over her. Right across from her were Captain Barron, and some guy from Internal Affairs named McClellan. Down at the other end of the table was a lawyer named Edwards, who represented the schmuck that made this whole thing necessary. Kara avoided everyone's stares, Barron's most of all. She didn't need to look to feel him boring into her, his eyes filled with contempt. *You're an embarrassment*, they said.

Kara hated that she had to go through with this whole process. Most of the cops she came across hated Internal Affairs with a passion. She saw real value in what they did. She just never thought she'd be on the receiving end of it.

"Detective Smalls," McClellan said, not once looking up from his form. "First, please understand that this is an official deposition and you are under oath. Any statements that are shown to be misleading can lead to a charge of perjury. And your statements here can be used should this case go to trial. He brought up his hand and flicked off a small piece of lint from his left lapel. "Do you understand?" he continued.

"Yes," Kara said with a small nod and steady breath. This whole thing felt surreal. Typically, she was the one asking the questions.

"Ms. Smalls," McClellan began. "Were you the lead detective in the murder of Rebecca Llewellyn?"

"Yes, I was," Kara replied, relieved to have the first question out of the way.

"Did any other detectives investigate with you?"

"Not in an official capacity."

"Meaning?"

"I consulted with some other detectives, but I was the only one assigned to it."

"So did all pertinent decisions related to the case come from you?"

"Yes."

"When were you first assigned the case?"

"The evening it came in, which would have been November 3 of last year."

"What did you observe when you arrived at the scene?"

"Ms. Llewellyn laid dead in the living room. She appeared to have been beaten to death." The whole thing shook Kara when she saw it. The entire left side of the victim's face had gone red and purple, swelling up to twice the original size. Her skull appeared lopsided, having been caved in. Beneath her, a pool of blood had congealed, creating a thick soup in which her head waded.

"What was your first impression of the scene?"

"That the scene was a robbery gone wrong."

"What led you to that conclusion?"

"The place had been ransacked. Furniture turned over. Door busted open. Jewelry box had been emptied." Her perception of the whole thing soon changed. Kara had seen more than her share of robberies gone wrong, and this screamed personal. On top of smashing her head in, someone had slammed her head against the ground repeatedly. Whoever did this had been full of rage, and they had wanted to hurt this woman.

"So, Ms. Smalls, when was it that you first began to suspect Mr. David Llewellyn?" McClellan asked.

"The night of the murder," Kara answered confidently. Just because she had been wrong, didn't mean she had done anything wrong. Besides, she had done this job for ten years, and her instincts on cases had become fine-tuned. And when a wife laid dead, one suspect always jumped to the front... the husband.

"And what first led you to suspect him?"

"When I first spoke with the neighbors, they expressed to me that the Llewellyns appeared to be having marital problems." When Kara had gone to interview the neighbors they had said that the couple could often be heard fighting. To the point that the shattering of dishes could even be heard.

"And how did you proceed from there?" continued McClellan.

"We retrieved Mrs. Llewellyn's cell phone and used that to make contact with her husband. Informed him of the situation. Asked that he meet with us at his home."

"Did anything occur there to make you suspect him?"

"His demeanor upon hearing that his wife had died."

"I object," Edwards said. "Detective Smalls is in no position to comment on my client's demeanor." The whole time his head didn't lift from his legal pad that had been filled with notes.

McClellan swung his head towards him. "Mr. Edwards, the whole purpose of this line of questioning is to determine Ms. Smalls's impression of the scene at that time and to establish her state of mind."

"Very well," Edwards replied.

"Please continue," McClellan said, clearly as annoyed by Edwards's general demeanor as Kara was.

"Mr. Llewellyn did not seem particularly upset to hear about his wife. And when we interviewed him, he still didn't. In fact, I don't even know if he inquired as to how she had been killed." The whole process chilled Kara. The whole time talking to him, he slouched in his chair and couldn't even make eye contact. Seemed bored by her questions. She'd interviewed plenty of grieving spouses, and most would at the least shed a tear or two. Not this one. His voice didn't even crack. So far she had a disinterested husband who was known to fight with the victim. And if there was one thing that this job had taught her... Occam's Razor was real.

"What kind of evidence was collected at the scene? And what, if anything, did you learn from this evidence?"

"Victim's skull had been caved in. The autopsy would later determine this to be the cause of death. Underneath the victim was a pool of blood. Spatter analyst determined that it collected like that for about an hour. Beside her lay a lamp with traces of the victim's blood on the bottom. This was determined to be the murder weapon. When we tested the blood collected, it was shown to all belong to the victim."

"Any fingerprints?" McClellan asked.

"Various prints all over the house and on the lamp. Only

ones that could be identified belonged to Mr. and Mrs. Llewellyn. Nothing which indicated a possible suspect."

"So to clarify," Edwards butted in again. "There was no physical evidence which pointed to Mr. Llewellyn as the killer?"

Kara inhaled, desperate to maintain her composure. She refused to look over at him, but sliding her eyes over, she saw that Edwards had a cocky little smile on his face. She wanted nothing more than to stand up and slap it off. But that would be frowned upon. "No. No physical evidence," Kara responded, making sure to put the extra emphasis on 'physical.'

"Since Mr. Edwards raises the issue," McClellan said, regaining control of the proceedings, "other than Mr. Llewellyn's demeanor, was there anything else that caused you to suspect him?"

"When we looked into his finances, we found that he had a large amount of debt. Appeared to primarily be due to a gambling addiction. From what we could gather, this appeared to be the cause of the fights that the neighbor reported."

"And was there anything that seemed to suggest that Mr. Llewellyn was innocent of the crime?"

Edwards perked up at this question, beginning to squirm in his seat. Kara expected him to start salivating and licking his lips, he seemed so excited. This whole process would be so much easier if that son of a bitch wasn't here. Everything about him screamed slimy douche. Jet black hair slicked back with so much grease that it would probably catch on fire if he got too close to an open flame. Wore a pinstripe suit that didn't have a single wrinkle.

"Yes," she forced out, hating that she was giving this bastard what he wanted. "He had an alibi for the time of the murder."

"And what was this alibi?" McClellan asked.

"A friend of his reported that Mr. Llewellyn was with him at his house at that time."

"And why did you not then exclude Mr. Llewellyn as a suspect at this time?"

"All we had to go on was the friend's word. And we didn't consider him completely trustworthy."

"And why not?"

"He had a criminal record from having stolen a car last year."

"And that means he can't be trusted?" Edwards asked.

Don't slap him. Don't slap him, Kara thought to herself. "It made his word suspect. Based on that, I didn't feel we could conclusively exclude Mr. Llewellyn."

"How did this case ultimately conclude?" McClellan asked.

"A man came in and confessed to the murder. He broke into the house to find drug money. Mrs. Llewellyn surprised him. In a panic he beat her to death. Gathered what he could and took off. When he came down off his high, he realized what he'd done and felt the need to turn himself in. In confessing, he had knowledge of a lamp having been used to fracture her skull. This wasn't public information, so the confession was determined to be legitimate."

"Do you have any questions?" McClellan asked, turning towards Edwards.

"Absolutely," he replied with a big smile. "Detective Smalls, is it true that you brought Mr. Llewellyn in for questioning?"

"Yes," Kara replied, trying to steady her shaking voice. She knew this was coming. "We were at a standstill on the case. I thought that if given time to properly interrogate, I could potentially get him to confess."

"And how long did you hold him?" Edwards continued.

"Twenty-four hours. As long as we're able to hold someone without charging them with a crime."

"And what information did you glean during this twenty-four hours?"

"Mr. Llewellyn admitted to his gambling habit and to having fought with his wife."

"And did he maintain his alibi?"

"Yes he did."

"And after you released him, were you given any instructions as it pertained to this case?"

Kara glanced over at Barron. His finger scratched into the table, wearing away at the finish, clearly fuming at what was to come. "Captain Barron asked that I pursue other leads and suspects other than Mr. Llewellyn at that time." Kara now looked down at the table, not able to take Barron's harsh judgmental glare.

"And did you?" Edwards asked.

"For a time."

"Meaning?"

"I spent another week exploring any other possible leads, but nothing came of it. At that point, I ordered a tail to be put on Mr. Llewellyn," Kara said. She had tried moving away from Llewellyn, but the whole time her instincts clawed away at her, demanding that she do more. So she had, and now she was here.

"And how long did this tail last?"

"A week."

"And what did you hope to gain from this?"

"We wanted to see if he would do something to give himself away."

"And did he?"

"Obviously not," Kara spat back. One of her union lawyers nudged her thigh, indicating that she had crossed a line.

"So, despite the complete lack of any hard evidence; despite the instructions of your superior, you insisted on harassing my client?"

Kara said nothing, not wanting to give the bastard the dignity of a response to such a condescending question.

Edwards just nodded, content with what he had gotten out of her. "Thank you. That's all I have," he said.

"Thank you for your time, Detective Smalls. We'll keep you apprised of the investigation."

Kara didn't say anything, she simply turned and walked towards the door. On the way out, she gave Edwards a wide berth, but it wasn't far enough to keep her from smelling the oil wafting up from his hair. Outside of the conference room a few people walked back and forth on some random errand. Kara went back to her desk and plopped into the chair. On top of it was a file box with a note on top.

Kara, Here's the case files that you wanted. Make sure I get them back. Cynthia

Cynthia worked in the file room in the department. Kara had wanted to see some of her old case files. She needed to look them over. Make sure that she had been right all along. She had been so sure that Mr. Llewellyn had killed his wife. She could feel it. But she had been wrong. And she couldn't help but wonder if that had been the case before. What if someone was wasting away in jail all because she'd become too focused on what her instincts told her? She needed to be sure.

Being a homicide detective had been what she had worked for her whole career. Hell, her whole life. She couldn't remember a time when she hadn't imagined herself solving murders.

When she was a kid she would consume every mystery book that she could get her hands on. Started simply with Nancy Drew, but by the time she was in 7th grade she plowed through all of Agatha Christie's books. Drove her mom nuts with it because for Kara, she couldn't just read it. She needed to solve it. While she read, she filled up notebooks with notes and clues that she left scattered throughout the house. Each time she picked up a book she was in competition with herself to see how early on she could solve it. Did the same thing with movies too. Her friends stopped watching them with her because about halfway through, she'd have figured it out and would yell out the answer.

By her third year of high school she had gotten bored with the mystery novels, often finding them too easy; so she moved on to true crime. With this it stopped being about solving the mystery. Now she'd become fascinated with the actual process of solving. She wanted to know how people actually figured this stuff out in the real world. Even with the most intricately plotted novel, there were still only so many people who could be the culprit. With real crimes, there were so many more possibilities. And the idea that someone could get to the bottom of it with so few details... She never really decided to become a cop so much as it just happened. And she wasn't too humble to admit that she was good at it. Had the highest clear rate of the department. Had a few commendations sitting on her desk. When it became time to look at a crime scene, she could read it like no one else. Looking at it she had a feeling of what the motive had been. There were certain telltale signs. Somebody in the middle of the street with a gunshot wound to the stomach? A robbery gone wrong. Single shot to the head, execution style? Victim had been targeted. Someone beaten to death in their home? Domestic dispute gone wrong. At least that's what it usually was.

Kara lifted the lid to the box of files when a shadow stepped over her. "How we doing, Smalls?" the shadow asked.

Kara looked up to see Brody Morgan, her partner, looking down at her. She felt like a small girl with Brody's hulking frame lurking over her. Standing, he'd be a whole head taller than her. His military style haircut and rigid goatee only added to the dominance he exuded. "Hey, Brody," she whispered.

"How was the interrogation?" He laughed as he pulled a chair over. Kara and Brody had been partnered together for the last two years, but during the Llewellyn case the department had been spread thin, so he got put on a different case. So now it was just her head on the chopping block.

"Like getting a root canal," Kara responded as she placed the lid back on the box.

"What's that?" he asked, gesturing towards it.

"My old case files."

"What the hell do you need those for?"

"I need to make sure that I was right."

"Oh my God. You're killin' me, Smalls!" he yelled.

Kara just shook her head at that. This was something he said to her all the time. From some movie from the nineties he said. She didn't know it.

"You're gonna do this to yourself all because some douche is pissy that he was inconvenienced? We both know that this thing isn't going to go anywhere. Shit happens all the time. Besides, I was with you on those cases, and I most certainly didn't screw anything up."

"It's not about that. It's about being able to trust myself."

"Kara," he muttered while hanging his head. She perked up at that. He never used her first name. "You can't do this to yourself," he continued.

"If this thing actually goes to trial, you know they're going to be looking into these anyway. I might as well do it myself."

"It's a waste of time. You were right on all of those. You usually are. I'll tell them that myself."

"I don't know if they'll care."

"Ouch," he said, feigning offense.

"That's not what I meant. Shut up."

"Detective Smalls," a voice yelled from across the room. Both

61

Kara and Brody looked up to see Captain Barron at the door of the conference room. "Please come back in here."

"Go with God my child," Brody said as he made the sign of the cross in the air towards her. Kara didn't say anything. She just stood and marched back towards the captain, feeling a bit like she was walking the green mile. Back inside, she saw that Edwards had left. Thank God for small miracles. She took her seat back in between the two union lawyers.

"Well, Detective Smalls," Captain Barron said, retaking his seat. "We have talked it over and we feel that it is in yours and the department's best interest if you were placed on leave until the conclusion of this lawsuit." Kara didn't say anything. She just stared straight ahead, not really looking at anything. Just taking in each word as he threw them at her. Kara knew that each one had to be a dagger in him, hating to have to be civil around her. But a good face needed to be put on for the union. God knows what he would have done if they hadn't been there to reign him in.

"It is a paid leave," Barron said. "And if all is sorted out, you'll be fully reinstated. I'm sorry to have to tell you this. Do you have any questions?"

"I understand," Kara forced out. It wasn't just that she didn't trust herself anymore. Apparently no one else did either.

7

Without a case to solve, Kara simply puttered around the house, trying to find something to do to fill her time, but she couldn't even remember the last time she had spent the entire day at home.

She eventually found herself on the couch, eyes glazed over as she flipped through the channels on TV, unaware of what was even there. That is until she happened to stop at the news. She saw an overhead shot of a school with a sea of people surrounding it. Kara sat forward on her couch, for once engrossed in what she saw.

"Details are just beginning to pour in," an off-camera voice said in a rushed tone. "It appears as if a gunman has laid siege to Stanford West High School. At this time we don't know how many casualties there are, but police have secured the building and victims are being attended to. As you can see there is a large crowd gathered around the front of the school. Students and teachers are being ushered out of the building now where they are being examined for any injuries." Kara looked on, her eyes not even blinking, taking in every detail, waiting for this all to be a part of one of those prank shows. "At this time," the voice continued, "we have no information about who may have been the shooter."

The overhead shot switched to a live feed from the studio and a blond goddess of a news anchor. "Thank you, Louis, for that report. Please stay tuned to Channel 5 News for more updates as they become available." Kara found herself taking a deep dive, wondering what could have happened. *Did some teacher or student snap? There was that protest today... Could that have had anything to do with it?*

Kara grabbed her phone and sent a text to Brody:

Are you on this?

And then she was left to await a reply. Just staring at the phone waiting for those three little dots indicating that a response was forthcoming. She felt like a teenage girl waiting to hear back from her boyfriend.

That reply never came. Instead, a phone call did. The name "Captain Barron" popped up on the caller ID. Kara did a double take, assuming that she had misread it the first time, but finally she answered it. "Hello?"

"Smalls. I assume you've seen," Barron said on the other end.

"Yeah. What the hell is going on?"

"We're still trying to figure that out."

"What happened?"

"It's complicated."

There was a pause before she spoke again. "What do you need?"

A heavy sigh followed by a few seconds of silence preceded, "We want you on the case." Sounded like he was only saying this because someone had him at gunpoint.

"You what? Why the hell would you need me on this?"

"That's the complicated part."

"Well... Don't keep me in suspense..."

"We don't know who the shooter was."

"YOU WHAT?!"

"Shooter was masked. And they escaped before the first responders got there."

"How the hell is that possible?" Kara ran her hand through her hair, floored by what she had just heard.

"Force was occupied with the protest. Delayed our response time."

"Jesus Christ."

"Yeah. So you can see what we're dealing with."

"Uh-huh. Still have a question though. Why me? Last I checked, I had been suspended."

"Placed on leave."

"Semantics."

"This thing is a big deal. Town is already on the brink with the Spaulding shooting. Now we have a mass murderer on the loose."

"Yeah, and I'm not the only detective on the force. Get to the point."

Barron let out a sigh. "You have the best clear rate on the force, okay? And there was that thing in KC." Before Kara had moved to Stanford, she'd been on the force in Kansas City. In her second year as a detective, she'd been put on the case of a gunman who ran through a shopping center, taking out ten people. People assumed it was a disgruntled employee, but when Kara looked at the crime scene she noticed something. The third person shot had been riddled with bullets, to the point that he was unrecognizable. Looking at him, Kara knew that something was off with this. Looking into the victim, she discovered that he'd been sleeping with his neighbor's wife. The whole thing had been planned just to kill that one guy. The other nine victims had just been to distract from that. When she went to talk to the husband, they discovered that he'd shot himself with the same gun used in the shooting. Kara ended up with a department commendation for solving the case.

"The chief going to okay this?" Kara asked.

"It was his idea."

"Why don't you just let the FBI take this? I assume they're reaching out."

"Brass would prefer to keep them on the sidelines right now. Just have them around for support."

"Why? They handle this stuff."

"Since the Spaulding shooting, the town is already against us. Chief wants us to regain their trust. And with the protests that are going on... he's worried about the optics. Thinks having the FBI all over the place will make it seem like we're under martial law or something."

"Jesus. This is a mess."

"Yeah. So what's it going to be? Clock is ticking."

"Fine."

"Good. Get down to the school ASAP and start coordinating." And with that the line went dead. Kara sat back, feeling the surrealism of the moment. She wanted to be working, but she didn't want it to happen like this.

8

K ara pushed her way through the crowd, coming up to the sawhorse barriers. A quick flash of her badge gave her entry. Every inch of the parking lot teemed with people. Parents being reunited with their kids. A few people seemingly in the middle of a panic attack. Uniforms going from one person to another to collect whatever small portion of the story they had to tell. She climbed the steps to the front of the school where a small group of cops huddled together, Brody at the center of it. As soon as he saw her, his face lit up and he worked his way through the crowd.

"Thank Christ, you're here," he said, walking up to her. "This whole thing is a fucking shit-show."

"Where are we at?" Kara asked.

"Trying to identify all the victims right now."

"What's the number?"

"We've got twenty-eight dead."

"Twenty-eight? Are you shitting me?"

"I wish I was."

"I see the interviews going on out there. Finding out anything?"

"Nothing useful. Principal is helping us pull up the security footage."

"Good. Let's take a look." Brody and Kara walked inside, heading past the body of Zach Levinson which still took up space behind the desk, a spray of blood on the wall behind him. Heading into the office, they passed by Sergeant Blake as pictures were snapped of him dead on the floor. They headed back into a small office off to the side. Inside was an older man with a head of silver hair sinking into his desk chair, his head buried in his hands. Behind him were five different monitors, two stacked upon the other three.

"Principal Devin," Brody said in a soft voice. "This is Detective Smalls. She'll be leading this investigation with me." Devin dragged his head up and forced a small smile. A spot of red ringed around his eyes. "We're ready to look at the security footage," Brody continued.

"Of course," Devin muttered as he stood and turned on the monitors behind him. Kara and Brody both gathered around, Brody producing a pen and notepad. A few clicks brought up the security footage, black-and-white images of various parts of the school popped into view, the time huddled in the corner. They all looked at the one on the bottom left, seeing Michael Myers come through the door and taking out Levinson.

"Timestamp says 8:30," Kara said, not looking away. "When is that during the day?"

"Second period," Devin replied.

"When in second period?"

"It had just begun."

"So halls were clear?"

"Yes." Everyone's eyes shifted over to the bottom right where Myers now charged down the hall. Devin punched a couple buttons and it now switched to a view from the library where

Myers began to lay waste. Kara and Brody gave each other a small nod, communicating exactly what they were thinking.

"There's a sign-in sheet for the library?" Kara asked.

"Yes. Of course."

The images appeared all around the different monitors; Kara's eyes darting from one to the other. Brody scribbled furiously, recording the times and the path Myers took. When they came to Myers's first classroom invasion, Kara called out the room number to Brody who jotted it down.

The footage kept rolling, and they arrived at Michael and Jason's uniting downstairs. "Who the hell is that?" Kara belted out at the sight of the second masked shooter. No one had mentioned this.

Devin paused the footage. All three of them looked on, all of them wondering how to proceed. Kara and Brody communicated silently again. *This is a whole new wrinkle to it.* "Let's proceed from here. See what happens. We'll go back," Kara said. The tape continued. Jason wrestled his way into what was Connor's room. The struggle played out and Jason went to the ground. From there they watched as Michael and Jason made their way and invaded what would be their final room. They saw nothing, but they could imagine what unfolded inside. And from there Michael came and waved his goodbye. Neither of the shooters showed up again.

"That it?" Brody asked. "They get out through the classroom?"

"It would appear so," Devin replied.

"You have cameras out there?"

"Some."

"Pull them up." A few outside shots came on screen, but no masked killers came into frame. "Shit," Brody muttered when it became clear that there was nothing to see. He pulled out a walkie-talkie and hailed one of the uniforms outside. "A couple of you head around back. Shooters escaped that way. Look for any signs."

"Roger that," a voice squawked back.

"Go back and find where the goalie came into play," Kara said. A search back through revealed Jason bursting out of the bathroom, taking out two of Kristin's students. "The fuck?" Kara let out. "Go back further." The tape rewound, and Kara looked on, not blinking, waiting to see when it was that Jason had headed in. But eventually they got to the image of a surge of students in the halls, with random kids heading in and out of the bathroom. "Goddammit!" Kara exclaimed. "What the hell happened here?"

"He must have headed in there during the passing period. And waited," Brody offered.

"Are students allowed to carry backpacks during the day?" Kara asked.

"No," Devin answered.

"Well, that means the gun and clothes were already there. Had to have been dropped off. Go back further. See if someone heads in there with a package or something." The tape rewound until the timestamp read 6:30. At that point someone stumbled into the building with a bag around their shoulder, a black hoodie draped over his head shielding him from view. He stalked through the halls, down the stairs, and into the bathroom from where Jason would emerge in a couple hours. He came out without a bag and slipped out the back door. "And there it is," Kara whispered.

All three of them turned and headed back outside. Brody still had his head in his pad and was scribbling away as he and Kara conversed in hushed tones.

"Is there a record of which students are issued a bathroom pass during class?" Kara asked.

Devin nodded as Brody tore off a piece of paper and handed

it to Devin. "This is what we need," he told him. Devin grabbed the paper and took a look at it. It read:

1. *Class roster and teacher names for Rooms 117, 15, 123, and 19.*
2. *Sign-in sheet for library*
3. *Attendance records for the day*
4. *Discipline records*
5. *Bathroom Pass Records*

Devin looked at it for a minute and then replied, "We can do most of this. Discipline records, I don't think can happen."

"Why not?" Brody asked.

"Those are confidential. I believe you would need a warrant for that."

"Dammit," Kara muttered. "But the rest will do?"

"I don't see why not. But why would you need a record of bathroom passes or the attendance record?"

"First shooter came in from the outside. So we need to know which students weren't in class at the time."

"So it was one of our students?" Devin choked out, sounding petrified at the idea.

"It usually is."

"But is it possible it was someone from the outside?"

"We're going to explore every possibility." The trio descended the outside stairs as a uniform cop hustled up to them, a book bag hanging from his arms.

"What do we have here?" Brody said as he peered inside. "What the fuck?!" he cried out as he threw his head back. A stench of bleach shot up out of the bag, stinging his eyes.

"Found it in the woods out back. Group of guns and some clothes," the uniform said.

"Well, I guess we know which way they went. Take us back there," Kara said as the group headed around.

They found the path the shooters took, but little else. The forensics team scoured the area, but discovered nothing of any use. Some slight indentations in the ground seemed to be where they had stepped, but not enough to get a print. From there they traced the steps of the shooters, seeing the bodies and carnage firsthand. They went to the library where they saw the deep stains of red in the carpet, enough to the point that one may think it was the natural color. They walked the halls where blood smeared the floor and lockers. They went to each of the classrooms that had been attacked. Bodies lay among a jungle of toppled desks. Bullet holes dotted the walls, some still hot to the touch.

Their journey ended at the room which marked Michael and Jason's escape, where the pools of blood seemed to be a couple of inches thick.

"Jesus Christ," Brody muttered, his typical wit having abandoned him at the sight of the slaughter. He and Kara tiptoed around, taking it all in. The air whistled as it came in through the open window. "How the hell did they get out of here anyway?" Brody asked.

Kara didn't respond, as she wondered the same thing herself. Then a glance over at the window revealed the answer. A rope had been tied around the window frame. She approached and looked out. The rope trailed down the side, ending right above the ground. "Looks like they climbed down."

Brody came over and saw for himself. "Who the hell are these people?" he asked to no one in particular.

"I don't get it. Why come up here just to climb out a second-story window? There's plenty of places to get out from down there. What's so special about this room?" Neither said a thing because neither had the answer.

From there, Kara and Brody took up residence in a conference room, the large table covered with various papers filled with all the information they had gotten from Principal Devin. They compiled a list of everyone that they needed to interview, which grew longer and longer with every passing minute.

"This is gonna take forever," Brody said. "Where do you even start with a cluster-fuck like this?"

"We'll get some uniforms to take statements from some of the students. We'll focus on the ones who were out of the classroom."

"Doesn't seem likely to me."

"What's that?"

"That the shooters were kids who ducked out under the pretense of taking a shit. They would have to have known we could track that."

"Well... they're kids. Kids are stupid."

"Does this look like the work of someone who's stupid?"

Kara sat for a moment in thought. "True. But we need to start somewhere."

The door to the room swung open and Captain Barron stepped in. "Brody. Smalls," he uttered in a cursory greeting. His eyes lingered on Kara for an extra second, annoyed at her presence. "Where are we at?"

"Somewhere around fuck all," Brody groaned.

Kara added, "We're making a list of who to question."

Barron glanced at the list which was forty names long and growing. "Looks like you have your work cut out. Lots of mistakes you could make along the way." His eyes settled on Kara. She wanted to curse him out but knew that her career wouldn't appreciate it.

"We're gonna do this right," Brody said.

"You better. This department has been reamed enough as it is."

"You usually have to pay extra for that sort of action," Brody blurted, not able to stop himself. Kara stifled her laugh.

"You about done? Cause the vultures are circling outside. We need to give them something."

"Give them the usual BS. We're pursuing all leads. We'll get the sons of bitches."

"I don't really think that's gonna cut it this time."

"Well, dealing with the press isn't really our job," Kara snapped. She zipped her mouth, wishing she hadn't said it. Brody looked around wishing he could be elsewhere.

Barron took a step back and regarded her. "No," he replied, "it's not. Your job is to find the killer. The right one." From there he whisked his way out of the room. "Come on!" he yelled behind him. "I'm not facing those bastards alone."

Kara and Brody shared a mutual look of disgust, and followed him outside. Along the way they passed a group of parents who were in a line of chairs. They were the ones who hadn't seen their kids outside. They prayed that their children had escaped. Prayed that they just hadn't made it back yet. A uniform would call them back into an office where he'd take down their information and in the rare instance that a victim had been identified, the bad news would be delivered. As the two passed, an unearthly shriek sounded from that office. A woman burst through the door, collapsing to the ground.

Kara turned away, this being one part of the job she struggled with. They arrived outside, the herd inside the impromptu hospital having thinned. Barron headed to the barrier where the media still stood at full force. As he stepped forward, reporters hurled question after question at him.

"Quiet down, everyone." He spoke with ease. Everyone obeyed. This was where he shined. "I will make a quick statement and then take a few questions." They all looked on in rapt attention. "At approximately 8:30 this morning, two masked gunmen took the school by force, resulting in the death of multiple students and faculty members. At around 8:50, a group of responding officers arrived and cleared the building. In the process it was discovered that the two shooters escaped prior to the officers' arrival." A murmuring began among the crowd. This was a horse of a different color. "We are launching a full investigation and hope to make an arrest soon." Barron's pause at the end signaled that he had finished. The questions unleashed yet again. Barron boomed his voice out again to add, "Any questions can be directed to our two lead investigators, Detectives Smalls and Morgan." He took off without looking back, but Kara could swear that she heard a chuckle as he passed. *That son of a bitch.*

"Detective! Do you currently have any suspects?" the first question came quick-fire.

"Can't comment on that at the moment," Kara said, trying to play catch-up.

"Do you believe the shooters were students?" came another.

"We won't speculate on that."

"Is there any reason to believe that this is related to the protests that were being held this morning?"

"Won't speculate," she repeated. The reporters continued to throw questions, and Kara realized that she couldn't dodge them all. "Listen!" she yelled. "We will be providing updates as the investigation proceeds, but we cannot comment on it at this time. Please respect that and the victims and families during this time. Thank you." Kara spun around and headed back towards the school, Brody nipping at her heels.

"Thought you handled that well," he said, catching up with her.

"Yeah. Thanks for all your help," Kara retorted.

"Looked like you had it taken care of."

"If that bastard is so pissed at me, he never should've brought me back."

"Are you complaining?" Brody asked.

Kara leered over at him. He shut his mouth. The two headed back into the school, hoping to find the needle at the bottom of the haystack.

Kara slugged her way back into her house, every detail of the case wheeling around in her head. She ticked off her mental list of things to do. Long list of interviews to conduct. God knew how long that could take. Track the serial number of the guns that were found. Wait for the forensic results of the clothes. But based on the smell of bleach that smothered every inch of it, that would likely result in jack shit.

While she thought it all over, the image of that mother writhing around in agony swam in front of her. She crashed onto her couch, trying to rid herself of the picture. She hated the view of it. Even now, hours later, it made her twitch. The sight of someone in that amount of pain made her feel so powerless. When she had been five years old, her grandmother had died. At the time, she didn't really understand what it all meant, so when it came time for the funeral, she was really just along for the ride. While the casket was lowered into the ground she looked around and smiled at the birds that flew from tree to tree. She wanted to go chasing off after them, but her parents had instructed her to be on her best behavior, so she stayed put. Her smile soon vanished when she heard the weeping coming from above her. She looked up to see her mother sobbing into her hands. Seeing her mother like that forced everything into upheaval. She cried plenty. When she fell and hurt herself.

When someone took her toys. But her parents, her mother... They were grown-ups. Grown-ups didn't cry. They were strong. So now that her mother stood here in tears... it didn't make sense.

Kara threw herself at her mother, wrapping her arms around her legs. "Mommy! Why are you sad?" She got no response. Her mother simply folded an arm around her and held her there. Kara began to cry herself now, heartbroken to see her mother like this. Confused by her inability to do anything about it. Of course, as she got older, it all began to make sense, but one thing that didn't change was the sense of helplessness that she felt.

9

All around Stanford that night people sat down stunned by it all. Eyes were glued to the television, taking in every bit of information that could be squeezed out. That evening, shots of Stanford could be seen on every news channel.

The main paper in Stanford was the *Stanford Tribune*. The story about the shooting took up the entire front page the following morning, the picture showcasing the parking lot jam-packed with people.

Tragedy struck at Stanford West High School yesterday, October 15. The school day had just begun when an emergency lockdown was called over the intercom. At 8:30 in the morning, two masked assailants charged into the school with firearms. For the next half hour the school was at their mercy as police response was delayed due to the protest being held concerning the shooting of fifteen-year-old Noah Spaulding.

Once authorities arrived, they conducted a full sweep of the building. However, the perpetrators could not be found, possibly having fled the scene. Authorities have made assurances that a full investigation will be made into the incident. However, they would not comment on any aspects of the investigation. Meanwhile, they have requested that citizens remain calm and allow them to proceed with the case.

Christopher Devin, principal of Stanford West High School agreed to speak to the Tribune. "The entire community here at West is devastated by this incident. While we pray that nothing like this would ever happen, this occurrence is something that we always make sure to prepare ourselves for. Several lockdown drills are held every year in keeping with federal and state standards. With this tragedy, we will definitely be looking into strengthening our security so as to make sure that nothing like this will ever happen again. But for right now, we just ask that everyone keep the West family in their prayers." The School Board for Stanford Public has announced that they are suspending classes for the entire district until further notice in order to ensure the safety of all their students and allowing families time to grieve.

By the end of the massacre, twenty-eight lives had been taken with fifteen more injured. The injured were rushed to Eternal Hope Hospital where they are currently being treated for injuries. Three of them are currently in critical condition. The rest are expected to make full recoveries. The names of the victims have not yet been released. The Tribune will provide updates as they become available.

The story stretched far beyond Stanford, and as is always the case with these incidents, it quickly became national news. A story would also appear on the front page of *The Washington Post*.

The eyes of the nation are now on the town of Stanford, Missouri, after it has suffered one of the worst mass shootings in recent history. With twenty-eight dead, many are waiting to see what effect, if any, this will have on the national debate surrounding gun control.

President Harris is expected to deliver a statement to the press later this evening. Many are speculating on whether or not she will address the issue of gun control in her statement, which was a major part of her platform when she was elected. There has already been a wide call for legislation involving firearms from both sides of the aisle. The Brady Campaign to Prevent Gun Violence issued a statement: "There is no reason that twenty-eight people had to lose their lives in such a senseless fashion. Unfortunately, tragedies such as this will only continue to happen if serious action is not made to limit access to dangerous firearms." The National Rifle Association also issued their own statement saying: "This shooting is only further evidence that teachers need to have access to firearms within their classroom. Had they been available in Stanford, someone could have prevented this tragedy before a single life had been taken." It remains to be seen if any meaningful legislation concerning guns will result from these events.

The evening of the shooting, President Danielle Harris stood at the podium of the White House Press Briefing Room. Just prior to her entrance the place had been abuzz with a barrage of shouted questions, but it immediately ceased once her presence was known. What follows is a transcript of this press conference:

Good evening. I will be making a brief statement regarding the events that transpired today, and then I will take a few questions. The nation was shocked by the events that transpired in Stanford this morning. The loss of any life is tragic, even more so when it's the lives of children. Our hearts go out to all those who were affected by this tragedy. We ask that your thoughts and prayers go out to the entire town of Stanford. Each and every time that this happens, we pray that it will be the last time. And I wish that I could promise you that it will be. However, no one can promise you that. All that can be promised is that we will come back stronger than before. I know that many people may be especially afraid since in this case the identity and motive of these killers are unknown. But I want to remind the entire nation that no criminal, no matter how violent, keeps their identity a secret for long. We will hunt this criminal down and see that justice is served. For as long as a single person in this nation feels unsafe in their homes and communities, then we are not truly free. And as we have always done, we will rally together. And as we have always done, we will look towards the future. And as we have always done, we will make our schools and communities stronger and safer. Thank you. I will now take a few short questions.

CNN Reporter: What role, if any, will the FBI be playing in the following investigation?

President Harris: The Stanford Police Department will be taking the lead in the investigation, but the FBI will be making themselves available to them, to provide whatever resources and manpower they may need.

MSNBC Reporter: Do you plan to introduce any legislation as a means to combat gun violence?

President Harris: Exploring ways to keep firearms out of the hands of dangerous criminals is definitely a step we need to take in going forward.

Fox News Reporter: With this shooting occurring during the protest about the Noah Spaulding shooting, is there any reason to believe that the two are connected?

President Harris: There is no reason to speculate that the two are connected.

Fox News Reporter: Is it true that during the protest a speaker made a threat on children?

President Harris: Investigators will be looking into any threats that may or may not have been made. That's all the time I have. We will keep you posted as more information becomes available. Thank you.

And all around the country, random citizens took to Twitter

and Facebook, offering their condolences, assuring the victims that they were in everyone's thoughts and prayers.

10

The sun had just started to peek over the horizon when Kara walked into the station. She hadn't gotten much sleep the night before. Not once could she shut her brain off long enough to rest. She'd decided to come in early and put her fevered brain to some use.

When she walked in there were just a couple desk jockeys who'd been saddled with the night shift, but besides that the place was a ghost town, and would be for about another hour. Kara sat at her desk where the box of case files she had requested lay undisturbed. From the moment she'd gotten the call about the shooting, they hadn't even crossed her mind, but now it became consumed with it. It just served as yet another reminder of her failure. And a reminder of how vital things were this time. An entire town, an entire country, would be watching this case unfold. Any mistake would be amplified. Any error would be the epitaph on her career.

But she had no time for that. She had to get down to work. She began by reviewing what case notes she had. The clothes were being processed through forensics. They'd relayed the information on the guns to the ATF, hoping to trace them. God knows how long that would take. She and Brody would need to visit the couple gun shops in town and hope they lucked out. Then came the laundry list of interviews that they needed to conduct. Kara reviewed the list, overwhelmed by the number of names on it. The scheduling alone would take a fleet of officers. Adding to that, most of them were kids, which only made it that much more of a headache. And once that was done, who knew how long it would take to actually get through them all.

Kara set down to work and had been at it for half an hour, when Brody walked in.

"Shoulda figured you'd be here already," he said as he slumped down in the desk across from Kara's. "Solved it yet?"

"Yeah. The butler did it," Kara responded without looking up. A minute passed without a word when she threw her head back and sighed. "Where the hell do we even start?"

"Well, I have one idea," Brody offered.

"I'm all ears."

"As I was on my way in, Hicks stopped me."

"And he is?"

"He's one of the officers that was at the protest yesterday. Said that during it, some lady from the SSPA made a threat against kids."

"She what?!"

"Yeah. Something to the effect that the privileged wouldn't care about them until their kids were the ones who were killed."

"Jesus..."

"Yeah. So I figured that that warranted us having a word or two with them."

"Why are we just now hearing about this? No one thought to say something yesterday?"

"Well... I think people had their hands full yesterday."

"Jesus. Well, I guess that just shot to the top of our never-ending list of things to do. Let's get to it."

"That's the spirit!"

Kara hoisted herself up from her chair, packed her notes back up, and headed towards the door with Brody in tow. Prior to heading out the door they stopped at the desk of Detective Dixon, who was new to Homicide, and gave him the unenviable task of getting started on setting up the interviews.

The headquarters of the SSPA sat across town, but it was really nothing more than a hole in the wall. A small splintered door interrupted the brick side of an office building. This door then led down a flight of stairs that would creak if so much as a feather happened to land on it. The cracks in them would widen with every step someone took. Brody stepped cautiously on them, sure that he would go through at any second.

Kara and Brody made it to the bottom without incident and landed in an open basement, with several desks placed at random on the floor. The moment they entered, an aura of tension filled the air as the four people who occupied the office stared over at them, looking like bulls ready to charge. At the back, Denise Liman stood up from a desk and plowed her way to where Kara and Brody stood.

"Do you have business here?" Liman asked. She strived to sound formal, but it still managed to come across as a threat.

"Are you Ms. Liman?" Kara asked.

"I am." *Fuck you* she seemed to say.

"We'd like to ask you some questions."

"Concerning?" *I said fuck you.*

"Is there, perhaps, someplace else we could do this?" Brody asked.

This time Liman didn't respond. She simply pushed past Kara and Brody and headed toward a small door tucked away in the corner. She opened it to reveal a supply closet that had been converted into its own office. Liman stepped aside allowing the two detectives to enter. Once in they took a seat, squished up against each other.

"The door remains open. So don't try anything," Liman said as she squeezed around to the back of the room and sat at the desk. "So what is it you need?" *You better not be wasting my time.*

"Were you at the protest concerning Noah Spaulding yesterday?" Kara asked.

"Of course."

"Well... It has been brought to our attention of some comments you made at that time."

Liman laughed with scorn. *I can't believe you're wasting my time with this.*

"Did you say something to the effect of...?" Brody began, pulling out his notebook.

"'It is not until their children are the ones left alone in a pool of their own blood that they will ever know our pain!'" Liman interrupted, quoting herself exactly. "Is that the comment you're referring to?"

"Yeah. That'd be the one," Brody replied.

"I stand by my comments. And last time I checked, I'm allowed to speak my mind."

"We're not interested in censoring you," Kara chimed in. "However, do you understand why those kind of comments may concern us considering what transpired yesterday?"

"You're referring to the shooting at West?"

"Something else didn't happen yesterday, did it?" Brody chimed in.

"And you think I had something to do with that?"

"We're just asking some questions right now," Kara said. "Given the reputation of your organization, I'm sure you get where we're coming from."

"What reputation would that be?"

"Have you ever been to West High?" Brody asked, ignoring the latest comment.

"I can't say that I have."

"What about other members?"

"I can hardly speak for them."

"Why did you make those comments in the first place?" Kara asked.

"Because it's true," Liman spat out, her voice dropping down. "If that school had been on this side of town. If those had been black children who were gunned down, would you even get out of bed?"

"So do you actually advocate that kind of action?"

"I advocate doing what is necessary to get the job done."

"And what job is that?" Brody asked.

"This figures," Liman groaned.

"What do you mean?"

"Someone gets shot and you go running to the brown people."

"Hardly without reason."

"And this isn't the first threat that has been linked to either you or your organization," Kara butted in.

"Has any crime?" Liman asked.

Brody threw his head back in exhaustion. "We're gonna need a list of your members," he said.

"No problem. Just let me see a warrant."

"Are you really going to fight us on this?"

"I just want you to follow the rules. Something some of your officers should be more conscious of."

Kara stared down at her feet wondering where they went from here. Liman may be a bitch, but that didn't mean she was wrong. She just needed to hope that she could appeal to the better angels of her nature. Kara looked up and in a somber tone said, "Twenty-eight people have died. Twenty-two of them were children. Some of those were African-American. Any help that you give is only going to help us get to the bottom of this."

"And I'll give you that help once a judge orders."

"For fuck's sake," Brody groaned as he sprang up from his seat and headed out of the closet/office.

Kara stood and offered a polite, "Thank you for your time." The two of them scaled the stairs, headed outside, got into the car, and took off.

"So what do think?" Brody asked.

"Well, she's a bitch. But a killer? I don't know," Kara responded.

"You don't think she did it?"

"You do?"

"Who the hell reacts that way when there are dead kids we're cleaning up after? Sure as shit seems like she has something to hide. And... Jesus... she might as well have said, 'Hey, let's go kill a bunch of kids!'"

"That's my point. Who the hell announces their plan in front of a bunch of cops an hour before carrying it out? That woman is a lot of things, but she certainly isn't stupid."

"It's a hell of a coincidence then."

"Stranger things have happened."

"So where do we go from here?"

"Well, we should at least try to get a warrant. Certainly can't rule her out. Keep pursuing our other leads in the meantime."

"Damn. And here I was, hoping we were going to crack the case in less than a day."

"No such luck. So what do you say? You want to go on a tour of the town's gun stores?"

"Ooh! Can we? Can we?" Brody squealed. The car headed off down the street.

11
———

Connor first woke up at 6:00 just like he did every other morning. He almost rose out of bed when he remembered that he didn't need to today. A brief smile formed on his face upon realization that he could go back to sleep, but a pang of guilt hit him when he recalled why it was. He winced as the gunshots popped off inside his head once again. Connor looked over to see Brandy still asleep beside him.

She now began to stir. Once she saw Connor sitting, she sprung up. "Connor, honey. Are you okay?"

"I'm fine. Internal alarm went off is all," Connor groaned.

"That it? You have any dreams or anything?" Last night, Brandy had taken to the internet and printed off pages and pages of information about post-traumatic stress. She pored over them with a highlighter, preparing herself and Connor for every eventuality. As they had laid down last night, one thing she had warned him about was that he may have dreams, reliving the whole experience. Connor shook his head, lying. The truth was that he had had a dream, but it wasn't something that he wanted to get into at the moment.

He had been back in his classroom, but alone this time. He

sat at a student desk and stared at the wall. From outside his room, came a pounding, like a stampede of elephants running into his door again and again. The whole time, Connor didn't move. He didn't even look over towards the source of the noise. He was a stone pillar. Next thing he knew, Jason Voorhees stood in front, his arm outstretched and ending in a gun. He pulled the trigger, and at that moment, time slowed down. A fireball erupted out of the barrel. A plume of smoke obscured Jason's mask. The bullet ripped through the air, making waves as it sailed towards Connor. Inside, he knew that he needed to move. He screamed at himself to do it, but nothing happened. Instead, he sat there as the bullet pierced his head. Globs of blood splattered in front of his face. Connor could feel his skull bursting into pieces. His brains were shredded. And still... nothing. As the bullet erupted out of the back of his head, darkness began to sweep over him. It was at that moment that Connor woke up. He kept it quiet, though, so as not to wake Brandy. It would be another hour before he drifted off.

"I'm okay. Let's just go back to sleep," Connor told her. He laid back down and she wrapped her arms around him.

They both slept for another two hours. Brandy insisted on cooking breakfast even though Connor hadn't actually eaten it once in the past couple years. But she was adamant, worried that unless she made him, he wouldn't eat at all. Connor sat at the table picking at his bacon and occasionally shoving a forkful of hash browns into his mouth. Years of waiting until noon to eat made it hard to have much of an appetite at the moment.

Connor looked down at the plate, the whole time feeling Brandy's eyes on him as though he was a puzzle that she needed to figure out. As though he was a cracked vase that threatened to shatter at any second.

"So..." Brandy started with a heap of trepidation. "I was

thinking that it might be a good idea to look into maybe seeing someone."

"Someone?"

"Like a therapist."

Connor threw his hand over his eyes and exhaled. "I don't know, Brandy. You know how I feel about that kind of thing." Brandy had been promoting this for him for a while now, concerned that he was depressed. She'd even suggested couples counseling for them a few times. Every time she did, he'd managed to duck the issue. He didn't imagine it helping at all. He'd attempted therapy for a bit in college at the pleading of his parents. It didn't do much good, so he soon gave it up and hadn't considered going back.

"I know. This is different though," Brandy said.

"Yeah... but..." He didn't know what to say.

"Just promise me that you'll think about it." Connor looked at her, the light shining off the glint of a tear in her eye. After all this time, she still amazed him. Amazed at her unwillingness to give up on him, long after he had given up on himself.

"Fine. I'll think about it," he said after a beat. Brandy didn't say a word. She just reached across the table and squeezed his hand. From there they finished their breakfast in silence. While they cleaned up the dishes a knock came at the door. Connor went to answer the door to find no one there. Instead, a plastic container full of cupcakes sat on the porch. On top of the container was a card with his name written on the envelope. He picked it up and brought it into the kitchen.

"Who was at the door?" Brandy asked.

"I don't know. This was just sitting there." Connor pulled the card out of the envelope to see "Thank You" printed on top of a floral pattern on the front. Opening it, he saw a handwritten message written inside:

Mr. Sullivan,

Christopher told us about what happened yesterday and what you did during the shooting. Our son, and other children, are alive today because of your bravery. There are no words to fully describe the love and appreciation that we feel for you right now. Please accept this small gift from us. There is no way that we could ever possibly repay you for what you've done. But please know that you will forever be in our hearts and minds for what you did.

Sincerely,

Tom and Clarissa Davion.

It was from the parents of one of the students who had been in his class when the shooter had come in. Connor didn't know how to react to this. He reread the note a few times and felt more and more uncomfortable each time. Connor had never been wonderful at accepting any kind of compliment. During his first year of teaching, the staff had done a team building exercise where they needed to go around and give different people compliments. Connor had just avoided it altogether, feeling embarrassed by the very idea of it. He didn't know why, but the whole thing just felt unnatural to him. So now, faced with something like this... he felt like a foreigner in his own skin.

Brandy came around, peered over his shoulder, and read the note herself. Connor couldn't stand it when someone did this, but now he barely noticed.

"Oh my God," Brandy gasped. "This is..."

"Yeah..." Connor cut her off. "What do we do with it?"

"What do you mean?"

"Well, should we return these or...?"

"Why would you want to do that?"

"I don't want them doing this. It isn't necessary."

"That's not the point."

"Then why?"

"Connor, you did a wonderful thing yesterday!"

"No I didn't."

"Connor... all those kids are alive now because of you."

"Please. I barely even know what happened there. I just reacted. I might as well have been pulling my hand away from a hot pan. Jesus, I'm not even sure I remembered that the kids were in there in the moment. I was scared for myself."

"But you did what you needed to do."

"Yeah," Connor said with a roll of the eyes. "Well, what about all the times that I didn't?"

"What do you mean?"

"Nothing." With that Connor took off out the room. He headed back to their bedroom where he flipped on the TV and shut out the world. Throughout the day, three more gift packages came. Flowers and two fruit baskets. Brandy would come up to the room and drop them off without a word. Connor read each card, all of them saying essentially the same thing as the first. He set all of them to the side and tried to wish them out of existence. Then at 1:00 came the phone call.

"Hello," Connor answered in a groggy voice.

"Is this Connor Sullivan who works at Stanford West High School?" the male voice on the other end asked.

"Yes."

"My name is Kyle Brennan with the *Stanford Tribune*. I was wondering if we might have a word."

"About what?" Connor asked, wondering why he even bothered.

"Well, we heard about what you did during the incident yesterday."

Connor wished he wouldn't tiptoe around the subject with a word like *incident*. "And?" he offered, hoping to get this over with.

"Well, I was hoping that we might set up an interview. It's an amazing story, and we would love to tell it in our paper. We think it's something that our readers would really respond to."

"I'm sorry, but I'm not interested."

"Is there another paper that you've agreed to talk to? Because if this is a matter of compensation, I think we could offer you something."

"What? No..." Connor spat out, thinking about the moral implications of profiting off the shooting. "I'm just not interested in talking about it. Besides, you've obviously heard about what happened, so why would you even need to talk to me."

"We want to hear your side of it."

"I don't have a side to it. I'm sorry, but no." With that Connor hung up and dropped the phone beside him. Would this be his life now? Constantly on the receiving end of adulation? If this is what happened while he held himself up in his house, what would happen when he dared to head out into the world?

Brandy came up into the room. "Were you just on the phone?" she asked.

"Yeah. It was a reporter."

"A reporter?"

"Yeah. They want to talk to me about the 'incident,'" Connor said with air quotes.

"Are you going to do it?"

"Of course not."

Brandy just smiled, knowing that this would be the answer. "Do you want anything for lunch?"

"No. I'm tired. I think I might take a nap." Brandy just looked over at him, an entire ocean between the two of them that couldn't be crossed. She turned and left Connor alone as he laid down and buried his head in his pillow.

He slept for two hours when his phone went off again. Connor shot out his hand and answered the phone while still keeping his head buried. He muttered what amounted to a greeting as he answered.

"Is this Connor Sullivan of Stanford West High School?" a voice asked.

"Yes..." he said as though he wasn't sure of the answer. *Who the hell is this? Fucking New York Times now*, he thought.

"My name is Detective Dixon with the Stanford Police Department."

Connor, caught off guard by this, hoisted himself out of his self-made cocoon.

"As you can imagine, we are currently in the midst of the investigation concerning the shooting from yesterday. To aid us we are setting up interviews with all relevant staff and students. And it is our understanding you had a confrontation with one of the shooters. Our lead investigators, Detectives Smalls and Morgan, would like to speak with you. We're just trying to get a full sense of what transpired."

"Yes. Yes. Of course."

"Would you be able to come down to the station tomorrow at 11:00?"

"Umm... yeah." Connor felt like one of his students with these disconnected responses, but having the police call him wasn't a typical occurrence.

"Great. Thank you for your time." With that the line went dead.

12

K ristin lay asleep in bed at the hospital. Her mother, Diane, sat beside her, book open in her lap. She looked down at the words on the page but didn't actually read any of them. Nothing could sustain her attention at the moment, her mind entirely occupied on her daughter as she wondered what, if anything, she could do for her.

She worked as an accountant at a law firm. Nearing sixty, she should have been looking forward to retirement, but with the death of Kristin's father last year, she needed the extra income. She had thought that nothing could compare to the dread she felt the day that he died. Until yesterday.

She had just gotten down to work when the entire office erupted. Missy, her secretary, came running into her office almost in tears. "Wha... what..." she stuttered.

"Missy, what's wrong?" Diane asked, feeling an ice pick go straight through her heart. Even though she hadn't heard the news at this point, in the back of her head she already knew. A mother always knows.

"What school does Kristin work at?"

With that she could feel the ice pick dig in deeper. "West. Why?" she asked, hoping that her instincts had betrayed her.

"There's been a shooting."

Once she heard those words, the entire world began to tilt and then turn upside down. Diane slipped out of her chair and collapsed onto the ground. Bile shot out of her mouth. Missy ran over to her and tried pulling her up from the ground, but she may as well have been lifting an anvil.

When she did finally lift herself, she gathered her things and ran to her car crying about how she had to be with Kristin. Missy insisted on driving her, worried that she was too hysterical to drive anywhere. Diane wouldn't even be able to argue had she wanted to. She hopped into Missy's car, the world still spinning the entire time. She had her phone out and called Kristin over and over again, but after a few rings it kept going to voicemail. If she wasn't answering her phone it could only mean one thing... that she'd been killed. That, and only that, ran through her mind the entire ride to the school.

A mass of people had already gathered there. Pushing through them felt like swimming through mud. She reached the front and would have jumped the sawhorses if a cop hadn't been there to stop her. "Please! Please! My daughter works here. I need to see if she's okay," she said through sobs.

"Okay, okay," the cop responded as he threw up his hands in a calming gesture. "Give me her name, and I'll see if we can find her."

"Kristin. Kristin Benson," she cried, feeling like she may vomit again.

He took off, leaving someone else in his stead. He had been gone for about ten minutes, and they were the longest ten minutes of Diane's life. When she saw him heading back she had to restrain herself from running towards him, not wanting to wait another second to hear the news. She studied his face, looking for an upward turn of his lips into a smile to indicate good news. But she couldn't make out anything, which, of course, could only be bad news.

"I just talked to the medics we have here," the cop began once he came up to her.

Oh no. The medics? She's been shot, hasn't she?

"She wasn't injured at all, but she was taken to the emergency room."

Another ice pick now dug itself into her heart as she attempted to sort out what she had just heard. "I... I... I don't understand. If she wasn't injured why would she be brought to the emergency room?"

"I'm sorry. That's all the information I have."

"But she is alive?"

"Yes."

"Thank you," she cried through a mass of tears. At this point she couldn't even tell if they were due to happiness at this news or devastation from the whole ordeal. Probably both.

After plowing her way through the crowd once again, Missy took her to the emergency room. It took a while for her to actually get brought back, but eventually she got to see her daughter. She charged into the room where a doctor hovered over Kristin, jotting something down on a chart.

"Can I help you?" the doctor asked, his head springing up.

"Tha... that's my daughter. What's wrong? What happened? Is she hurt? Is she going to be okay? Why is she here? What is she doing?" Diane's string of questions had been interrupted when she looked over at Kristin to see her staring ahead blankly and moving her lips ever so slightly. A subdued whisper emitted from her.

"I'm Dr. Christensen. You said you're Ms. Benson's mother?"

Diane just nodded her head, not taking her eyes off of Kristin for a second. The small bit of relief that she felt when she heard that Kristin hadn't been killed vanished when she saw her lying in bed like this. She barely recognized this girl in front of her as her daughter.

"Physically she appears to be fine," the doctor continued. "However, she is in shock."

"In shock? What happened?"

"Not really sure. We haven't gotten the story yet."

"What is she doing with her lips?"

"She appears to be saying something over and over again."

"Saying what?"

The doctor leaned in close to Kristin's mouth. "I believe she's saying, 'I'll be behind you.'"

"What does that mean?"

"Again, I don't know."

"Well, is she going to be okay or what?"

"We're going to give her some fluids and something to calm her down and let her sleep. Hopefully once she wakes up after getting some rest, she'll be back with us."

"Can I stay with her?"

"Of course. Take a seat." And so she did. She would only move to go to the bathroom. Other than that her eyes didn't leave her daughter. At 7:00 that night, Kristin had finally stirred.

"Mom?" she croaked. "Where am I?"

"You're in the hospital, sweetie," Diane replied as she reached forward and took Kristin's hand. "Do you remember what happened?"

"Something happened at school, didn't it? Oh God, the kids!" Kristin screamed as she began to rise from the bed.

Diane reached forward and pushed her back down. "It's okay. Just relax. Can you tell me what happened?"

She didn't reply. She just turned away and began to weep into her pillow. The only time she would look up was when the doctor came back in to check on her. Soon after, she fell back to sleep and didn't rouse once during the night.

She still slept when Diane's phone began ringing the next morning. She didn't recognize the number but went ahead and answered.

"Is this Diane Benson?" the voice on the other end asked.

"Yes," she uttered with hesitation.

"Are you the mother of Kristin Benson who works at Stanford West High School?"

"If this is a reporter, my daughter has zero interest in speaking with you." She kept waiting for one of those scavengers to come for her.

"No. This is Detective Dixon with the Stanford Police Department. We understand that your daughter had an interaction with the shooters during the lockdown yesterday."

What was this interaction? Did this cop know more about what happened with her daughter than she did? "Yes, I believe so."

"Well, our lead investigators, Detectives Smalls and Morgan would like to schedule an interview with her to discuss what transpired. We've attempted contacting her directly, but there hasn't been an answer; so we contacted you. Could you please connect us with your daughter?"

"My daughter is in the hospital right now. And she's sleeping."

"Well, do you think it would be acceptable if our detectives came by to speak with her?"

Diane wanted to say no, afraid of how Kristin might deal with this, but knew that it was something that would need to happen. "Yes. I suppose."

"Would 12:00 on Friday be okay?"

"Sure."

"Thank you for your time." With that, the voice on the other end was gone and Diane sat alone in silence once again.

13

———

Julie and Brian had both taken the day off today, not wanting to leave Terry alone. From the moment they had gotten home yesterday, Terry had collapsed into bed and only woke up long enough to eat dinner. From there he shut himself off in his room again. The time neared 11:00 and Julie kept checking the time, wondering when her son would emerge into the world of the living.

"You need to calm down, honey," Brian said, looking up from the newspaper.

"How can he be sleeping so much?" she asked, looking towards the stairs, hoping she'd see Terry descend any minute.

"After yesterday, can you blame him for being exhausted?"

"No. It's just..."

"What?"

"I already feel like he's been drifting as of late. He doesn't talk to us much anymore to begin with. I'm worried he's going to keep all of this to himself. Won't let us help him." This had been shuffling around in the back of her mind for the past couple years. When Terry had been younger, they had been so close. She could remember when he had been about five years old, and she couldn't even leave the room without him running right behind her. She knew better than to expect that to continue as he got older. But even as recently as a couple years ago she still felt like they had a closer relationship than most parents had with their teenage kids. When he'd first started high school he would still come home every day and give her a recap of all that had happened. He still came to her for help on homework and even more amazingly, for advice with girls, but not as of late. Any time she asked about his day it would be a miracle if he gave a verbal reply. When he went out with his friends, he would be cagey about what he'd be doing. More than that, though, there would be times when it seemed that he could be borderline hostile towards her. Not that he would cop an attitude with her, but the glances that he would throw her way seemed to be filled with something akin to scorn. Any time she would raise her concerns to Brian, he would brush it off saying that it was to be expected. That she was paranoid to think that Terry could be upset with her about something.

"Jesus Christ! Is this true?" Brian suddenly cried out from behind the paper.

"What's that?" Julie asked, being shaken out of her obsessive stupor.

"I'm reading about that protest from yesterday." Typically, the story would have been front page, but now it had been pushed back to page three.

"Yeah..." Julie offered, waiting for him to get to the point.

"Did some woman make a threat against the schools?" he asked, getting to Liman's now infamous quote.

"Oh Jesus. I had nearly forgotten about that."

"So it's true?"

"Well, I don't know that it was a threat against the schools exactly. She did say something about the privileged needing to know what it was like for their kids to be killed."

"Who said that?" a voice from the living room said.

Julie looked behind her to see that Terry had finally emerged. "You're up. How are you feeling?" she asked, ignoring his question.

"Fine. Who said that about kids being killed?" he asked, getting back to his earlier question.

"A woman from the protest yesterday. She's with that Stanford Society something."

"The SSPA?"

"Uh-huh," Julie uttered, a bit concerned about how he knew about them.

"So... are they thinking that they're behind what happened?"

"I have no idea. Are you hungry? Can I make you anything?" Julie asked, desperate to change the subject.

"No. I'm fine. I think I might hang out with Johnny in a little bit."

Julie tried to hide her dissatisfaction at this. She hadn't admitted it to Brian, much less Terry, but she did not really care for Johnny. Terry had started hanging out with him late in his freshmen year, and his detachment soon followed. More than that, she didn't think Johnny a wonderful influence. She'd seen him sitting around the police station a couple times. Typically for things like trespassing or vandalism, but no matter why, she didn't like the idea of her son hanging around someone with a record.

"No, no, no. Come on and have something to eat before you go anywhere. We want to talk to you," Julie insisted.

"Mom. I told you I'm fine. I don't think I even knew anyone who died yesterday."

"But still. To have been in the midst of it. There's nothing wrong with being upset. With needing to talk to someone or..." The sound of the house phone ringing cut her off. Julie stood up and went over to answer. "Just please don't go anywhere right now," she told Terry as she picked up the phone. "Hello?" she said, answering it.

"Officer Lipton?" a familiar voice said.

"Yes?"

"This is Detective Dixon from Homicide." Julie knew the man but hadn't had much interaction with him.

"Yes?"

"Your son Terrance is a student at West High School?"

"Yes."

"Could I speak with him, please?"

"What is this concerning?"

"We're just setting up interviews with a number of students and staff from the school as part of our investigation."

"I understand. He's right here. I'll put us on speaker." She knew she didn't need to be worried, but she wanted to be a part of any conversation that Terry had with the police. She flipped on the speaker as she explained to Terry what was happening.

"Terrance?" Dixon said on the other line.

"Uh-huh," Terry replied with nervousness.

"My name is Detective Dixon. We're investigating the shooting at your school yesterday. And we were just hoping that we could speak with you. It's just a matter of routine, I assure you. Nothing to worry about. And your mother can sit in on the interview as well. So do you think you could come in tomorrow?"

"Umm... yeah, I guess," Terry said with a gulp.

"Would 2:00 at the station be okay?"

"Sure." His voice hardly went above a whisper.

"Great. Thank you. We'll see you then."

Julie hung up the phone and looked over at her son. He looked down at his feet before saying, "I'll be in my room." Julie went to call him back, but before she could utter a word, Terry had vanished. She wouldn't see him again for another hour when he came down the stairs to help usher Johnny into the house. They both started upstairs when Julie came into the room.

"Hello, Johnny," she said, daring to inch towards the two boys.

All Johnny offered in exchange was a tilt of the head accompanied with a noise akin to a grunt and a laugh. Not only that, but the look in his eyes could only be described as loathsome.

"Are you doing okay from yesterday, Johnny?"

"Uh-huh."

Julie resisted the urge to go off on a rant about simple manners, but held back, not wanting to embarrass her son.

"What are you two planning on doing?" she ventured.

Johnny looked away, refusing to dignify that question with a response. All that Terry offered was, "Dunno. Just hang out, I guess."

"Can I get you something to eat, maybe?"

"No. We're fine." At that, the boys didn't give her a chance to say another word, retreated upstairs and behind a closed door.

14

_____

Stanford had four different gun shops. Kara and Brody had visited two of them in the hopes of tracking down where the guns had come from. So far they hadn't come up with anything. The two pulled up to the third, Stanford Firearms and Ammo. Once they entered, Kara felt like she'd walked into the NRA's wet dream, every inch of the store covered with various kinds of guns. Along the side walls were a variety of rifles and shotguns. The back wall had been covered with assault rifles. A few aisles showed off the pistols. The glass counter showed off more guns along with what seemed to be a never-ending supply of ammunition.

Behind the counter, the store's lone clerk sat at the register. He sported a thin beard over a bony face with a jutting chin. With the ringing bell of the door, he snapped to attention. "Morning. What can I do for you today?" he said in greeting to the two detectives.

"I'm Detective Morgan. This is Detective Smalls with the Stanford PD," Brody said as they both flashed their badges. "We're investigating the shooting at Stanford West High School yesterday."

"Damn tragedy that is," the clerk offered.

"Yes. Well, we recovered the firearms used and we're attempting to trace them. See if we can't find out the owner."

"You think he got 'em from here?"

"We don't know. We're checking with all the retailers in town hoping to get lucky. We have the serial numbers of the weapons used and were hoping that you might take a look at your past sales."

"Be happy to. What have you got for me?"

Kara brought out a sheet with the makes, models, and serial numbers of the guns recovered. The clerk took it while putting a small pair of glasses on. "What do we have, what do we have?" he said to himself. "Looks like two Uzis and a couple Glocks." He moved over to his computer and he began typing away.

Kara and Brody stood in silence as the clerk went about his work. Kara had little hope that this would lead anywhere. Who knew if these guns had even been purchased in town at all? And if they had, who knew whose hands they had turned up in now?

The clerk got through with his search and chimed in, "Ding, ding, ding. Looks like we got a hit on those Uzis." Kara and Brody both snapped to attention. "Looks like they got bought a year ago by a Jeremy Farrah."

"Can you tell us if he's bought anything else?" Kara asked.

"Oh definitely. Man must be a collector."

"Could you print out what you have?"

"Will do." Both detectives couldn't help but feel a tinge of excitement and hope that this would prove to be a worthwhile lead.

Kara and Brody arrived back at the station where a horde of reporters had gathered outside. The moment they noticed the familiar faces of the detectives from the impromptu press conference yesterday, they all pounced.

"Detective Smalls!" one yelled, shoving a microphone in Kara's face as a camera hovered right behind her. A barrage of questions came, all of it sounding like garbled mush.

Even if she had wanted to answer them, she didn't know where she'd start. Instead, she shoved against the crowd, squirming her way through. Brody didn't have as much trouble, though, his large bulk forcing a parting of the crowd like the Red Sea. The two stepped inside, the roar of the reporters now dulled.

"They're persistent. You gotta give them that," Brody said as they made their way back to their desks.

"They're a pain in the ass," Kara replied. Taking their seats, they pulled out the notes they had so far. "So what can we find out about this Farrah guy?"

"I'm on it," Brody said as he went away at his computer. Meanwhile, Kara looked at the printout from the gun store, reviewing all that Farrah had bought. From the look of it, the guy must have been either preparing for war or stockpiling for the apocalypse. Over the years, this guy had bought ten different AR-15's, five 12-gage shotguns, and a host of pistols including Sig Sauers, Glocks, and Magnum revolvers. And that's just what had been bought at that store. God knew what else he had. "Goddammit. Who the fuck is this guy?" Kara wondered aloud.

"Jeremy Farrah. Age forty-five. Address is 4351 Clifford Boulevard. Divorced twice. And from the looks of it the guy is quite the asshole," Brody chimed in.

"Why's that?"

"Well, we have a host of domestic disturbance calls. Neighbor complaints of arguing. Concerns that he was abusive towards his wife. And, of course, there are those DUIs."

"If the guy is a wife beater, how in the hell did he manage to collect this kind of arsenal?"

"Never got charged. Went out there only for the missus to say that she wouldn't be pressing charges. Damn thing happened about half a dozen times. Asshole was basically an episode of *Cops* in and of himself."

"Jesus Christ. So what are we thinking here? You think he was behind this?"

"I don't know. Based on what we've seen so far it sure as hell seemed like it would have been a student. And do you go through the trouble of disguising your identity to only leave behind guns you know can be traced back to you?"

"I guess not. Well then what? Did he sell the guns to whoever did shoot the place up? If you're buying in bulk like he does, it would stand to reason that he's got his own little business on the side."

"Don't people usually scratch off the serial numbers when they do that?"

"Goddammit, I don't know! I'm spit-balling here."

"Yeah, yeah. Well, we're gonna want to get the guy in here to have a chat anyway, so hopefully we'll get our answers."

"Speaking of getting people in here," Kara said as she turned behind her to see Dixon at his desk. "Dixon, how are the interviews coming?"

"It's a big pain in the ass. Thank you for this esteemed honor."

"You're welcome. Now can you answer my question?"

"We're about halfway down the list. Got 'em scheduled from about 8 till 3 tomorrow so far."

"Oh my God. Maybe we'll get lucky and someone will come in and confess. Save us all the trouble."

"The likeliest of scenarios," Brody said.

"Let me have this, please," Kara pleaded before continuing. "So do we know where Farrah works?"

"Last we had was Leeson's Trucking. That was from two years ago, so who knows."

"Well, that's easy enough to find out. Give me the number." Kara picked up her phone and dialed as Brody recited Leeson's Trucking's number to her. The conversation only lasted about thirty seconds before Kara had gotten the information she needed. "Well, no shocker there," Kara said. "Got fired a month ago for coming to work drunk."

"Real winner we have here. Well, we might as well try to go by his house."

Kara and Brody pulled up to a small ranch-style home. Right away, one could see that the place hadn't been cared for much over the years. The gray shingle sidings were stained with dirt that had worn in so much over the years that it might as well have been a paint job. The little grass that still occupied the front yard had become long and patchy. The front door had been painted an orange that didn't go with the rest of the house at all. Looked like there had only been one coat, too, because the white underneath still showed through the streaks. The two walked up to the door without a word, both of them with their badges ready. Brody reached out and knocked. A couple minutes passed and he knocked again. After another couple minutes the door creaked open a bit and Farrah poked his head out.

"Yeah?" he said with a hoarse voice.

"Mr. Farrah. I'm Detective Smalls..." Kara began as she raised her badge. But as soon as it came in view Farrah disappeared as he turned and ran towards the back of his house.

"Fuck!" Brody cried as he took off to the side of the house

and hustled to the backyard. While he did that, Kara ran back to the car, hopped in the driver's seat, and took off. She peeled around the corner and headed towards the other block hoping to cut off Farrah.

Brody ran into the backyard, Farrah having busted out the back door and being a few steps ahead of him. Farrah ran right towards the fence and leapt over it. Brody followed close behind and vaulted the fence himself. "Stop!" he shouted as he gained on him. The two men flew through the yard coming up on a gate which led to the front yard and street beyond it. Farrah threw his shoulder against the gate and busted through, stumbling to the ground in the process. He jumped to his feet in a second and sprinted into the street.

Kara had made it around to the next street over in mere seconds. She pulled up to Farrah's location by the time he had made it halfway across the street. She slammed on the brakes and jumped out of the car. She ran for a few steps before throwing herself forward and tackling Farrah to the ground. He tried to crawl away, but by that point Brody had caught up and hauled Farrah to his feet and slapped cuffs on him. He led Farrah to the car and threw him in the back seat.

"Well, we certainly earned our pay for the day, didn't we?" Brody joked before going around and climbing in the passenger seat. Kara got in as well and called for additional officers to come out and help search the house. From there they drove Farrah back to his house and led him inside.

The state of the indoors made the outside look well kept. A dirty, moth-eaten carpet covered the floor. Paint peeled along the walls. Stuffing poured out multiple holes of a couch that seemed to occupy a no-man's land of the living room. A stench filled the house that Brody would later describe as being a cross between shit and B.O.

Brody led Farrah to the couch, undid the handcuffs and had

him sit. Kara went into the kitchen and retrieved two chairs. Once she and Brody sat down on them, the legs creaked, threatening to break any second.

"So, now that all that bullshit is over, let's continue where we left off," began Brody. "I'm Detective Morgan. This is Detective Smalls. We want to ask you some questions. And I'll clue you in right now, you just made me run. And I hate running. So you're not my favorite person at the moment. So it'll be in your best interest to cooperate."

"I didn't do a goddamn thing," Farrah barked.

"So is that why you ran?" Brody asked.

"I just don't mess 'round with cops."

"We're investigating the shooting at Stanford West High, yesterday," Kara said.

"I didn't have a fuckin' thing to do with that."

"Well, it would appear you did."

"How's that?"

"Mr. Farrah," Kara started as she produced the printout from the gun shop and handed it to him. "Did you purchase these weapons?"

"That a crime?"

"Just answer the question, please."

"Yeah I did. Big fuckin' deal."

"Well, two of those were used in the shooting yesterday." Kara leaned forward and pointed out the Uzis in question. Back at the station she had highlighted them.

"Motherfucker," Farrah uttered, more to himself than anyone else.

"So now you see why we're here," Brody said.

"I didn't do that shit."

"Can you tell us where you were yesterday morning?"

"Here. Usually am."

"Since you got fired, you mean?"

"That illegal now too?"

"Can anyone verify that you were here?" Kara asked.

"Yesterday? No, I don't..." Farrah trailed off. "No wait!" he jumped back in. "I was with my cousin."

"Doing what?" Brody asked.

"Nothin'. He'd stayed over the night before."

"We'll need his name and contact information," Kara said, handing over a pad of paper and pen. Farrah grabbed it and jotted it all down.

"So how the hell did two guns that are registered to you end up being used to kill twenty-eight people?" Brody asked.

"How the fuck should I..." Farrah stopped himself mid-sentence as he looked back down at the sheet. "Oh shit."

"What's that?"

"Those guns were stolen."

"Stolen?"

"That's what I said."

"Well, we don't have a report of any stolen guns from you," Kara said.

"Cause I didn't report it."

"Why wouldn't you?"

"Well..."

"Well?" Brody cut in, his patience having run out along with his breath.

"I don't know how much more I should say."

"Motherfucker." Brody sighed in exasperation.

"Mr. Farrah. You're already getting brought in for running earlier. It will go a long way towards helping your cause if you cooperate."

From outside, two cop cars pulled up and four officers walked into the house. "Thanks for coming, boys," Brody said. "Take a look around and see what you can find."

"What the fuck? I don't want ya snooping around," Farrah

objected. A quick look from all the cops in the room shut him up. The four officers then began their search.

"Wait a minute," Kara called after them. A young, baby-faced officer ran up to her, looking eager to please. "Check this out. Find out where he was yesterday morning." Kara handed him the sheet with Farrah's cousin's information. The officer ran out the door. With that done, Kara and Brody turned back to Farrah who attempted to avoid eye contact.

"So you gonna help us out?" Brody asked. "If those guns were stolen, why wouldn't you report it? You didn't think having those out in the open like that was something the police should be aware of?"

Farrah remained silent for a full minute. The whole time his eyes darted around and his mouth moved as though he couldn't figure out how to form the words he wanted to say. Kara and Brody just watched him the whole time, not saying a thing.

"Fine," Farrah finally said, apparently realizing that he didn't have many options. "The reason I have all those guns is that I sell 'em on the streets. I didn't report those stolen because I figured that'd put you onto me."

"Is it possible that you just sold those guns and lost track of it?" Kara asked.

"Nah. I keep track of that shit."

"How long ago were they stolen?" Brody asked.

"Maybe a month?"

"They stolen from here?"

"Uh-huh."

"Any other guns stolen?" Kara asked.

"Couple pistols, I think," Farrah said.

Kara nodded, assured that all the guns used had come from here.

"Well, good going. If you weren't more concerned about your

little side business, maybe we could have tracked these things down. But now twenty-eight people are dead," Brody said.

At that, Farrah's face cracked. Slowly and then all at once. His eyes began to glass up as well. "I didn't mean for nothin' like that to happen. I didn't want that."

"Well, why do you think people would be buying a gun on the black market?"

Farrah just looked on in shame. By this time a couple more units arrived. Kara and Brody had one of them take Farrah back to the station for processing. From there they joined the search of the house. They made their way to the basement where stacks of guns had been piled high. Sacks filled with cases of ammo sat in the corner. Over on a side table was a lockbox laying open. It had been stuffed with cash in no discernable order.

"What the fuck? How the hell does this happen?" Kara said. She, Brody, and the other cops went about their search.

It was pushing 8:00 when Brody finally walked in through his doorway. He felt like he'd fall asleep the second he laid down. But first things first, he needed a drink. Right next to his kitchen stood the bar that Brody had built himself a couple years ago. He had taken up woodworking. He found that the order that came with it went a long way towards keeping his mind off all the crap he saw every day.

Brody had come to the force later in life than most other cops had. He had just turned thirty when he decided to join the academy. Prior to that he had a few odd jobs, the most recent being bartender. Married too. Wife's name had been Christine. His college sweetheart. And then there was his daughter, Mandy. Things had been happy enough for the three of them until...
Ten years ago, Mandy had gone missing.

Brody's shoes had begun to fall apart and despite his hatred of having to buy new ones, he couldn't deal with Christine's nagging him about it anymore. So he relented to her wishes and headed off to the mall to buy a new pair, Mandy in tow.

He sat on a bench perusing through the different pairs, unable to find any in his size. Christine always enjoyed teasing him about his "clown feet." All around him, Mandy hopped up and down, squealing.

"Daddy, I want to go!" she begged.

"You and me both, sweetie," Brody responded. "Not much longer."

"But you said that you'd take me to the park!" she whined.

"And I will. Please stop." He continued to search the shelves, trying to ignore the headache she had started to give him. It proved a futile endeavor as she began tugging on his arm and whimpering. At that he dropped the pair he was looking at and whipped around to look at her. Christine often got frustrated with him saying that he spoiled Mandy, forcing her to play the bad guy. At this moment, he usurped that position as he made himself look every bit the bad guy. Eyes narrowed, lip quivering, vein bulging out of his forehead.

"Mandy," he uttered, making sure to hit every syllable, "you need to stop right now. Do you understand me? If you don't shut it, the only place you're going is your bedroom when we get home." Without even realizing it, Brody made it through the entire speech without blinking once, exposing his daughter to every ounce of subdued rage that laid within him. Her eyes widened and the dam broke. Brody's face softened at the sight of his daughter welling up. He started to apologize, but she turned and ran off out of the store. Brody hopped up to take off after her, but just as he stood, he clipped the shelf, sending a stream of shoes cascading onto the ground.

"Fuck!" he screamed out, looking on at the mess he had just

created. That brief delay proved to be the death knell for Mandy. Brody would never see her alive again. The last words he would ever speak to her would be ones of anger.

He and Christine had never been a couple that fought much but they went at one another that night once the police had left.

"How the fuck could you let this happen?!" She screamed at him. Brody sat before her, cowering as though he were a kid in the principal's office. He wanted to say something in his defense, but found that he couldn't muster it. All he could do was imagine what horror his daughter was experiencing, and wondering if she cried out for him. Or maybe he had scared her too much. Maybe she was glad to be rid of him.

"You son of a bitch. I can't even look at you right now." Christine left the room. The two of them barely spoke to one another for the next week. It was at that time that the police found Mandy. Her body at least. She'd been stabbed a dozen times and left on the side of the road. Brody and Christine's marriage died a month later.

For a whole month, Brody did nothing but drink himself to sleep every night. The brief moments of sobriety were filled with his fantasies of what he would do if he ever came across the sick fuck who had hurt his daughter. Thinking back to it now, Brody felt disturbed by the things that occurred to him. Things that would have been over the line in torture porn. That came to an end once the bastard had been caught above board.

Two things struck Brody when he finally got to see him in court. First, the man seemed so pathetic. Thin and wiry. Hair that had started to thin even though he was only in his twenties. Not the diabolical mastermind he had envisioned. Just some asshole with a history of kiddie porn for whom the pictures no longer sufficed. Then when it came down to it he panicked and figured killing the little girl was his best bet. Still didn't bother to wipe his prints off her. Second, seeing him in shackles, face in panic when the life sentence was handed down, provided Brody with a sense of relief that he hadn't thought possible. Soon after, Brody decided that he needed to become a cop himself. He found the thought that he could find people like the bastard who killed his Mandy more satisfying than those thoughts of revenge had been. And so become a cop he did, only to find that it suited him more than any of the other bullshit jobs he had held.

Brody threw back a couple fingers of whiskey. Once he had joined the force he'd made a point of limiting his drinking. With this case, though, he needed it. Seeing all those kids torn apart with bullets, lying in their own blood, brought images of Mandy back to him. Every time he saw one of those kids, he saw Mandy in their place. Hell, if things hadn't been cut short for her, she would have been there. With Farrah right in front of him, Brody had been tempted to wring his throat, blaming him for each of those deaths.

15

Kara and Brody readied the interrogation room. They weren't likely to get much time outside of it today, so it needed to be comfortable and stocked with anything they may require. Kara set out all their notes while Brody prepared the TV setup they had wheeled in. Their tech department had been given the unenviable task of compiling and organizing all the security camera footage so that they could pull up whatever they needed.

Kara examined the list of people they had coming in. From nine to five they had twenty different interviews. They figured most of them would go by quickly. Couldn't imagine that many had much useful information, but if this job had taught her anything it was not to assume anything. Hell, she'd just had to learn that lesson the hard way.

~

Connor sat waiting for someone to call him back for his interview. He didn't know why, but he felt guilty just being around all these cops. He'd seen other teachers and some students filter in and out the whole time he'd been sitting there. No words were spoken between any of them. Only a polite nod. To exchange hearty greetings at such a time seemed gauche.

"Connor Sullivan," a soft voice called from behind the main desk. Connor put up his hand as though he were in school and then rose to follow the officer back. He knew that Brandy must have been going nuts waiting for him at home. She had said she wanted to come with him, but he insisted that he go by himself. He needed the time alone to sort out all that happened so he could recount it accurately.

The officer led Connor to the interrogation room where Kara and Brody waited for him. They both rose from their seats to greet him.

"Mr. Sullivan. I'm Detective Smalls. This is my partner, Detective Morgan. We're leading the investigation into the shooting. Thank you for coming in," Kara said, shaking his hand. "Please take a seat." Connor took a seat across from the two. He felt even more uncomfortable coming into this room. Whole place was a small square and a dingy gray all over. A slight chill caused him to shiver as he sat down in the chair. Connor hoped this wouldn't take long. The little bit of cushion in the chair didn't go far in protecting him from the hard steel underneath.

"Can we get you anything? Coffee, soda?" Brody offered.

"I'm okay," Connor replied.

"Okay, well let's get started," Kara said as she pushed play on the recorder that sat in front of her. "First, let us assure you that this interview is entirely a matter of routine. You should not take your presence here as a sign that you are under any kind of suspicion. We just ask that you be open and honest with us because it will aid our investigation. Do you have any questions?" She rattled off the spiel that she had been reciting all day. It had already begun to lose meaning.

"No, ma'am," Connor said.

"Okay. To begin with, please state your full name and occupation."

"Connor Brian Sullivan. I teach 10th grade English at Stanford West High School."

"How long have you been working there?"

"For the last five years."

"Would you please state in your own words, your experiences during the shooting?"

Connor, hoping he wouldn't need to tell this story too many times in the days to come, began speaking. "Well... the second period had just begun and..."

"What time would that have been?" Brody interjected.

"Uhh... let's see... that would've been about 8:30."

"Okay, please continue."

"So, second period had just started when the call came over the intercom that there was a shooter in the building. So I jumped up and locked the door to my room. Shoved a cabinet in front of the door. Turned off the lights. Had the kids get against the wall." He stopped talking and replayed everything in his head, trying to figure out if there had been anything else. "Oh, and then I called 911, but they'd already been notified." Connor stopped there and watched the two detectives scribble down illegible notes on the pads in front of them. He knew they expected him to go on to the more dramatic events. He hesitated, a bit embarrassed by the whole thing.

"Please go on," Kara said, only looking up for a brief second before returning to their pad.

"So I heard someone unlocking the door..."

"How long after the announcement was this?" Brody asked.

"I don't know. Fifteen minutes or so. I wasn't really keeping track," Connor said. "Anyway, the door opens up and I see a gun. And from there it's kind of a blur." Connor's voice began to shake. "I know a couple shots went off, and then the next thing I knew, I was facing the shooter, and I... I... just sorta pushed him out of the room."

"Was it just the one shooter?" Kara asked.

"Yeah. That's the only one I ever saw. It wasn't until later that I found out that there had been more than one."

"Did you notice anything about the shooter? Height? Weight? Anything?"

"No, not really. I remember he had a mask on but I couldn't even tell you about what kind."

"That's okay. Now, we are looking at any students who may have been out of class at the time. The bathroom pass from your room listed a... Dennis Clements," Kara said, referencing her notes. "What can you tell us about him?"

"You think Dennis did this?" Connor almost wanted to laugh at this. On most days Denny looked like a breeze would push him over. The idea that he could've gunned down thirty people... it just didn't fit.

"We're simply looking at anyone whose presence we can't account for during the time of the shooting or immediately following."

"Well, he's a pretty good kid. Quiet, but smart. Never had any problem with him."

"How quiet?" Brody asked.

"Umm... very?" Connor said, unsure of how to answer. "I don't really know of any friends he has. He rarely speaks up in class. Seen him around school, though, and he's a nice kid. Helps out other people and... I... I don't really know what else to say."

"Okay. Well, did anything strange happen that morning before the shooting?"

"Well, I teach high school. Most days are kinda strange."

Brody smiled a bit at that. "Sure. But anything that stuck out that morning?"

"No. Not really."

"That's fine. We just have to ask," Kara said with a smile. "Now we have security footage of the shooting. Would you mind taking a look at the footage from outside your room with us? We just want to see if maybe it helps you remember anything else."

"Sure." Connor turned to the TV as Brody clicked away at the laptop. The screen sprang to life with the grainy black-and-white footage. Connor's story played out on the screen. He saw the shooter approach, remembering now that he had been wearing a hockey mask. His door opened up and the struggle ensued. From this angle in the hallway, you couldn't really tell what went on. Not even a whole minute had passed before the struggle ended, and the shooter fell into the hallway.

Brody stopped the video and turned to Connor. "Help you remember anything else?"

Connor hesitated, as in the back of his head some small detail called towards him. He attempted to make it out, but a dense fog clouded it from sight. "No," he finally answered, assuming that if it were all that important, that he would remember it.

"Okay. No problem," Kara said as she and Brody stood. Connor followed their example. "Thank you for coming in. Is it okay to contact you if we have any further questions?"

"Yeah. Sure."

"Great. Well, if you think of anything else, please let us know." Kara held out her card with her phone number on it. Connor took it, placed it in his wallet, gave a polite nod, and left the room.

～

Terry sat leaning back in the interrogation room chair with Julie sitting right beside him. She nudged him and motioned for him to put the legs down. Julie struggled to compose herself as she became increasingly frustrated with her son. He did not seem to be taking this very seriously.

"So, Terrance," Kara began. "You're enrolled at Stanford West High School?"

"Uh-huh," he muttered, not even looking at Kara or Brody. Julie wanted to say something but knew it would be frowned upon if she began inserting herself into the interview.

"Please answer yes or no," Kara said.

"Yes, I am," Terry told her.

"Age and grade?"

"Sixteen. I'm a junior."

"Now we have a bathroom pass here that said at the end of first period you left Ms. Merrin's government course?"

"Uh yeah, I guess I did."

"Had you made it to class by the start of second?"

"No, I hadn't."

Julie began to squirm in her seat. It almost sounded like they were accusing Terry of something. She wanted to stand up and announce that she wouldn't stand for this, but forced herself to stay seated. She knew these two were just doing their jobs.

"So when you left Ms. Merrins's class, did you head to the bathroom?" Kara asked.

Terry opened his mouth and then hovered over his words for a moment. "Yeah," he finally said.

"Which bathroom was that?"

"There's one a few doors down from her room. That one."

"Were you in there when the lockdown happened?"

"Yup."

"What did you do?"

"I was heading out of the bathroom when I heard it. That's right near a staircase, so I ran down and went outside."

"That's a long time to be in the bathroom," Brody said.

"I was taking a dump." At this Julie hung her head, not able to hide her annoyance anymore.

"Fair enough. Well, we have some security footage. If we played it for you, would you be able to point yourself out on it?"

"Ummm... yeah." Terry once again seemed confused as to how to answer. Brody clicked away and brought up a file with videos of students in the hall from shortly before the shooting. The file switched from one to another with no sign of Terry even when it landed on the camera from just outside the bathroom he had claimed to be at. As the video went on with no sign of her son, Julie looked over at Terry with a mixture of anger and confusion. She turned back to the video just as a clip of Terry walking towards an exit popped into view. She whipped her head back to him, waiting for him to say something. When it became clear that that wouldn't happen, she finally spoke up.

"That's him," Julie said while pointing at the screen. Kara and Brody looked down at the timestamp to see that the video was from 8:23am. Everyone in the room turned to look at Terry.

"Terrance. Is it possible that you were mistaken about the time that you left?" Kara asked.

"Well... I..." Terry's eyes darted everywhere as he attempted to find a way to explain himself.

"Tell them the truth, Terry," Julie directed at her son in a measured tone.

Terry lowered his head now. "I didn't go to the bathroom. I was skipping."

"Why?" Kara asked, seeming genuinely fascinated.

"Johnny and I were meeting up to smoke."

"Who's Johnny?"

"Johnny Lemming. A friend of mine." Both Kara and Brody flipped through their notes.

"We don't have a record of him being out of class," Brody said.

"I didn't end up seeing him out there. I don't know where he was."

"Anything else you want to tell us?"

"No."

"Are you sure?" Julie said again, fury rising in her eyes.

"I'm sure. I'm sorry."

"Okay then. Well, we'll be in touch if we need anything else," Kara said with a quiver in her voice. The agitation emanating from Julie towards her son had become palpable. Julie and Terry stood. She led her son out of the room assuring him that they would speak about this at home.

Dennis took a seat and hunched over the table in front of him, his hair hanging over his eyes. His mother hadn't been able to get off of work to be with him here, and his dad still hadn't gotten back from his errand to get cigarettes ten years ago. Prior to leaving for work, his mother had given him a pep talk, telling him that all would be okay. As long as he told the truth, he'd be fine. After all, he had nothing to hide.

"Would you mind looking up at us, son?" Brody asked.

Dennis lifted his head and threw his hair out of his eyes.

"So you are a student at Stanford West High School?" Kara began.

"Yeah," Dennis replied, his voice ready to shatter.

"Age and grade?"

"Tenth grade, and I'm sixteen."

"So please tell us about what happened on Tuesday morning from your point of view."

"Well, I was in the bathroom when I heard the announcement." Kara and Brody offered each other a glance. This seemed to be a popular story today.

"Yes, we have that you left Mr. Sullivan's first period to go to the bathroom. That's a long time to be in there."

Dennis didn't know how to respond, so he didn't.

"So what did you do when you heard the call for the lockdown?"

"Well, I thought of making a run for it, but I was worried the shooter would see me. So, instead, I climbed out the window."

"There's a window in the bathroom?" Brody asked, a hint of doubt in his voice.

"Yeah. It's a little high up, but I climbed up on the urinals and was able to squeeze out."

"What did you do once you got out there?"

"I ran back to the rally point and joined the other classes there."

"So there would be others that could verify that you were there."

Dennis's eyes popped open and he began to bite his lips at the realization that they may suspect him. Even just a bit. "I... I don't know. I didn't really talk to anyone. I just sorta joined the crowd."

"Okay. Well we have some security footage. Would you mind looking at it and pointing yourself out?" Kara asked.

Dennis nodded and then watched as the clips ran. Once he saw himself going into the bathroom, he told them so. From there, Kara and Brody wished him a good day and gave their cards in case he had anything else to share. He took it, jammed it into his pocket, and rushed from the room. Kara and Brody both laid their heads down on the table, grateful that their day of interviews had finally come to an end.

"I swear to God that I am never stepping foot in this room again," Brody groaned.

"So are you just never going to interrogate anyone again?" Kara said with a laugh.

"I'll do them in the damn shitter if I have to, but this room is evil."

"Well, let's not get too comfortable. We need to convene now," Kara said as she stood and gathered her materials.

"Please. Just five more minutes," he whined.

"Now," Kara said, kicking one of the legs of his chair. Brody stood, gathered his own things, and then stumbled out of the room. They headed to the conference room where a host of other officers waited, having conducted some of the interviews themselves.

"So," Kara said as she walked in. "Anything worthwhile?" One by one the officers went around and recounted the highlights of their interviews. By and large everyone told the same thing. Some kids gave some basic descriptions of the shooters. Most of it boiled down to average height and weight. In other words, nothing to go on. Some students did offer their own theories on who was responsible.

"Any names that popped up more than once?" Kara said, realizing that she was grasping at straws.

"One name that came up a few times was Dennis Clements," one of the officers called out. "Several kids described him as being quote, 'creepy as fuck,' 'a fucking weirdo,' and 'a total whack job.'"

"Well that just about cracks the case," Brody said. Still, the name stood out.

"Anything else?" Kara asked. Some mumbles and shaking of heads indicated that there wasn't. "Okay then. Leave the tapes here. Good work everyone." All the officers deposited their recordings on the table and then filed out. Kara and Brody began organizing and packing it all up when Charles, the officer who had been manning the front desk walked in.

"Detectives, we have someone here to see you," he told them.

"We don't have any more scheduled for today," Brody told him.

"It's not one of your witnesses. She says her name is Sharon Handel. Says she's with the Black Lives Matter Chapter. She was wondering if she could just have a few minutes of your time."

"Send her back," Kara said in exhaustion. Charles left to go get her.

"But we were done!" Brody said while pretending to cry.

"It shouldn't take long. We at least need to hear what she has to say." Sharon Handel walked in, dressed in a finely pressed suit. Her jet black hair hung down straight from her head. She stood in the doorway and smiled.

"Thank you for seeing me, detectives," Handel said.

"Please have a seat, ma'am," Kara said. All three of them took a seat around the table. "So what can we help you with?"

"It's our understanding that you met with Denise Liman the other day," she said.

"We can't really discuss an ongoing investigation," Brody told her.

"Well, she informed us that you did. And I just wanted to make something clear. Despite her appearance at our rally the other day, we do not condone the comments that she made. We did not know that she was going to say such things, and if we had, we never would have allowed her to speak. Those views are not shared by our movement or our organization."

"We understand that," Brody said.

"Good. We don't want anyone to think that we had anything to do with that senseless tragedy. The very thought that our rally may have delayed a police response makes us sick. And if there is anything we can do to assist in this investigation, we are happy to help."

"We appreciate that," Kara said. "Is there anything else you may need?"

"No, ma'am. That's all I needed. Thank you." Sharon Handel got up and walked out of the station. As they are wont to do, several reporters hung around the front hoping that they would catch any updates as soon as they were made available. Sharon Handel thought nothing of this at the time, but she would soon wish she had. The reporters out there noticed her exit the station and couldn't help but begin to speculate about her possible reason for being there. Could she be a suspect? Was there a connection between the rally and the shooting? Of course, they didn't have any answers to these questions, but in the age of a twenty-four-hour news cycle, only the question was needed. By the morning, all outlets had reported Sharon Handel's presence at the police station. The talking heads on Fox, CNN, and MSNBC examined this small bit of news from every possible angle. Could the shooting have been revenge for the death of Noah Spaulding? Could the rally have been scheduled for the purpose of delaying the police? And from here the social media activists jumped on the story and began inserting their views. Whether any of it was true mattered very little. It had become what everyone believed.

16

"You go in and take a seat. We are going to have a talk," Julie told her son as she ushered him into the house. Right away, Brian could see outrage painted on her face.

"What's going on?" Brian asked, walking into the living room.

"Why don't you ask your son how the interview went," Julie said, her gaze directed entirely at Terry.

"Jesus, Mom. It's not a big deal!" Terry yelled.

"Hey! Watch your tone," Brian told him.

"It is a big deal. You lied to the police! And you lied to me!" Julie yelled back.

"What is she talking about? Someone please tell me what's happening," Brian insisted.

"Terry told us that he left class to go to the bathroom and headed outside as soon as the lockdown was called. But that's not what really happened."

Brian, typically very stoic, morphed his face into one of restrained rage. "What did happen then?" he asked, trying to keep his tone in check.

Terry hesitated but finally said, "Johnny and I were skipping class to go smoke. I had left the building before the lockdown was ever called."

"Why would you lie?"

"I knew I'd get in trouble for skipping class."

"And for smoking."

"Yeah and now you are in trouble," Julie said, her voice getting louder with every syllable.

"Really, what are you going to do? Arrest me? Shoot me?!" Terry yelled back at her.

"What is that supposed to mean?"

"That's what the police do, right? Shoot kids that look like us?"

"Terrance! Watch how you speak to your mother!" Brian yelled.

"That isn't fair, and you know it," Julie said to her son. "And that has nothing to do with it."

"Sure. Brush it under the rug," Terry snapped.

"Do you think for one second that I'm okay with what happened to Noah Spaulding? It makes me sick to my stomach. I would have no problem with that idiot being locked up for shooting him. But that's not my call! I work every day to make sure those kind of things don't happen. So don't lump me in with those trigger-happy assholes!" Julie typically made it a point not to curse or yell in front of her son, but she had lost control now. It broke her heart that her son would say these things, much less think them.

"Whatever. I'm getting the hell out of here," Terry said, heading for the door.

"And where do you think you're going?"

"Over to Johnny's."

"Oh I don't think so! Come back here right now!" But by the

time Julie had finished her sentence, the door slammed shut. She headed towards it, wanting to get her son back.

Brian's hand descended on her shoulder. "Let him go. We all need time to cool off," he told her.

"Brian, he lied to us. He lied to the police. You can't tell me for one second that you're okay with that."

"Of course I'm not. But yelling at him isn't going to change anything."

"For God's sakes. Thanks for the support." Julie turned her back and headed upstairs. She went right into Terry's room. She knew now that he was smoking. God knew what else. She began to rummage around his room, kicking aside dirty clothes that were strewn all over the floor. Looking under the bed that had been littered with trash. She went over to his dresser and opened up the top drawer. It had been filled with a random assortment of pens and various knick-knacks Terry had collected over the years. Along with a pill bottle filled with marijuana. That only captured her attention for a moment because underneath it was a familiar red pamphlet. She picked it up to see "Stanford Society of Police Accountability" plastered on the front. She'd seen them around town while on patrol. Julie picked it up and went through it, reading their mission statement. The line that most caught her eyes read, "*We will meet violence on our people with violence. We will make them feel our pain.*" Julie's stomach dropped at that. *Does Terry actually believe this*? she thought. She never had any delusions that she was a perfect parent, but until this moment, she'd never felt like she had failed him. She'd always taught him that violence solved nothing, but apparently she hadn't taught it well enough.

As Julie reeled from what she'd just found, a small thought passed through her mind. It sat there for only the briefest of moments, but thoughts, especially the dark ones, often act like a virus. It latches on and refuses to let go. It may lie dormant for weeks, days, and years, but it is always there. And it begins to multiply and infect us and all that we do. For the briefest of moments, Julie wondered if Terry may have had something to do with the shooting.

17

W hile Stanford may not have been a small town such as Mayberry, in the age of social media it may as well have been because stories from the shooting had spread like wildfire in only a couple days. One of the most popular stories was that of the young teacher, Kristin Benson, who had led her students into the line of fire, getting two of them killed. Some lamented how she must feel. Some damned her, blaming her for those deaths. All were fascinated by it. For that reason, the first interview would be a huge story, and every reporter in town wanted it.

Some well-placed sources revealed that Kristin was completing her stay in the hospital. Kyle Brennan, the same reporter who had called Connor, stalked the halls, looking out for Kristin's room. On the second floor he came across it.

Inside, Kristin threw on her jacket, getting ready to leave. Beside her, Diane stood, with the look of concern that hadn't left her face since she first learned of the shooting.

"Do you want to grab something to eat on our way home?" Diane asked. She had insisted that Kristin stay with her for a few days. She felt pleased when Kristin agreed without argument.

"No. I just want to go home," Kristin whispered. She hadn't said anything above a whisper the last couple days. She appeared as though she had aged twenty years in that time. Her brown hair was now streaked with bits of gray. Crow's feet formed around her eyes. Kristin headed towards the door, her shoulders hunched. Her eyes and cheeks were a dark red from the tears she had cried during her police interview this morning.

Kristin hadn't been happy to hear that her mother had scheduled it but understood that it needed to happen. When the two detectives had entered, she refused to even look them in the eyes. Brody and Kara took a seat next to Kristin's bed and spoke in hushed tones, not wanting to upset what was clearly a troubled young lady.

"We're detectives Morgan and Smalls," Brody told her. "We just want to get some information from you. It shouldn't take long." Brody looked at Kristin with a kind face that had a small but unmistakable bit of love in it. Kristin looked to him what he imagined Mandy would look like had she been given the chance to grow up. He needed to hold back tears as he spoke to her. "Does that sound okay?" he continued.

Kristin merely nodded.

"Okay. Please tell us what happened."

Kristin looked away, staring at nothing for a couple minutes before she began speaking. "My second period had just started. The call for lockdown came on. My room was only a little ways down from the exit, so I decided we'd leave the building. I started pointing the kids out of the room and towards the door. They were going. They were almost all out when something happened." At this point, Kristin broke down and began to sob into her hands. No one said a word. They let her cry, which she did for two straight minutes before she started trying to speak again. From there her words came in hard gasps.

"Is there any way we can do this later?" Diane asked.

Brody opened his mouth to respond when Kristin finally regained control long enough to say, "No. I want to get this over with." Everyone in the room nodded and then looked down at the ground until she spoke again. "I wasn't even sure what happened," she continued. "Suddenly there was a loud bang inside my ears and two of the students dropped to the ground. And then I had red all over me, and then... and then... I'll be behind you. I'll be behind you," she began to repeat again. Those words then gave way to deep heaves.

Brody and Kara looked at each other and nodded. They both stood and Brody offered a polite, "Thank you for your time." The two left the room as Diane stood and wrapped her daughter in a deep hug.

An hour passed before Kristin felt ready to leave. Diane opened the door for her and Kristin headed into the hall, head sunk down. Right outside the door, Kyle Brennan waited for them.

"Kristin Benson?" he said, leaping out in front of her. She jumped, almost falling back into the room. "Name is Kyle Brennan. I'm with the *Stanford Tribune*. I was wondering if I might have a few words with you." Kristin stared at him in shock as though he had just threatened her.

"Leave my daughter alone!" Diane yelled as she edged her way out and pushed Brennan back. "Who the hell do you think you are?! Leave my daughter the fuck alone!" Diane screamed.

"Please, I don't mean any harm. I just want a couple minutes of your time," Brennan pleaded.

"Mom. What's going on?" Kristin asked, not able to make any sense of the situation.

"Hey!" a voice called from down the hall. "What's going on?" Everyone turned to see a security guard hustling down towards them. Diane took advantage of the distraction, grabbed her daughter by the arm, and escorted her away. On their way through the halls and the parking lot to the car, people stole glances at Kristin followed by whispers. Her image had been circulated enough by now that there were few places she would be able to go in town without being recognized. She did nothing but look at her feet the entire way. She continued to during the car ride.

Diane let her be and didn't attempt to say anything until they got home. Once they walked in the door, she said with some hesitation, "Honey, why don't I make us something to eat and we can sit down and watch a movie?"

"No. I want to lie down," Kristin said. Diane started to protest, wondering how Kristin could possibly still want to rest after all that time in the hospital but then thought better of it. Kristin headed back towards her childhood bedroom. She pushed open the door and looked at what lay before her. Multiple shelves lined end to end with books. Photos of her with her friends taped to the walls. Right now it all meant nothing to her. The only thing that interested her was the bed which she headed towards. She wrapped herself in her blanket and promptly cried herself to sleep.

Later that day, Kara and Brody took up residence in the interrogation room once again. This time, Johnny Lemming sat across from them. They both felt glad that they got turned onto Johnny in the first place. With him not showing up on attendance, they would have missed him on the security footage altogether. He leaned back in his chair and looked up at the ceiling as though two cops weren't trying to ask him questions.

"Johnny, would you mind, son?" Brody said.

"Uh-huh," Johnny replied, coming back to the ground.

"So we understand that you chose to skip second hour

yesterday. Terry Lipton told us that the two of you planned on leaving school to go smoke?"

"Gonna arrest me for that?" Johnny said as he drummed his knuckles on the table.

"Why didn't you get counted as absent?"

"How the hell should I know? Attendance probably hadn't been entered."

"Terry also said that he never saw you out there," Kara said.

Johnny just shrugged.

"So where were you?" she asked.

"How long is this going to take?" Johnny responded, ignoring the question.

"Until you answer all our questions. So where were you?"

"I ducked into a classroom during passing time so no one would see me ditch. Heard the alarm, so I hid out in there."

"You were on the ground floor. Why not slip out the window?" Brody asked.

"For all I know, someone was waiting out there to pop me."

"Let's see," Brody said as he brought up the security footage. "When you see yourself, let us know."

Johnny stared on at the images with a glaze over his eyes. After a few moments, he elicited a sound to indicate that he'd seen himself on screen. Kara and Brody looked on, seeing that Johnny really did hide away in a classroom as he'd told them. Fast-forwarding to the end of the shooting, Johnny was seen escorted out of the same room by a policeman.

"Did you see anything?" Kara asked, frustrated at another dead end.

"Nope," Johnny said, popping the "p" sound.

~

As soon as they let him out, Johnny raced towards the exit, not wanting to spend another second in this "pig pen." He chuckled to himself as he thought of his little turn of phrase. He'd have to remember that. As he descended the outside stairs, Terry sauntered up, having waited around the corner for him.

Johnny took one look at his friend, and muttered, "Motherfucker." With that he turned around and headed the other way. Terry took off after him. The two boys traversed a whole block before Johnny finally turned around. With a brusque shove, he directed Terry into a small alley.

"What the hell do you want, man? And what the fuck are you doing hanging around outside like that?" Johnny demanded.

"I wanted to see how it went. What'd you tell them?" Terry asked.

"Hell of a lot less than you did, that's for sure."

"They had me on fucking camera. And my mom was right there. I didn't have a choice."

"Whatever, man."

"So, I think we need to put a stop on things."

"Why?"

"We just got questioned by the cops. Not really a good time to be starting shit. Especially with my mom breathing down my neck."

"To hell with that. And them. And your mom."

Terry bristled a bit at that last dig.

"Get me those cop's addresses like you said you would. With every one chasing their tails, now is perfect." Johnny didn't wait for a response. He was done talking to the snitch in front of him.

18

Howard Park stood in the center of downtown and had been named after Clifford Howard, Stanford's longest serving mayor. It stretched to a little over three acres and served as a popular attraction to Stanford families. Teenagers would often occupy the baseball field while the younger kids would run around on the playground.

On the Saturday following the shooting, what drew a crowd was the memorial service being held for the victims. A group of seniors contacted Principal Devin for help in organizing it. A Facebook invite went out and the town rallied together. So now a group of around 200 gathered at noon and stood in silence waiting for Principal Devin to begin speaking. He stood at the front of the crowd, a board featuring the pictures of all the victims had been erected behind him. Towards the back, Connor stood, keeping his head down. Over the past couple days, additional care packages had ended up on his doorstep and other reporters had called. He hoped to avoid attention and then be out before anyone noticed.

"Thank you all for coming out today," Principal Devin said, speaking into the microphone that had been set up. "At times of such tragedy, it is very easy to fall into despair. But it is by coming together like we have today, that we get through these hard times. Right now we all have many questions. Who did this? Why? Could we have done something to prevent it? I wish I had answers to these questions, but I don't. However, there is something that I do know. I know where we go from here. We go forward, and we do it together. But in going forward, we must always remember those who have been left behind. And that is what we do today. We remember. So now in honor of those we have lost, let us share a moment of silence."

For the next minute, all that could be heard amongst the crowd were the few stifled cries of those who mourned. Connor looked on at it all and tried not to think of a similar memorial he had attended a few years ago for a student.

Once the minute came to an end, Devin spoke up again. "Now I would like to invite people in attendance to come up and share a few words in remembrance of those who have been lost." At first, no one moved, as though each person dared everyone else to be the first to speak. Eventually, a young girl did walk up front and spoke at length about her boyfriend who had been killed. After that, student after student came forward and shared. Some shared their experience from the shooting. Others spoke about their friends who had died. Others just spoke at length about the tragedy of it all. Over the course of an hour, thirty-two different people addressed the crowd.

After everyone had spoken their piece, Devin took up the microphone. "Thank you everyone. Those were all wonderful sentiments. Now as you can see behind me, we have a poster in remembrance of the victims," he said, gesturing behind him. "Before you leave, please come up and write a message. It will be displayed in the main hall at school so that generations to come can honor and remember those we have lost. The Stanford West community is a strong one, and we will not be brought down.

Thank you, everyone, for coming." With that the crowd began to break up. Some departed immediately. Others took to the poster and waited their turn to write their message.

Connor turned to head back to his car when he saw Richard idling by himself. He stood beneath a tree simply staring straight ahead, a look of frustration on his face. "Richard. You okay?" Connor asked, walking up to him.

"Hey, Mr. Sullivan," Richard replied, not even looking at him. "Whole thing is bullshit."

"How's that?"

"We don't honor anyone by doing this. Just do this to make ourselves feel better."

"Well, we need to make ourselves feel better at times like this."

"Not working for me. I came here hoping it would help, but it doesn't. Natalie is still gone. I could sign a thousand posters and it won't change a thing."

"People grieve in different ways. You just need to find what works for you."

"I don't know that anything will."

"Pour yourself into something. Must have some college applications you can fill out."

"What's the fucking point? I just... I don't know."

Connor sighed, feeling helpless. "Listen, Richard, I really shouldn't do this, but if you need someone to talk to... give me a call." Connor recited his number and Richard typed it into his phone.

"Thanks. I'll see ya around." With that he took off.

Connor turned and walked to his car. He opened the door and began climbing in when from behind him he heard someone call his name.

"Mr. Sullivan! Wait!" a young girl cried out.

Connor turned and saw Theresa Marrow, a girl from his

second hour, running towards him. Right on her tail, an older woman waved. "Hi, Theresa," Connor said, having a bad feeling of what this would entail.

"Hey. This is my mom," Theresa said, motioning to the older woman who had caught up with her.

"Mr. Sullivan," Theresa's mother said in a soft, admiring voice. Connor expected her to continue, but instead, she just stepped forward and wrapped Connor in a hug. "My daughter is alive because of you. You're our hero."

Connor gave her an awkward pat on the back before pulling away from the hug. "Ms. Marrow, thank you. But I really didn't do anything. I'm just glad that she's okay."

"Well, if there is ever anything we can do for you, please let us know," Ms. Marrow continued, wiping a tear from her eye. Right beside her, Theresa looked over with an ear-to-ear grin on her face.

"Thank you," Connor said, forcing a smile. The three of them stood there for a moment saying nothing before they all seemed to give silent consent to moving on. Connor slipped into his car and drove off.

19

―――――

"Okay, so where do you stand so far?" Captain Barron asked. The force had gathered in the bullpen of the station for an update. It was Monday now, about a week after the shooting. Barron's eyes became fixed on Kara, expecting to hear good news from her. She had spent the entire weekend reviewing the evidence. All of Saturday itself spent reviewing every inch of security footage. She hoped to see anything that might hint at someone. But there wasn't anything there. Nothing concrete at least. Except one thing did stand out. It came from the footage of Jason being pushed to the ground outside of Connor's room. As he got up, Michael walked towards him. Jason almost seemed to flinch at his presence. Michael's simple point over his shoulder appeared full of wrath. Could he have been the one calling the shots? From there she went to the moment right outside of Kristin's room. In it Jason busted from the bathroom and it looked like he might jump from out of his skin. The shot he fired went wild. Had those two students not been right in front of him, he probably wouldn't have hit a thing. And then he just took off running, leaving an easy victim sitting there. Whoever laid beneath the mask didn't seem fully committed to what they were doing. If they could find Jason, it might not take much to get him to flip on Michael. She felt happy to find this but knew she would need more for Barron. Every time he walked by her, she could feel his judgment.

She also looked around at everything preceding the shooting and right at the very end. She stared at the images of students heading in and out of bathrooms and classrooms. Every time she looked it over, something felt off. She couldn't put her finger on what, but knew something was wrong.

From there, she looked at the end where Michael and Jason charged into the final classroom, not to be seen again. Kara remembered seeing this classroom when she and Brody surveyed the building. Just standing in that room and looking at the carnage made her feel light-headed. *Why did this entire classroom get wiped out?*

Kara shuffled through her weekend activities, but knew that she couldn't offer up feelings as a measure of progress. "We finished up interviews Friday. Have plenty to go through from them still," Kara said matter-of-factly to Barron, attempting to display more confidence than she actually had.

"Anyone stand out?"

"Nothing concrete, but there are a few who theoretically could have carried it out."

"Their names?"

Brody glanced down at the pad in front of him and read off the names. "Dennis Clements, Johnny Lemming, Terrance Lipton, William Holland, and Larry Stuart." At the back of the room, Julie bristled at the sound of her son's name. She could feel a few eyes fall upon her, but thankfully no one said anything. And the name didn't seem to register with Barron.

"So what about this Farrah guy?" Barron asked.

"His alibi checks out, and I find it hard to believe that a guy like that could have carried out the kind of organized shooting we're looking at. Guy can't even piss without getting half on the floor," Brody reported.

"So do we believe that his guns were stolen?"

"It's certainly possible. An infant could probably get into that house unsuspected."

"So who would have known that he was stockpiling?"

"Sweep of the neighborhood suggests it could be just about anyone," Kara answered. "Sounds like most everyone suspected that he had something illegal going on."

"What about the SSPA?"

"Still waiting on a warrant to search the place."

"I'll see what I can do about getting that moved along."

Kara stared over at Brody in surprise, thinking, *Is he actually being supportive?*

"What about forensics? Anything?" Barron continued.

"Everything on the clothes came on Friday. Nothing useable," Kara answered.

"Nothing?!"

"The bleach made sure of that."

"Who the fuck are these people?" he wondered aloud. Everyone looked around, wishing that someone had the answer.

"Anything else?" Barron asked.

"Not at the moment," Brody said. Kara felt relieved that he said that, not wanting to see the righteous indignation of Barron's face if it had come from her. She looked to offer Brody a thankful glance, but he barely even noticed her. He hadn't even looked her in the eyes this morning. When they had come in, he shielded his gaze and only extended cursory greetings. Very different from his usual nature. Kara felt taken aback by the haggard man that sat in front of her now. Dark bags sat underneath his eyes and his lips were chapped.

What Kara didn't know was that while she spent her weekend engrossed in security footage, Brody had spent his deep in a bottle. He had begun it looking over his case files. He reviewed the photos from the school but every time he saw Mandy lying there instead. He didn't understand what was happening to him. He had seen plenty of dead bodies in his time on the force, and it had never had this kind of effect on him. But he had just never had to see something quite like this before. Most of the cases he investigated were robberies or domestic disputes gone horribly wrong. But seeing all these kids torn in half by bullets... it just didn't happen here.

Originally, he had only meant to have a couple drinks to take the edge off. Those couple soon became several, however. Those several became enough that he lost count. Brody laid on his couch, plowing through his bottle of bourbon. The world swam before him and then the next thing he knew, he held his phone and heard Christine on the other end.

"Hello?" she said from wherever the hell she lived now.

"Christine?" Brody said, surprised to actually hear her voice.

"Brody, is that you?"

"Umm..." That was all he could manage.

"Brody, what's wrong. Have you been drinking? You can't call me when you're like this." The line went dead. The next morning, Brody didn't even remember calling until he looked at his phone. He debated whether he should call her back and explain himself. Try a little mea culpa. But best to let sleeping dogs lie. He laid where he was and thoughts on her and the train wreck of their marriage. The way she refused to even acknowledge him in court when their divorce had been finalized. That is until the end when she walked up and in a voice like she was reading from a textbook, said that she never wanted to see or hear from him again. He kept meaning to delete her number from his phone, but he knew the second that he did, she really would be gone. Those seven digits were all he had left of her. And she was all he had left of his daughter.

He had considered calling out today, but knew that wasn't an option in the midst of all this. Still, he felt like an ass coming in like this for all to see, most of all Kara. He had never told her about Mandy. Hell, she didn't know that he had ever been married. He could only imagine what she thought of him at the moment, so all he offered her was a small frown, and then he looked away.

"So where are you going from here?" Barron asked, snapping Brody and Kara's attention away from each other.

"We're going to look into the few kids who could have done it. And once we can, we're looking further into the SSPA," Kara said.

"What's the actual likelihood that they really orchestrated this?"

"Won't know until we look. Maybe one of the members has some connections to the school. We'll see."

"Okay. Get to work." Kara looked down at her desk, but Barron soon interrupted her with a brisk, "Smalls, come back into my office." Kara and Brody both stood up but Barron then clarified with, "Not you, Morgan. You stay here and get down to it." Kara tried to express her worry to him but he simply sat back down and dug into a drawer, pulling out some Tylenol.

Kara stood and made the walk back to Barron's office. In reality, everyone busied themselves with their own work, but in Kara's mind they all watched and judged her. Once in the office, she took a seat and stared straight ahead.

"So," Barron belted out as he fell back into his chair, "we heard from Mr. Llewellyn and his attorney. They've made an offer."

Ugh. I really don't have the time to deal with this bullshit. "Yes? What is it?" Kara asked.

"They'll settle for 500K and your badge."

"Jesus Christ. You can't be serious."

"That's what they want."

"He's just being a vindictive little shit."

"Let's tone it down a bit, okay? While that may be true, it doesn't mean this isn't something that we have to deal with."

"Well, let them bring this to a judge. He'll laugh them out of the courtroom and then he'll be left with nothing."

"Well, I've discussed this with our attorneys and they don't feel like that's wise at this point in time."

"What, so I have to hand in my badge because some spoiled rich boy says so?"

Barron gave a sharp tsk and continued, "I didn't say that. But we can't afford to let this go to court at the moment."

"Why not?" But the moment she asked, she thought, *Of course they can't.*

"Do you mean besides the twenty-eight dead people and the entire country watching us to make sure we don't fuck it up? Plus, it's only a matter of time before Noah Spaulding's parents bring a suit. We don't need any more fucking publicity."

"I understand," Kara said, finally looking away.

"Yeah. And so does he. He knows we're desperate to end this, so he's going to try to exploit it."

"Well then he's a sociopath."

"Granted. Anyway, we're going to make a counter-offer. Haven't decided the details, but it will probably entail offering more money in exchange for you keeping your badge."

"Fair enough."

"In the meantime, get this damn thing solved. And soon."

"Yes, sir," Kara said, swallowing her disgust.

"All right. You can go now." Kara stood, exited the office, and walked back to her desk. Brody still sat at his desk, poring over the case file, a bottle of water beside him.

"So what's going on?" Brody asked.

"I don't want to talk about it," Kara told him.

"Whatever. So where do we go from here?"

"Let's see what we can find out about these five kids."

"It would be helpful if we could see the file the school has on them."

"Yeah, well we can't do that without a warrant now, can we?" Kara barked at him, still seething over her conversation with Barron.

"What the fuck is the matter with you?"

"Me? You look like a horse trampled you on your way in today. We've got a fucking job to do."

At that Brody began to dig around on his desk.

Kara rolled her eyes and said, "What the hell are you doing?"

"Looking for my proctologist's number, so he can remove that stick from your ass."

"Not everything needs to be a damn joke. I don't know about you, but I'd like to find the SOB who gunned down twenty-eight people."

"Fair enough. Go do it, Serpico." With that Brody stood up and headed towards Julie who prepared to set out on her patrol.

"Lipton," he said as he approached her. "I was wondering if I could have a few minutes before you take off."

Julie shut her eyes, and stifled back a moan. She wanted to take a run for it, avoid the issue, but knew that wasn't an option. "Sure," she said, resigning herself to the situation. The two of them walked back to an interrogation room. Both of them took a seat.

"So you can probably assume what this is about," Brody told her.

Julie merely nodded.

"Okay. Well, I don't want you to think that we're considering your son a suspect or anything at the time. We just can't entirely rule anyone out until we're sure of their whereabouts at the time of the shooting."

"I understand, but I know as much as you do about what he was doing."

"Of course. I was just wondering if you might be able to help us understand him. What is he like?"

"Are you asking me to incriminate my son?"

"Hardly. We just want a clear picture of who he is. His interests, his..."

"My son isn't an angel, but he's certainly not a killer."

"Not saying that he is."

Julie stood up and continued, "So unless you have something concrete, I don't really have anything to say."

"Fine. I'm sorry to bother you," Brody said while flopping his head down onto the table listening. He sat there motionless, letting out a groan. He felt like a garbage truck kept backing up onto his head.

Back at her desk, Kara had just received a phone call from Stanford's Superintendent Sherri Hill. "Ms. Hill, nice to hear from you. What can I do for you?"

"Well, the school board just met to discuss when classes can resume at our schools. As you can understand, we are concerned about the possibility of them returning when we don't even know who was behind this incident," Sherri said.

"Of course. I can understand that."

"So, can you give me any indication of when it might be safe for our students?"

"Ms. Hill, you understand that I can't discuss the investigation with you while it's still ongoing. And even if I could, there's no guarantee of when it would be resolved."

"Yes. Understandable. But should we be worried about further attacks if classes were to resume prior to you solving this case?"

"Ms. Hill, again that's almost impossible to say at this point.

We have no reason to believe that further attacks are planned, but nothing can be ruled out at this moment."

Sherri said nothing to this, just sighed in exasperation. "Okay," she continued after a moment. "Well, there are students who are in need of materials that were left at school. Would it be possible for us to allow them in to do that?"

"I would recommend having a police presence there just in case," Kara said, and then a switch flipped in her head. How the hell had she not thought of this before? Maybe they didn't have enough for a warrant to see any student's record, but they didn't need one to search a locker. "But there is one thing I ask for before anything is done. There are some lockers that we'd like to search first."

"What are you looking for?"

"We won't know that until we find it, I'm afraid."

"Well, I don't see that being a problem. When would you like for this to happen?"

"As soon as possible."

"I'll talk to Principal Devin, but I imagine we could arrange for that to happen tomorrow. Will that be okay?"

"Perfect. Thank you very much, and I'm sorry that I couldn't be of more assistance to you." They both hung up. Kara jumped from her seat and ran back to the interrogation room to find Brody sitting slumped down in his seat. He didn't even look over at her when she entered. Kara shook her head at the sight. "Busy?" she asked.

"Extremely. What can I do for ya?"

"We're searching lockers at West tomorrow. With any luck we'll find something worthwhile."

"Sounds like a blast. Can't wait."

Kara opened her mouth to say something else, but stopped herself, wanting to avoid another spat with him. Instead, she headed back to her desk.

After a bit, Brody came back to their desk and both of them went about the task of looking busy. An hour passed before Barron headed up to them.

"Morgan and Smalls. You have your warrant," he told them, waving a sheet of paper in the air. "So get off your ass and go do some actual work." Neither wasted a moment as they rose out of their stupor and headed towards the door. They gathered two officers to assist in the search and were on their way.

On the ride over, Brody and Kara didn't say a word to each other, just accepting the tension that rode with them. They pulled up to the crack in the wall that was the SSPA and charged inside, the two officers right behind them. They ignored the creaking and splintering of the stairs, both determined to find something in the midst of all this. At the bottom of the stairs stood Denise Liman, glaring them down the entire time.

"Was there something else you needed, detectives?" she asked.

Brody presented the warrant. "We have that warrant you requested. Now if you would please stand aside while we have a look around."

Liman grabbed the warrant from him, read through it with a look of doubt on her face. Everyone else just headed right past her and searched the tiny basement. Kara headed to a set of filing cabinets and yanked open the drawers. In one cabinet, every drawer had been lined with files about different police shootings through the years. She pulled each one of them out and instructed one of the officers to begin perusing them for anything that stood out. From there she moved on to the next cabinet. There seemed to be no rhyme or reason to what this one had been filled with. She started to rummage through it as well.

"Okay, Ms. Liman. So how about I get a look at a list of your members," Brody said at the other end of the room. Her only response was a glare of derision before she headed into her office and began digging around in her desk. She extracted a single sheet and handed it over. Brody looked it over to see a list of ten names. "So you're not exactly bursting at the seams with people trying to get in are you?"

"We make do with what we have, Detective Morgan," Liman told him.

Brody looked it over, looking for any standout names. "Is this really everyone you have?"

"Other people come and go. Volunteers and such. Those are the ones who have contributed and are full members."

"So these volunteers and such... Any list of them?"

"We may have sign-in sheets from some of our meetings. I can't guarantee anything though. We don't hang on to them for that long."

"Well, let me see what you do have," Brody said with a smirk.

They sifted through all the basement had to offer, packing up what they deemed valuable enough to take a closer look at. As all these materials got hauled out to the cars, a crowd had begun to gather to see the action. People clambered for a view, eager to see the proceedings, so they could relate the exciting story to their friends. None of them could truly say what was happening or why, but to everyone gathered, that didn't seem necessary. The mere presence of the cops here said all that needed to be said. Why else would they be here unless it had to do with the shooting? For many who had had their doubts when the story first broke, this would prove enough to convince. For those who believed it straight away, this was the confirmation they so desperately wanted.

20

The next morning, Kara and Brody got an early start and had arrived at West High by 7:00. They stood at the front doors waiting for Principal Devin to meet them. Other than a perfunctory greeting once they showed up, nothing was said. For the second day in a row now, Brody showed up looking like he'd had the shit kicked out of him. Meanwhile, Kara just tried to stave off the cold, this morning being far more brisk than it had been as of late.

Devin strolled up to the two, pulling out a set of keys. "Good morning, detectives," he said as he passed by them and unlocked the doors. "Do you really think you'll find something worthwhile?"

"Maybe. Maybe not," Kara said. She and Brody followed him inside. They went straight into his office where Devin flipped on his computer.

"It feels strange being back here. Haven't stepped foot in here since the morning of. I can't even imagine how we'll finish out the year. Whenever we do get back here that is," Devin said as he waited for the computer to warm up. "So whose lockers are we going to be taking a look at today?" he asked as he signed in to his computer. Kara handed over a list with the five students' names on it.

"What makes you want to look into these five?" Devin asked.

"Can't really get into that," Brody said, his voice sounding like a cement mixer.

"I find some of these names a little hard to swallow for this."

"Like who?"

"Well, Brandon Hoffman and Terrance Lipton are honor roll students. Plus, isn't Terrance's mother a cop? Larry Stuart and Johnny Lemming are the only ones who are frequent flyers, discipline-wise." Devin typed away at his computer and brought up the records of lockers. He jotted down the locker numbers next to the names and then stood up. "All right. Here we go."

The three of them went around to the different lockers. The first one they came to belonged to Brandon Hoffman. He had been listed as absent the day of the incident and had stated he'd been home alone during the shooting, so they couldn't rule him out. Devin pulled out a small key and opened the locker. Inside, a stack of books were all arranged, getting smaller as the stack grew. Tucked in beside the books were a series of folders. Brody stood, writing down all they found while Kara looked through them. Certainly nothing in there to suggest a psychopath in hiding. All of it got put back and they moved on.

The next locker they came to belonged to Larry Stuart. Once it got opened, it seemed as if Larry was the Goofus to Brandon's Gallant. Larry also hadn't been at school the day of the shooting, but he seemed to have just decided to not show up. When interviewing him, his answer to why he hadn't gone to school was a, "I don't know." Far from a neat pile, only a couple books were in this locker and looked to have been tossed in. The cover on one of them had started to rip away from the binding. Other than that, various papers sat in there, most of them torn or crumpled up. Kara went through them, seeing that they were mostly some incomplete homework assignments.

Johnny's locker had a backpack stuffed inside along with a few books. A couple notebooks filled the backpack that Kara threw to the side, but what did catch her eye was a flyer for an SSPA meeting. Kara held this up to Brody. He responded with a smirk and a nod and recorded it.

Terry's locker offered little of interest. Last, they came to Dennis's locker. What they did find here was a sketchpad. As Kara flipped through it some of the pictures caught her attention. In one of them a man lay in a pool of blood with a large sword sticking out of his chest. In another, the Marvel character, The Punisher stood atop a pile of bodies with two assault weapons in his hands.

"Well, that's a bit disconcerting," Brody mentioned. Kara turned to finish the search. She reached in and pulled out a small book. Looking at it, it didn't appear to be one that she recognized at all. The cover read *Rage* by Richard Bachman. The image sent a chill down her as it featured a young man sitting on what appeared to be a teacher's desk with a pair of legs on the ground, presumably belonging to a dead woman.

"Any idea what this is?" Kara said, passing it off to Brody.

He took it and turned it over, glancing at the plot summary. As he read, his eyes grew larger and larger.

"What is it?" Kara asked, concerned that he seemed to be going pale.

"This thing is about a school shooting," Brody said, his eyes never leaving the book.

"Are you shitting me?" Kara asked. Behind Brody, Devin shifted from foot to foot as if he might take off running at any moment.

"I think this would certainly elevate the kid to a person of interest, wouldn't you?" Brody asked as he handed the book back to Kara. She put it all back in place feeling a bit disappointed by what they had found.

~

The next day, Brody walked in half an hour late. Kara looked him up and down, noticing that his 5 o'clock shadow now seemed to be an 8am shadow. His clothes conspicuously the same ones he'd had on yesterday. As he passed by Kara, it smelled as if he'd spent the night at an oil refinery.

"Good of you to make it," Kara said, not bothering to look up at him.

"I looked up that book," Brody said through a phlegmy throat.

"And?" Kara said, looking up.

"It's a Stephen King book. Wrote it years ago under a pen name."

"Yeah. Okay."

"Thing has been out of print for a long time. It was found connected to a few different actual shootings so he asked that it get pulled. You can't find it anywhere."

"Shit. But..."

"But what?" Brody asked as he sank into his desk chair.

"Whoever did this," Kara responded as she sat. "They covered their tracks. They knew where to go. Knew where they wouldn't be seen. Do you really think after going through all of that, he would leave a book like that in his locker? He'd have to have known we'd end up looking."

"Maybe he thought he'd have time to get it out of there. Maybe he forgot it was in there."

"Yeah. Possibly. What about the Lemming kid? He had the SSPA flyer in his locker. We've been looking for a connection between this and them. Maybe this is it. And besides, there's two shooters. If the Clements kid is one of them, who the hell was the other? From what we hear, he's not exactly the star quarterback."

"Get with the times, Breakfast Club. The dynamics have changed."

"Whatever. My point is, that we already know that Lemming is friends with Lipton. We can't account for either of them at the time of the shooting."

"Well, we also have Lemming on video as having come out of the same classroom he went into. The shooters got out of the building."

"Maybe he climbed back in."

"You don't think any of the outside cameras would have caught him if he'd done that?"

"Not if he knew to avoid them. Which he certainly seemed to."

"Well shit. So basically we're still back squarely at having fuck all. Where the hell do we go now?"

"You think there's a snowball's chance in hell that we get a warrant based on any of this?"

"Based on a book and some drawings? Hell no. Based on a flyer? Fuck no."

"So what do we do then?"

"Bring them back in, I guess. Maybe we can get them to talk."

"I don't like Clements for this."

"Why not?"

"I have a tough time buying him as a cold-blooded killer. Looks like if you touched him he'd break."

"It usually is the quiet ones."

"I don't know. Just doesn't feel right."

"Has any part of this case felt right?"

21

From the moment that Kristin got back from the hospital, other than to go to the bathroom, she had come out of her room four times. The first time was Friday night when her mother had demanded that she come eat her dinner at the table with her. She ate the entire meal in silence. Every comment Diane threw at her bounced off like a ball hitting a brick wall. For an hour, Kristin picked away at the pasta on her plate. She'd barely gotten half of it down when she announced that she felt full and headed back to her room. From inside the living room Diane would occasionally hear the sound of the TV. Seemed as though it never stayed on one channel for long. The steady beat of bass would thump the door. Beneath it the sound of Kristin's tears bled through.

The second time Kristin emerged from her cave was two days later. Diane's knocks on the door had been ignored, so on Sunday Diane let herself into the room.

"Kristin, I want you to come out with me today," she announced.

Kristin's only response was a groan into her pillow.

"I understand what you're going through here, but..."

"No you don't!" Kristin screamed as she snapped into a sitting position on her bed. "You have no idea what this could possibly feel like!"

It took everything Diane had to keep from crying. She choked back the tears and responded with a strained voice, "Fine. That's fair. But you cannot spend all your time in your room. You need to get out of the house. Establish a routine or something so that you can start to feel normal again."

"Normal? Who says I want to feel normal? I don't *deserve* to feel normal."

"So what are you going to do then? Spend the rest of your life in here?"

"Why not?"

"Because it isn't an option. Whatever you do, you still need to live your life. And that starts today. Put on your coat. We're going to go shopping."

Kristin looked across the room, her eyes dead. "Fine. Whatever." She trudged her way out of her bed and put on some clothes. Diane looked on the entire time racking her brain, wondering if she had handled this well. Guilt had already seeped in for getting upset. It didn't feel right, but she didn't know what else to do. She just knew that the girl that stood before her now did not resemble her daughter. The walls had been adorned with pictures of Kristin with her friends from college. In each of them, she had a huge grin, oftentimes making some sort of goofy face. Diane remembered how rarely she ever saw Kristin during her college days. When Diane asked her if she felt like coming in for a weekend, Kristin would go on and on about the plans she had and how much fun she was having. It seemed as though every time they talked, Kristin was in the midst of some activity.

And then there was when Kristin announced that she planned on becoming a teacher. Kristin had called her one evening, practically shouting. She had started volunteering at an after-school program where she tutored kids. She went on and on about this kid who came in every day in tears because he didn't understand anything and felt convinced that he would fail every class. Every day she'd take him through his work and then one day he ran in waving a paper in his hand. He'd gotten his report card back and what had been straight F's at the start of the year had become all A's and B's. The sight of this made her weep. In that moment she knew that she wanted to be a teacher. That she needed to be a teacher. She wanted to make this moment possible for all kinds of kids. But now... now if Diane couldn't see Kristin's chest rise and fall she might very well had assumed her daughter had died. Because there certainly didn't seem to be any life behind those eyes.

Diane watched as her daughter threw on a baggy hoodie and hid her face away. From there she stomped out to the car and slipped into the passenger seat. The two of them drove off. Diane had attempted to put on the radio, but Kristin turned it right off, apparently content to listen to the voices in her head.

When they got to the mall, Kristin followed Diane around, always a few paces behind. Every time Diane asked where she wanted to go, the only response she got was, "Home."

The two walked around for all of about fifteen minutes when the staring began. Just because no reporter had gotten the much coveted interview with Kristin didn't mean that they didn't print the story. It didn't take long for Kristin's face to become instantly recognizable around town. So now all looked upon her as though Scarlett Johansson had graced them with her presence. And while it began with simple stares, the whispering soon followed. People would lean over to their companions and relay a message about this local celebrity, all the time never letting their gaze leave Kristin.

With every turned head and hushed conversation, Kristin

fidgeted more and more as though a cascade of bugs had crawled on her. And then she noticed a stare not from some random person, but from a woman whose hair hung down in greasy clumps from having not been washed in days. Her outfit consisted entirely of stained sweats. A look of confusion soon transformed into one of absolute hatred. Her name was Ms. Perry. Kristin recognized her from the Back to School night at the start of the year. She was the mother of Kevin Perry, who had last been seen having his brains splattered on the wall outside of Kristin's room. Kristin had led this woman's son to his death, and now it appeared as though his mother would soon be knocking at the same door. Kristin sank into Ms. Perry's eyes, the blue of them washing over her like an ocean. An ocean that threatened to drown her. And Kristin was inclined to let it. It hadn't just been those two kids who had died, but so many more. A line of bodies piled up, and it all led right back to her. She wished she'd never stepped foot into that school, into their lives.

Ms. Perry's mouth began to drop open, looking as though a scream would soon emit. Kristin didn't wait for this. She just took off at a run and headed back to the car. Diane struggled to keep up, but once she did they headed home. Once there, Kristin retreated back to her sanctuary.

The third time that Kristin emerged was three days after that. Those days had been filled with the ceaseless ringing of the phone with reporters once again begging for the opportunity to speak. They even offered money now. Diane wouldn't even entertain them, hanging up immediately.

One evening, Diane awoke to the sound of a soft beating against her door. She headed downstairs and peeked her head outside. Running down the door and the sides of the house was egg yolk mixed in with bits of shell. She threw open the door to scream at whoever had done this but they had vanished into the night. She knew that she should call the cops, but bringing more people around the house wouldn't be good for Kristin. So, instead, she cleaned up in secret and didn't say a word about it to anyone.

The next day, Diane sorted through the mail and found a letter addressed to Kristin. She walked over to her room and knocked on the door.

"Kristin, honey. You have a letter out here," she called.

"Just slip it under the door," Kristin yelled back.

Diane reached down to do so, but then she froze and stood back up. She couldn't encourage Kristin's self-imposed exile like this. "No, honey. You need to come out and get it."

"Seriously? Just put it under the fucking door!"

A single tear leaked from Diane's eye. Her daughter had never cursed at her before. "No! You come out here and get your damn letter!"

The door swung open and Kristin stormed out, yanking the letter from her mother's hand. She ripped it open, unfolded the letter inside and read. As she read, her face turned into something ghastly. It almost seemed as though a gun had been stuck right against her forehead. Her mouth began to open and close as she attempted to catch her breath. Finally, she took in huge gulps as though she'd just surfaced from being stuck underwater. Kristin crumpled the paper in her hand and took off back into her room. The door slammed and this time even locked behind her. She had now barricaded herself inside leaving Diane feeling more helpless than ever.

The fourth time would come a little further down the road.

Fear may be the strongest emotion of all. It has the power to drive the best of friends apart. Fear has been the underlying cause for many of the terrible acts that have been done throughout history. It can force people to do irrational things; things that hitherto would have been unthinkable.

One thing that could be said about Stanford at this point in time, is that it was a town gripped by fear. Since the shooting of Noah Spaulding and the protests, things had become tense. The shooting at West had only added to this. The idea that people that walked their streets could have gunned down so many, made them feel vulnerable. It could be someone that passed them in the supermarket, at the movies. All of it was a vice squeezing tighter and tighter around their skulls. At times of tragedy, people need someone to blame in order to feel safe, and if someone has not been made available to blame, they will find someone.

Most people in the town couldn't have indicated any evidence that existed to implicate the SSPA in the shooting, but they had seen the headlines. And that was enough to light the match, igniting the fear that had spread through them like methane.

Eight days had passed since the shooting when Toby Henlon walked the streets of downtown at midnight, a backpack slung over his shoulder. Ever since he saw that sickening display of a protest, he dreamed of ways he could make his voice heard. Then with the shooting happening that very same day, he knew in his heart that all those black sons of bitches were to blame. But still they stood, protected, because these days everyone was too afraid to offend. Well he wasn't. He would do what needed to be done. So he stuffed his backpack with a can of spray paint, a can of lighter fluid, and some matches.

He stalked through the streets, making his way towards the SSPA headquarters and leaving a trail of beer cans in his wake. He didn't waste any time once he got there, knowing that the second someone came along he would be done for. Out came the can of spray paint and he went to work. Right on the door that led into the SSPA's basement headquarters, in dripping red paint, Toby wrote the message, *"Fuck You Niggers!"* With that done, he dropped the spray paint and pulled out the lighter fluid and matches. Toby drew two intersecting lines on the sidewalk, lit a match, and threw it down. A flaming cross erupted, throwing light onto Toby and his message. He admired his work for a moment before heading off for home.

PART III

A TOWN ON THE EDGE

22

The shooting of Noah Spaulding had brought a number of national reporters to Stanford. After the shooting, even more made the pilgrimage. After more than a week went by without much in the way of developments, most started to leave. Any articles about Stanford had started getting pushed back a couple pages in the paper. The TV reports started appearing in the second half of any program if at all, so it no longer required the man on the ground. However, they were soon given a reason to stay.

One such reporter was Heather Morrison with CNN. Thursday morning, she stood outside the SSPA headquarters with a microphone in hand and a camera in her face.

"This is Heather Morrison with CNN. We are here, live, outside of the headquarters for the Stanford Society for Police Accountability here in Stanford, Missouri. This place appears to have been the subject of a hate crime. Last night, an unidentified man came here to spray paint a racist message on the door. In addition, a cross was made with lighter fluid on the sidewalk and lit ablaze. Over here, we have Mr. Thomas Conway who lives across the street and was the first to report the incident."

Heather headed over to an older man who stood up straight and kept trying out a different smile on his face.

"Mr. Conway, will you please tell us what you saw?" Heather asked as she placed the microphone near him.

"Well, I had just gotten up in the night to get a glass of water," Thomas said, his eyes darting all over the place attempting to find a place to fix them. "I saw someone out front of the... the..." Thomas pointed behind him, trying to make sure his hand went in the right direction. "I saw him drawing something on the door and then messing around on the sidewalk. Then all of a sudden, this cross just went up in flames right over there." Thomas turned to show off the area he spoke of. Then he realized he should still face the camera and turned back around. "It, it was so scary. Then I ran and called the cops."

"And did you get a good look at the vandal?"

"No, it was really dark, so I couldn't see much."

"Thank you, Mr. Conway." Thomas stepped away as Heather took center stage again. "This town has been rocked with controversy as of late. First there was the shooting of fifteen-year-old Noah Spaulding which sparked nationwide protests as part of the Black Lives Matter movement. This was then followed by what has been called the Stanford Massacre when twenty-eight people lost their lives in a school shooting, which has yet to be solved. Many have wondered if the SSPA could have been connected with the shooting due to some controversial remarks that SSPA head, Denise Liman, made at a protest being held at the time of the shooting. We're here with Ms. Liman now. Ms. Liman, how do you respond to this vandalism?"

Liman stared down the camera like it was the barrel of a gun. She struggled to keep a dignified face on, but the fire behind her eyes could not be masked. "This isn't just a case of vandalism," she said. "This was a hate crime. And it appears to be indicative of the kind of attitude towards people of color that pervades every inch of this town. It is that same kind of attitude that led to Noah's death."

"Now, Ms. Liman. Your name has been mentioned in relation to the Stanford Massacre due to some comments that you have made. Did you or any member of the SSPA play any part in the shooting?"

"Absolutely not. I'm offended by the assumption."

"There have been reports that the police have looked into your organization as part of their investigation. Is this true?"

"They will investigate anyone and everyone. I can tell you that they won't find a thing. I can only hope they show the same determination in finding the bigot who has disgraced our property."

"Thank you very much for your time, Ms. Liman." Heather took her place center lens of the camera again. "Time will tell what effect this will play on the cultural climate of Stanford. As updates on this situation and the Stanford Massacre become available, we will have them for you. Stay tuned to CNN."

Around town, people sat horrified by what they saw. Many felt heartbroken to see all of this happen in their town. The only comfort that they gave themselves was the assurance that things could not possibly get any worse. But if human nature has taught anything, it's that things can always get worse.

23

The cliché says that "idle hands are the devil's playthings." This often proves to be particularly true for children and with Stanford's youth, that was the case. Without the daily routine and structure of school in place, they found other ways to occupy their time. It began innocuously enough with some calls of disturbing the peace. The kids found themselves celebrating the fact that they had time off school, oblivious to how inappropriate it might be to engage in frivolity at a time like this. Parties were thrown and students went around at all hours of the night causing a cacophony on the streets. From there, some started engaging in various forms of vandalism. While not hateful in nature like Toby Henlon's, it still resulted in plenty of property damage. Kids drove around town smashing mailboxes, tossing rocks through the windows of abandoned buildings, even slashing the tires of some cars. The most dramatic incident happened the night after Henlon left his message. Several kids from West went around town driving and throwing back some beer. Failing to pick a designated driver, they ended up getting into an accident with another car. Thankfully, Stanford's death toll didn't rise. However, of the five kids in the accident, only two didn't have prolonged stays in the hospital.

This accident ultimately convinced the school board that having school suspended might be doing more harm than good. Fearing that more students may be injured or worse, they decided that they needed to explore how they could send everyone back to class. Of course, this decision couldn't be made without first addressing the public. The Monday following the accident, a school board meeting was held. Prior to this, the record turnout for a meeting had been about a dozen people. This time, that number increased to over 100. While the meeting would typically be held in a conference room of the central office, it was now moved to the auditorium of East High School.

The board arranged a table on the stage while the crowd filled in all of the seats. Sherri Hill banged her gavel and called everyone to order. The talking in the crowd died down and they all looked up at the board. Many eyes hung low as they drilled into each person on the stage, abhorring every word that they had yet to hear.

"Thank you for coming, everyone. This turnout is quite impressive," she said with a nervous laugh. No one else joined in. "So as we mentioned in the announcement for this meeting, we are exploring the possibility of resuming classes for Stanford Public Schools. Now we obviously understand that there is some trepidation among the community over this, which is why we asked to hear from all of you. We would never dream of making any important decision without first hearing the thoughts of the community." While this hadn't been intended as a joke, there were a few laughs from the crowd. Probably in response to the numerous times over the years that the board had cut programs for schools without asking a soul.

"Before we open it up to your questions and comments, we would like to explain to you the basis for our decision. First, we must acknowledge that we cannot keep the schools closed indefinitely. While we would all be more comfortable with this once the people behind this terrible tragedy have been brought to justice, there is no guarantee of when this may occur. We have been in contact with the police, but they can't comment on the investigation one way or another. Second, with the recent spate of incidents involving our students, we believe that it is in their and the community's best interests to make sure that a routine is established for our students once again.

"Our plan would be to begin classes one week from today. We understand that returning to school after such an incident could be troubling to our students. We are sensitive to this and want to help our students through this difficult time. We are in contact with several grief counselors who will be available to students throughout the first week back should they feel the need to talk to anyone.

"Also, we are in arrangement with the Stanford Police Department for an increased security presence at the school in order to make everyone feel safe and secure. We are even exploring the possibility of having metal detectors at the entrance to the school. The safety of your children is and will remain our number one concern. Now we know that many of you have your own questions or comments, so we would like to open it up to you to share your thoughts. We have microphones on either side of the room, so if you have something to share then please line up, and we will get to each of you in turn."

Once Sherri stopped speaking, about half of the people in attendance stood and lined up behind the microphones. An unnerving silence palpitated throughout the room. Looking at the long chain of people ready to pounce, Sherri swallowed and took a look at the other members of the board who all tried to avoid looking at the onslaught that awaited them.

A young woman stepped forward, her eyes bloodshot, her

hair unkempt. It was the same woman whose presence at the mall forced Kristin to break down. "My name is Helen Perry. My son Kevin was killed in the shooting, and it seems to me like you want to sweep all of that aside just so you can go about business as usual."

"Ms. Perry, I can assure you that we have no desire to sweep anything aside. We are gathering a number of school officials to determine what is the best way to honor the memories of all those lost, including your son," Sherri responded.

"Uh-huh," Helen Perry said, doubtful of the veracity of what she had been told. "Well, another thing I want to know is what you plan to do about Ms. Benson?"

The name rang a bell with Sherri, but she couldn't place it at the moment. "Would you please remind me who Ms. Benson is?" Sherri asked, cursing herself for this.

Helen Perry almost exploded at hearing this, but at the last moment, she regained composure. "Ms. Benson is the reason that my son is dead."

With that, it clicked into place who Ms. Perry was talking about, the story having been relayed to her. She could understand why Ms. Perry would be upset, but also knew that she wouldn't like the response. "Yes, I know who you are talking about, Ms. Perry, and while I can understand why you may feel upset at her, according to district policy and the law, Ms. Benson cannot be held accountable for the deaths of those students. When we train our teachers in the lockdown procedures, we tell them that they are to take whichever steps they feel is necessary for protecting the students. From my understanding of the incident, she did exactly that."

"If she had, my child wouldn't be dead right now!" Helen Perry screamed as she finally broke and ran from the auditorium crying. It seemed as though everyone in the room looked down at their shoes, unaware if they could or should continue with the meeting after that. One by one, people began to look up and around again. The proceedings continued when someone at the microphone on the other side of the room stepped up.

"I understand why it's beneficial to get the kids back in school, but is there no other solution other than sending them right back there? Having students go into that building, seeing where their friends were killed. How can we expect them to learn in that kind of situation?"

"Yes, absolutely. That is a concern that we have had as well," Sherri began, relieved that she didn't feel under attack this time around. "We looked into the possibility of moving West's students into our other schools, or even having them transported out to another district's school. However, the fact of the matter is that the room simply does not exist in any of those buildings to hold a significant number of our students. So what we are going to be doing during the course of this week is making sure that the building is entirely cleaned of the remnants of the shooting. We are even exploring closing off certain rooms in the building where students may have been killed. We want the students to feel safe in our schools, and we mean that in every sense of the word. We have also discussed doing major renovations during the summer in order to transform the school."

That speaker left and they switched back over to the other side of the room where another question was ready. "I just wanted to say that I think you and the entire board should resign! We trust you with the safekeeping of our children and you failed! How can we possibly ever trust you again?!" A smattering of applause filled the room.

Sherri had expected this kind of demand be made, so thankfully she came ready with an answer. "I can speak for the entire board when I say that we feel terrible for this incident. I have spent many a sleepless night over the past couple weeks wondering if we did somehow let down our students in not properly preparing for such an occurrence. If there was something that we did or didn't do that contributed in any way to this horrible tragedy, then I would never be able to express my deep regret and guilt that would come along with that. I can only give you every assurance that we are going to double our efforts in every way possible. We are going to re-evaluate our preparedness for such things. We are going to offer more outreach to students who may be in crisis. And if anyone has suggestions for things that we can do better, then please tell us. We are a community, so we must move forward together." Sherri paused for a moment when she concluded her speech, pleased with how it had come out. She expected her own round of applause, but it didn't come. Instead, the questions and attacks kept coming.

"I think that if our children are going to feel safe in school, then we need to arm the teachers. If they had had their own weapons, then this tragedy could have been ended before it really began!" another parent demanded. This was met with a mixture of applause and boos. Sherri put an end to it with a simple declaration that teachers would not be provided with firearms in the schools. The boos and applause happened again, but reversed.

"I just wanted to say that I have no intention of sending my daughter back to that school while these monsters are on the loose," someone else stated. A flurry of agreement came from the crowd. A series of questions, demands, and accusations were lobbed at the stage for the next hour. Sherri and the other board members managed to answer or at the very least deflect all that the crowd threw at them.

As the lines grew shorter, it appeared as though things would turn out okay, but then a man stood up out of his seat and ensured that all would be ruined. "We all know who's responsible for this," he shouted. "It was those goddamn niggers from downtown!" he bellowed. At that moment, the entire auditorium became a vacuum, all sound and air sucked out of the room.

Everyone looked around wondering who would be the first to respond. Not a word was spoken though. Instead, a young black man popped up next to him and without saying a word, reached back and gave a hard jab with his right fist and knocked the bigot on his back. And with the sound of his body hitting the ground, an invitation was sent to the rest of the crowd to erupt in violence. Some rushed to the bigot's defense while others jumped up and clashed with them.

About half of the crowd rushed to the doors and ran outside. Up on stage all the board members jumped to their feet. Sherri banged her gavel, but even she couldn't hear it over the ruckus that now filled the entire room. Insults and additional racial epithets were shouted at each other. Punches and kicks to the face landed. Blood splattered to the ground. Many of them didn't even know why they were fighting each other. They had no quarrel with one another. For many of them, they probably couldn't even tell you the person's name. But that didn't matter. Violence had erupted around them and their instincts demanded that they take part in it.

The moment the fighting began, multiple people phoned the police and within several minutes they had arrived and began the long process of breaking up the fight. People were hauled up out of the crowd and put in handcuffs. In some cases, batons were taken out and used to subdue those who wouldn't comply.

All in all, it would take fifteen cops and another twenty minutes in order to end the fighting entirely. In total, thirty people would be arrested that evening and face charges ranging from causing a public disturbance to assault and battery.

∼

The next morning, *The Stanford Tribune* ran a story detailing the events of the previous evening. The headline read, "VIOLENCE ERUPTS AT BOE MEETING."

Violence has struck Stanford Public Schools again. Last night, the Board of Education held a meeting to discuss the possibility of ending the suspension of classes. After the shooting that rocked Stanford West just a short two weeks ago, the Board decided to cancel classes until further notice in the interest of protecting the students. However, a spike in youth crime in that time has convinced them that classes need to resume.

Last night, the Board held a meeting in order to address any concerns that parents may have about this decision. Over 100 people attended, forcing the meeting to relocate from its usual location to the auditorium of East High School. Tensions were already high as many of those in attendance expressed dissatisfaction with the decision, feeling that no classes should be held until the people behind the shooting were apprehended. Board President Sherri Hill attempted to address their concerns by promising an increased security presence at the school.

Towards the end of the meeting, a man took to the microphone and using racial slurs, placed the blame of the shooting on African-Americans in the community. Presumably, he was referencing reports that police have looked into the Black Lives Matter affiliate, the Stanford Society for Police Accountability as part of their investigation into the shooting. In response to his comments, another man retaliated causing a fight to break out. Many joined in, resulting in a group brawl which the police then had to break up. In the end thirty people were taken into custody. The police have not currently released the names of these individuals.

Tensions have been high within the community since the

*shooting. Just last week, an unidentified man vandalized the SSPA
headquarters with a derogatory statement and flaming cross on the
sidewalk. Many seem convinced that the SSPA played a role in the
shooting, however, the police have refused to comment on the current
state of their investigation. It remains to be announced if the Board
will proceed with their plan to resume school.*

People around town read the story. Many of them knew those
that had been arrested. The mere fact that this could happen
made them fear what would come next. The events of the past
month had transformed the town into a place that they no
longer recognized. They felt like they could no longer trust even
those that sat next door.

24

By the end of last week, all that had been taken from the SSPA had been sifted through and categorized. Kara and Brody went through the report, focusing on the members. The worst they could find for anyone was a charge of assault that ultimately got dropped. And they didn't find a single connection to West High School. Johnny Lemming's and Terrance Lipton's names didn't appear anywhere. Not even on sign-in sheets for a meeting. For all they knew, Lemming had just found the flyer somewhere. Who knows how into it he really was. And now with the battle royale at the board of education meeting, Barron had called them in for another one of his gripe sessions.

"So what's happening?" he asked the two of them.

"Coming up dry," Brody said.

"You're telling me there wasn't anything useful from the SSPA?"

"'fraid not."

"Well you don't have much longer, I'm afraid."

"I didn't realize there was a running clock," Brody responded.

"There is now. Hate crimes. Public brawls. Mayor isn't exactly enjoying the headlines as of late."

"We're not exactly getting off to it either," Brody said.

"Yeah, well, it does seem like you're holding your dick lately."

"You want to do it?" Brody shot back.

Having little time to waste knocking heads, Barron chose to pull past the comment. "Mayor says that if you don't bring someone in soon, he's asking for the FBI to come in."

"Come the fuck on," Kara finally piped in. "We're tracking down every damn lead we can. There's only so many ways to skin a cat."

"Well, you better start inventing some new ways. If you don't have a solid lead by the end of the week, then you're off the case." Not another word was spoken. Kara and Brody marched to their desk hoping a piece of evidence would fall out of their ass.

"Seriously, where the hell do we go from here?" Kara half shouted as they left the office.

"Keep looking into those kids. Still haven't ruled them out."

"How are we going to do that?"

"Maybe we can get one of them to confess."

"The likeliest of scenarios."

"Well you tell me then." Kara and Brody eyed each other, both of them feeling like they may flare up again at any moment. They both had opted for ignoring their spat from the other day entirely, but it still sat there. And from the look of him, Kara could tell that Brody had yet to climb out of whatever bottle he had found.

They just sat there going back through the report when Kara lifted her face and said, "Hair."

Brody looked back at her and replied, "Skin. Teeth. See, I can name body parts too."

"Shut up, smart-ass. We still have hair that the lab collected from the clothes that got left behind."

"They've already tested it. We can't get anything from it."

"Maybe we can't get any DNA, but we should still be able to compare. We bring those kids in and give a sample. By looking at them, we should at least be able to tell if there's a possible match."

"Oh shit. I hadn't thought of that."

"That's because I'm smarter than you."

"Oh damn. Smalls has been unleashed."

"Thanks. Okay, let's check with the lab." The two headed to the forensics department and checked with the technicians. They were told that with samples to compare, that a match couldn't be confirmed but could possibly be ruled out of if the samples were different enough. That weekend they had gotten all five students to agree to come in and provide a sample. And now they just needed to wait and see what the results would be.

25

C onnor read the story of the board meeting gone awry as he sat down at his kitchen table the morning after. He threw back his cup of coffee feeling exhausted at the account of the fight. He sometimes wondered how the hell his students could show such ugliness in class. If this is the kind of stuff that happened when their parents gathered, it stood to reason.

Brandy came in, having just woken up, and joined him. "What's going on in the paper?" she asked.

"You should read it for yourself. No way I could do this justice," Connor told her as he handed over the paper. Brandy took the paper and read about the meeting.

"What the fuck?" she whispered. "Is this real?"

"Unfortunately."

"Jesus Christ. What the hell is happening? I don't know that I want to be around here. You know things are only going to get worse before they get better."

"What are you saying?"

"Maybe we should get out of town until things calm down."

"Where would we go?"

"Well... we could go down to St. Louis and stay with my parents."

"Is that somehow supposed to be less hectic?" he said with a chuckle.

"Oh that's very funny," Brandy replied with a smirk. "So are they going to restart school?" she said, changing the subject.

"I have no idea. I guess they'll call if they decide to actually go through with it."

That call would come later that same evening. Connor recognized the number and answered, hearing the recorded voice of Sherri Hill: "Good evening, Stanford community. After much discussion the school board has come to the decision that classes will resume at all schools, this coming Monday, November 4. In spite of recent events, including those of last night's board meeting, we think it is in the best interest of our children and our community that we begin the process of getting our children back to work. We understand all the concerns that people have about the possible dangers that this may cause, and I want to ensure everyone that we are fully committed to the health and safety of our students. We are coordinating with the Stanford Police Department in order to make sure that all campuses are properly secured. Thank you all very much for your time." Connor put down the phone and felt surprised by the sense of relief that he had. It had been quite some time since he had looked forward to going to school, but he had to admit that it would do him some good. He had had little sense of what to do with himself being at home. All day he puttered around the house attempting to make himself look busy. He'd watch TV or read a book but found that his brain wouldn't turn off. He kept reliving the whole experience and imagining if things had gone just a little differently. Those few shots that the shooter had managed to get off... What if one of them had actually hit a mark? What if one of his students had ended up dead... again? He tried getting out of the house and going around town but everywhere he went people stared. Some would even come up to him, talk about how much they admired what he'd done. But what had he done? He got lucky.

Brandy headed downstairs, taking a break from her writing. "Did I hear your phone ringing? Who called?" she asked.

"It was from the district. They're starting up school again on Monday."

"Oh wow. So they're really doing it. You feel okay about it?"

"Yeah. I think so."

"Really? You'll be able to go back there after all that?"

"Well, I'm going to have to eventually."

"Yeah, but you don't want to rush that kind of thing. Things will only be worse if you..."

"Brandy, I'm fine. You can take off the kid gloves."

"Is that what you think I'm doing?" She began to bite her lower lip which Connor recognized as the sign that a fight was on its way.

"Well no... it's just..." he sputtered, trying to take back what he'd said.

"It's just that you seem content on excluding me from this."

"I hardly think that's fair."

"Really? Because you barely say a word about it unless I ask. You don't let me be with you for anything. Your interview with the police. The memorial service. You insist on doing all of it alone."

"It's because I'm doing fine."

"No, you're not. And you know what..." Brandy inhaled and looked to the side, wondering if she should actually go through with this conversation.

"What?" Connor asked, realizing he couldn't run out on the argument this time.

"You haven't been *fine* for a while."

"What is that supposed to mean?" He wondered why he even bothered asking. He knew what she meant, and he knew she was right.

"When was the last time we had an actual conversation?"

"What are you talking about?"

"For the last couple years, I feel like I'm living with a reluctant house guest. I ask you how your day is and you say, 'fine.' I ask what you want to do on the weekend and you shrug your shoulders."

"We've been together all these years. Do you expect us to still act like newlyweds?"

"No. But I'd rather that we not act like strangers. And then there's the fact that you won't even discuss the..." She trailed off in hesitation yet again.

Connor shut his eyes as if in preparation for a hit.

"You won't even discuss having a child," she continued through a choked sob.

"I... I just... don't think I'm ready."

"Not ready? You've devoted your life to working with kids, but somehow you're not ready?"

"Yeah, and I'm not even any good at that," he blurted out, surprised to find himself actually saying these words. "I can't even tell how many times I've screwed up. Kids that I've failed. And that's with kids that I work with for about seven hours a day, nine months out of the year. How badly am I going to fuck up when it's someone that I have to guide through their entire life? What's going to happen then?"

"What do you mean you failed them? Just because they didn't do well..."

"That's not what I mean," he interrupted her. "I mean that I let them down."

"Connor, I've taught too. And you should know that you're not responsible for everything that happens to them."

"Well, when one of them offs themselves, it's gets a little more complicated." With that, Connor decided that the conversation was over. He headed up the stairs, went into the bedroom. He wanted to avoid any further argument and the memories that came with it. He slammed the door as though he could keep it out, but it leaked through and as he collapsed on the bed he relived it all.

It happened right towards the end of his second year of teaching. He had loved that year. He had good classes. He got to teach some of his favorite books. He saw test scores go up for about seventy-five percent of his kids. It had been during that year that he knew that he had made the right decision in becoming a teacher. He even came close to admitting that he was good at it. Then at the start of the final week of school, all the teachers were called into the auditorium.

"Thank you for meeting on such short notice," Principal Devin told them. "Unfortunately, I have some awful news to share." Connor sat forward, wondering what had happened.

"One of our 10th graders," Devin continued, "Bradley Neuman, took his own life this weekend." Connor felt his stomach drop. He'd had this kid in class. He pictured him sitting in his seat tucked in the back corner, and now lying in a coffin.

"We don't know any details about how or why it happened or anything. Whatever information we get, we'll be sure to share with you. We wanted to make sure all of you were aware, though, as the students will probably be talking. So please don't allow anyone to engage in the spreading of any rumors about this. And if any students should need help processing this, please send them to the counselor's office. Right now the school is reaching out to his family to see what we can do for them, and we're looking to organize a memorial service for him. If you have any questions, then please let us know. Thank you."

The group of teachers broke up in silence and headed to

their rooms for the start of the day. When Connor got back to his, he sat in his chair and stared at where Bradley sat. Where he wouldn't be sitting anymore. This didn't make any sense to him. He couldn't imagine any of his students actually doing something like this. He liked to think he could've helped if only he'd known... and it was at that moment that it all came back. He thought back to the last time he'd actually seen Bradley. It had just been a few short days ago. It was the previous Friday, and Connor was rushing to get out of the building because he had a doctor's appointment right after school. As he slipped his bag over his shoulder, Bradley walked through the door of Connor's classroom.

"Mr. Sullivan," the boy said in a deep voice that didn't match his mousy demeanor.

"Hey, Brad. What can I do for you?" Connor asked.

"I was wondering if I could talk to you for a second."

"I'm kind of in a hurry. Is it important?" Connor asked, anxious at the thought of running late.

"No. I guess not," Bradley answered.

"Okay. I'm sorry. Why don't you come by Monday morning? Can it wait until then?"

"Sure." With that both Bradley and Connor exited the room. It would be the last time that Connor would ever see his student. Connor tried to look back on that day. What had Bradley been like? One second Connor would swear that he seemed happy and carefree like a teenage boy should be. The next moment, he was convinced that a large frown had been painted on the boy's face. And what was he coming to talk to him about? Had he already decided to take his own life? Was he looking for someone to talk him out of it? Maybe if Connor had bothered to stay behind a few minutes, things could have turned out differently. Unfortunately, he could never really know.

From there the entire year ran through Connor's mind like a

movie on fast forward. Every day, Bradley had come in, never making eye contact with anyone. Every day, he stayed in the corner and wouldn't say a word to anyone. Bradley wore long sleeves every day, even when it was ninety-five degrees outside. Could that have been because he had been cutting himself? And could Connor really have been so goddamn blind? Had he really not noticed that something had been wrong with the kid?

Every year he became convinced that he'd end up failing his students. When Brandy broached the subject of them having kids of their own, he felt convinced that he would fail them too.

When the school held a memorial service he found that he couldn't even look at Brad's parents. While many of his teachers went and gave their condolences to them personally, Connor couldn't bring himself to face them. Any time Connor passed the memorial plaque that got put up for him, he couldn't bring himself to look at it.

All of that was part of why he hated being called a hero now. In that moment he'd just reacted. But he hadn't been proactive when it counted. When it counted, he'd just let the cards fall where they may. He'd let one of his students die.

For the rest of the week, little was said between Connor and Brandy. Meals were eaten in silence. They gave each other small greetings at the start of each day. Connor could tell that Brandy wanted to continue their conversation, but he felt like he didn't really have anything else to say. He felt awful treating her this way. He knew she didn't deserve being kept at arm's length. He kept waiting for the other shoe to drop. He kept waiting for her to get wise and take off. Each time she walked up to him he expected her to say that she'd be staying with her parents for a while. But, instead, she'd usually just ask him what he wanted for dinner or ask him to do something around the house. And that only managed to make him feel even worse.

Then the day came for him to finally head back to school. She offered him a kiss on the cheek and wishes for a good day, seemingly resigning herself to the fact that all would be ignored. Connor headed to school, driving in silence the entire way there. He trotted through the halls, the whole place feeling so much bigger than he remembered. New pictures of people from around school had been placed in odd places. Connor assumed they had been put there to cover up bullet holes. When he stepped into it, his classroom felt like a ghost town.

When the students arrived, all the teachers were asked to supervise in the hallways. A long procession of students filtered in through the doors. Each one of them passed through a metal detector. Once they did, a security guard waited for them and gave a quick search of their backpacks. When they had all been cleared, they headed towards the auditorium where Principal Devin would address the entire school. The whole process of getting the students from the door to their seat for the assembly took about an hour. As Connor observed the whole thing, he couldn't help but be struck by a couple things. One, everyone was eerily quiet. On a typical day all the talking and shouting made it sound like a three-alarm fire. Of course, this day was anything but typical. Second, there seemed to be a relatively small number of kids coming in. Once they were all seated, he noticed that they only seemed to take up about three-fourths of the seats in the auditorium. Later, he would find out that attendance for that day had been at seventy-three percent. Many parents refused to allow their kids to go to school so soon afterwards. He couldn't exactly say that he blamed them.

Connor and the rest of the teachers made their own way to the assembly and took their seats. Principal Devin came to the stage and stood at the lectern.

"Good morning, everyone, and welcome back to West," he said in a somber tone. "I don't need to tell all of you of the tremendous struggle that we all have in front of us. The school has gone through something which cannot be adequately expressed. Tragedy does not even seem to convey the feelings that come with having been a part of this. Moving forward won't be easy, but move forward we must. Today we begin that process.

"Now, first I want to give you all an idea of how we'll proceed. While we are in session today, we won't be having classes. The morning will be held right here. We have a few people here to speak to you that we'll get to later. This afternoon, you'll break up into your first period classes. And that time will be for all of you to speak and share your experiences. We want you to consider that a safe space where you can say whatever you need to."

The afternoon session in the classrooms had been awkward for Connor. Once everyone got settled, Connor let them know that this would be an open forum. Anyone should feel free to share their stories and their feelings. At first not a syllable would be uttered. Every student looked around, daring each other to break the ice. Five minutes passed, and Connor thought that it might stay like that all afternoon, but then one person spoke up and rattled off their experience. Then another and another. Some cried and some yelled. Some even spouting off about what they thought the solution should be. The moment things got political, Connor worried that fists might get thrown. Thankfully, it never came to that.

Through all of it, Connor's eyes would periodically land on parts of the wall that had been spackled over. Parts of the wall where bullets had been lodged. He wondered whether they were still in there. He shook at the image of them having hit somewhere else.

One thing that stuck out for Connor during the whole thing was the student who didn't say a word. He just stayed in the corner and kept his head down. When the final bell rang, Connor called him up to his desk.

"Dennis, you doing okay?" he asked. "Did you want to make an appointment with one of the grief counselors?"

"No. I'm fine," Dennis answered, only looking up for a second.

"You know, there's no shame in admitting that you need some help. At a time like this, we all…"

"I said I was fine," Dennis blurted before heading out of the room. He rushed outside and made his way to his car. In all honesty, he hadn't been feeling good since he'd been called in to give a hair sample. After all, why would they want something like that unless they thought he had done it? And now, even on the first day back, the rumblings had begun, just as he suspected they would. When he had gotten called back to the police station, Johnny and Terry had been there as well. And it didn't take long before they shared the tale with everyone else, including Dennis's presence there. Dennis knew what would come next. Everyone said he was a psycho before the shooting, and this did nothing to shed the image. He had stayed quiet during class because he knew the second he said anything, it would get turned around on him. Even as he slid behind the wheel of his car, he could feel people watching him, could almost hear them judging him. He raced home where he would be safe from it all. For now.

Connor was left alone in his classroom, not liking what he had just seen. He sat down at his desk and looked up Dennis's home number. He wanted to call his mother to let her know about his concerns. All he had been able to do was leave a message for her. He would need to keep an eye on him as the week progressed. So now he packed up his stuff and began heading back towards his car. On his way down the hall, he thought of something and took a detour. He realized that he hadn't seen Kristin today at all. Given her behavior the last time he'd seen her, he could only imagine how she was coping.

He headed towards her room wanting to see how she had been. When he got there, Kristin was nowhere to be seen. Instead, a woman with gray hair pulled back in a ponytail walked around the room picking up trash. Connor recognized her as Mrs. Turner. She had been a teacher here during Connor's first year but had retired. She still came around fairly regularly as a substitute teacher now. Connor never quite understood why someone would come right back into a building they just escaped from. At least he felt like it would be an escape for him when he finally retired.

"Mrs. Turner?" Connor said as he walked in.

"Hi, Mr. Sullivan," she replied as she looked up with a smile. "Can I just say that I am so impressed by what you did during the lockdown? You really are a..."

"Please. That's fine." Connor knew what word was coming and didn't want to hear it. "Did you sub for Ms. Benson today?"

"Yes. Quite a shame about her."

"Yeah. It is."

"I'll actually be here all week for her. At least."

"All week?"

"Yes. Maybe she's just not ready to come back."

"No. Guess not. Well, you have a good day."

"You too, Mr. Sullivan." Connor left her alone and exited the building. He hadn't given Kristin much thought since the day of, but it now occurred to him that what he saw in the back of the ambulance may not have fully passed for her.

Julie had the day off so she insisted on driving Terry to and from school. She had always prided herself on her willingness to give Terry as much space as he needed. Her mother tended to smother her as a girl, so she felt adamant that she wouldn't do that to her son. But lately she had started to cling. Ever since she found that flyer in his dresser she demanded to know where he was at all times. Particularly if he said he would be with Johnny. Now that she pulled up she saw him sitting out front with Johnny, both of them hunched over and whispering to each other. As she stopped out front, she chugged down her fourth cup of coffee that day, desperate to stay awake. She tried to remember the last time she actually slept through the night.

Julie went to honk the horn to call out to her son, but hesitated as she saw him commiserate with his friend. *What could they be talking about? Is this what it feels like to not trust your own son?* Ever since he'd gotten called in to give a hair sample, it seemed like everything made her jump. Every ring of the phone, every knock on the door. She felt convinced that that would be the death knell for Terry. Her stomach felt like it had been fed through a meat churner. Everything inside her said that she should tell someone about that flyer. A student with no alibi having a connection to an organization under investigation... that's the kind of thing Smalls and Morgan would want to know. But if she did that, her son might be taken away, just like her father had been. But if she couldn't even approach her son with it, then how could she ever approach the police. Hell, she hadn't even shown the damn thing to Brian. She just felt like the moment she said it out loud it would become real. The moment you say the words, "I think my son may have committed mass murder," you can't take them back. Even if you insist that you didn't mean it, everyone will know that you did. No matter what you do with the rest of your life, you will be known as the woman who ratted out her own son.

Julie honked her horn, grabbing Terry's attention. He stood up, gave some final comment to Johnny and then dragged his feet to the car.

"How was the first day back?" Julie asked as he slumped into the passenger seat.

"Fine," Terry shrugged.

"Is that it? Come on. You need to give me more than that," she pleaded. "Did everything go smoothly? There weren't any fights, were there?"

"Nope."

"Terry," Julie said as she stifled a whine.

"What?"

"I just wish you would talk to me."

"We're talking right now, aren't we?"

"I guess that depends how you define it. You're just a mystery to me, Terry. Me and your father."

"Stop worrying about me."

"Stop giving me a reason to worry." She started saying something else but choked it back. She wanted to ask about the flyer. She wanted to ask about everything. But then what? Where would they go from there?

26

Dennis went through the rest of the week attempting to keep an even lower profile than normal. On Tuesday he sat by himself at lunch like he usually did, but the entire time he could feel the glares of the entire student body. After that, Dennis began to eat his lunch in the bathroom. And even though he had never been one to skip class, he began staying in there for some of them.

Wednesday morning, he stopped by his locker. He opened it to see a white piece of paper fall out, having been slipped between the slits on the door. He unfolded it, his hands trembling the entire time. He could already see red letters that had bled through the front of the sheet. Once it was opened, he saw the large block letters spelling out the message: *Go to hell you fucking psycho! I hope you die.* Dennis crumpled up the piece of paper and looked around him, convinced that someone would be sneaking up behind him, but he only saw people come and go in the halls offering nothing more than the typical stares.

The entire week, Connor tried to keep a close eye on him. Dennis not showing up to class didn't make it any easier. He never did hear back from Dennis's mother either, not realizing that Dennis had heard the message first and erased it.

Starting on Tuesday, the school attempted to begin easing the students back into actual classwork. For that whole first week, students only had half of their classes every day. Between each period they had free time so as to allow people to check in with the counselors. The teachers had also been instructed not to assign any homework at all that week.

For Connor, the whole thing slogged by, feeling as if the entire school year happened in that one week. It didn't help that each morning began with the thorough search of each student. Shrines to the students who had been lost were erected on many of their lockers. On more than one occasion, Connor would see someone break down crying when they passed by one of these memorials.

The teachers had been warned that there may be a number of fights breaking out due to the pressure of coming back into the building, but thankfully there were few discipline problems at all that week. It seemed that most kids felt too exhausted to even bother. And those that didn't knew better than to start something. Connor did witness one fight, however.

Classes on Thursday had come to a close and Connor sat at his desk reviewing assignments from the week. He had thought better than to jump right back into reading *The Chocolate War.* Something about school violence seemed far from appropriate. Instead, he had shifted his classes towards creative writing, wanting to give the students a chance to express themselves. As he went through some rough drafts to give feedback, Connor heard something that sounded like arguing come from the halls. Someone seemed on the verge of yelling but kept trying to hold back. Connor headed towards the hall to see what it was.

"Why? Why the fuck did you do it?" the first voice demanded.

"I didn't. I swear to God," the other pleaded.

"Don't fucking lie to me. Everyone knows you're a little freak. Just tell me why you killed her. Natalie never did shit to you!" A metallic clang punctuated this.

"Please. I'm telling you the truth." Connor rounded the doorway and for a moment assumed his eyes were playing tricks. He saw Richard with his hands gripping the collar of Dennis's shirt and holding him up against the lockers. Dennis stood there flinching for a hit he kept assuming would come. His feet wriggled on the ground, ready to take off running the moment he had been set free.

"What the hell is going on?" Connor asked. The question wasn't entirely rhetorical either. He almost assumed the two must have been rehearsing a scene for a play or something, because right now he saw a side to Richard he didn't think existed. He'd known the kid for four years and as far as Connor knew, he'd never even been tardy. Both boys whipped their heads around to look at their teacher. In the process, Richard loosened his grip ever so slightly which gave Dennis the chance that he needed. He slipped away and took off running, not looking back once. Richard started, ready to go after him but thought better of it.

"Hey, Mr. Sullivan," he said with a casual nod. He began walking away down the hall.

"Hey!" Connor yelled after him. "Get your ass in here, right now!" A sharp point of his finger directed the young man into his classroom. Richard threw his arms up as though he couldn't understand what the problem was. Still, he walked in all the same.

"Take a seat," Connor told Richard as he walked in.

"I'll stand," Richard said in defiance.

"Suit yourself." Connor walked right by him and hoisted

himself onto his desk. "You want to tell me what the hell is going on?"

"Nothing."

"You looked like you were about ready to kill him."

Richard raised his eyebrows as if to say, "So what?"

"Really? Is that all I get? I want an explanation."

Richard still said nothing, but his eyes began to water up.

"Fine. You can go and I'll just get this written up. You're probably looking at a couple days out of school suspension." Connor hopped off his desk and walked around to go to his computer.

"What?!" Richard burst out. "That's bullshit!"

"Excuse me?" Connor's voice went up a couple octaves.

"I barely touched him!"

"You assaulted a student and threatened him. And I find it hard to believe that Dennis did a damn thing to you."

"Didn't do anything?! He killed Natalie. He killed all of them."

"Don't give me that. You don't have any idea who was responsible. No one does."

"Oh come on! Everyone knows it was him. Kid is a fucking freak. And it's all over school that the cops are looking at him. Put two and two together."

"I don't want to hear it. First of all, I can tell you right now that that kid doesn't have it in him to do anything resembling what happened here. Second, even if you saw him do it with your own eyes, you don't get to go around attacking people. And with all of this happening on campus, you haven't really left me much choice."

"You can't do this." Richard's voice cracked, making him sound ten years younger.

"Why not?" Connor's voice softened.

"I don't even know who I am lately. It's just that since Natalie died, nothing makes sense. We hadn't been together long, but I felt like... She and I were the real thing. I wanted to marry that girl."

"Richard, I can understand that, but it doesn't change what just happened."

"I know. I acted like an asshole. And I'll apologize to him myself tomorrow. I swear to God, I will. But I can't get suspended. I'm looking into Princeton, and if I have something like that on my record, it isn't going to look good." Richard dug his fingers into his scalp. He gave off loud sobs and gasps. Lines of spit dangled from his lips. His legs began to tremble, looking like he might crumble at any second.

Connor looked on, once again seeing someone that didn't resemble the student he knew, but in a different way this time. He had brought up the discipline form on his computer, and as he looked at it, he found he couldn't bring himself to type anything. Kid had lost his girlfriend. Did he really want to pile it on now? What good would that do? Plenty of people had died, and he'd be damned if he contributed to killing this kid's spirit.

"Fine," Connor said. "I'll look the other way. But I'm gonna check to see that you actually apologize. And if I see anything resembling that crap you just pulled, I won't be so nice next time. You understand?"

Richard nodded his head as he wiped his eyes. "Thanks," he croaked as he shuffled towards the door. Connor watched every step, and the moment that Richard was out of sight, Connor brought his head down onto the desk. It wasn't just Richard that had changed. There was nothing of this school that he recognized anymore. Nothing of this town that he recognized anymore. And he knew that if things ever went back to normal, it wouldn't be for quite some time.

27

While tensions simply simmered at the school, they were ready to boil over out in town. After the incident at the SSPA and the fight at the school board, a number of small protests began to crop up all over the downtown area. Around ten or fifteen would gather outside City Hall or in the park demanding that the racist attacks end.

Typically, the police would never comment on the status of an open investigation, but found it in the town's best interest to do so this time. Captain Barron conducted a press conference where he called for peace and made it clear that no connection had been found between the Stanford shooting and the SSPA or Black Lives Matter. But at that point the damage had already been done. Tragedies have the ability to bring out the worst in people, and that's what it had done here. People around town had become convinced of the SSPA's involvement and now their own ignorance wouldn't allow them to believe anything else. Long, festering prejudices had been laid bare. For many, they had been given an excuse to do things that they had always wanted to do. So while the protests ended after Barron's announcements, the attacks only intensified.

First, more racial slurs would be hurled out on the streets. From there the assaults began. On three separate occasions, as young black women walked the streets, someone would jump out, shove them to the ground, while screaming at them. One of them even got kicked in the head and put in the hospital. The house of a black family, who had had the temerity to move into a predominantly white neighborhood, had a brick thrown through their front window.

With that, Sharon Handel had decided that the time had come for another rally. She wanted to send a message to Stanford's black community that they had friends in town. It had been scheduled for Saturday, November 9.

The next day a crowd of over 200 gathered at Howard Park. The sight of everyone here made Sharon's heart swell. Her apprehensions began to slip away as she felt filled with hope. This many people would go a long way to sending a clear message to everyone. And with the rally being held on a Saturday this time, she needn't worry about anything else happening at the schools. Sharon headed up onto the small stage and went to the microphone. Despite her joy at the turnout, she suppressed her smile, knowing this whole rally to not be a cause for celebration. The crowd broke into cheers and applause as Sharon got ready to begin her speech. She held up her hand, motioning for them to quiet down, which they eventually did.

"Good morning, everyone," Sharon began. "Thank you for coming. I can't begin to tell you how impressed I am with today's turnout. However, I am heartbroken over the mere fact that any of us need to gather at all, but with recent events, we have been left with no other choice. I don't need to recount to you the different hate crimes that have been committed over the past couple weeks. Now nothing can undo the hurt and pain caused by those crimes. And try as we might, we can't make sure that they never happen again. But we gather here today in order to send a message. To send a message that no matter what the monsters of this world do, no matter how much they hurt us, they will never make us cower in fear. They will never break our spirit. No, all they will do is bring us closer together. And it is together that we are at our strongest!"

The crowd erupted into applause again, and this time Sharon allowed herself a small smile. Granted, if she knew what waited for them she wouldn't have smiled at all. And not a person would be cheering. In fact, not a single person in attendance would have been there. And when it was all over, all would wish they hadn't been.

Julie stood towards the back of the crowd not believing that she had to be back at another one of these. She looked on at everyone raising their signs and heard them shout out support. All of it sounded like white noise to her, her mind still back at home thinking about Terry. All week it seemed that no matter what she did, he was the only thing on her mind. She drove around on patrol, but she couldn't even notice anyone speeding. Her radio would go off, and she would need to ask for the message to be repeated. Yesterday, she had been off work and had used the opportunity to look around his room again. If Terry had really done what she feared, there had to have been something lying around to prove it. She'd been at her share of crime scenes and even the smartest criminals left a trace of some sort. So she did another search, looking in his closet, between his mattress and box spring. Each time she looked somewhere, she would hold her breath, terrified of what she might find. News clippings of the shooting? A mapped-out plan? But after an hour of it, there was nothing. She went right to her bed where she laid down and cried. She cried tears of joy that her worst fears hadn't been realized. She cried tears of shame for what she had just done. She cried tears of terror because she still didn't feel convinced.

Once the speeches concluded, the march towards City Hall began. The crowd moved as one appearing like a flock of birds. They hoisted signs in the air, and began their cheers and chants. Julie followed, attached to the crowd's hip the entire time.

As they made their way down the street, the sun had begun to dip below the horizon. A shade was pulled over the sky. As she walked along, she kept waiting for her radio to announce some emergency, convinced that lightning would strike twice. Of course, her worries should have been placed on what waited for them down the street.

Julie looked out onto the pack as they progressed down Main Street. Less than 100 yards remained before the final stop of City Hall, and that was where it all began.

One of the buildings along the march route had office space which had been vacated for over a year. This made it the perfect spot for Toby Henlon to lay in wait. Watching the reaction to his art show at the SSPA had been the most exhilarating experience for him. To see all those damn coons go on and on about how they'd been wronged. Their cries were music to his ears. Except it hadn't been enough. By the next day, they'd already covered up his message. So now he would need to send a stronger one. One that no one could ignore. One that would have a lasting impact. This gathering below him served his purpose. A whole crowd of insects asking to be snuffed out.

Around his feet was a collection of Molotov cocktails and a complete arsenal of guns. He picked up a pistol and readied it, taking a moment to caress the cold steel. From within his pants,

Toby could feel himself harden at the anticipation of what was to come.

~

The first pop came. Initially, it sounded like nothing more than a car backfire, so no one thought anything of it. That was until one of the crowd became disentangled from the rest and went face down into the street. From there another pop. And another. And another. By that point it had become clear to all that those pops were gunfire. The crowd scattered like ants under a spotlight. One person after another bumped into Julie as her head darted around like a bird. She looked for the gunfire's origin, but in the midst of downtown the sound echoed, making this impossible. Bodies got knocked over like bowling pins, specks of blood splattering up, some of it sprinkling Julie's face.

"Get down! Get down!" Julie screamed into the mayhem, but she could barely even hear herself. The chants of the crowd had now turned to mindless screams. She had her gun drawn but knew not where to fire. With the ever descending night, the likelihood of seeing the attackers seemed slim. But then a sliver of red and yellow appeared in the air. Julie looked up to see a flaming bottle spinning end over end. The Molotov cocktail hit the street, the shattering of the glass being heard over the shouts. Fire erupted in its place. Another twirled through the air after that. And one more after that, the third actually hitting someone, turning them into a flaming pillar. Julie looked up, finally able to see the window from where the bottles were spit out. She raised her gun and began to let off shot after shot hoping she may hit her mark. Later on, she would realize that this would be the first time she had ever actually discharged her weapon while on duty.

The slide on the gun slid back signaling an empty chamber. Julie reached down and fumbled on her belt for another clip. It would only have taken her but a moment, a few seconds. But with the rapidity of it all, that proved to be too much time. As she went to jam in another clip she felt a sledgehammer against her chest as a bullet found its mark, hitting dead center of her vest. She could swear she could actually feel her ribs fracture. The force of the shot forced her gun from her hand. Instinctively, she went to grab her chest when another bullet hit home. This one got in her side, just underneath the Kevlar. Julie went to the ground, dropping as though she had been yanked down. Clutching her side, her hand became beet red. Then the crowds, the flames, all faded, leaving only the sound of the screams and gunfire. Soon that would fade too.

When the smoke had cleared, three people had lost their lives. Seven more were injured, including one man who would never feel anything below the waist again. And as much as he would have liked to look down on his masterpiece, Toby had slipped out into an alley once he had shot his wad of weapons. For the next two days, Toby had taken to his basement room where he watched the aftermath of what he considered to be his masterpiece. He laughed and even shed a few tears of joy. Upstairs, his mother went about her business none the wiser about what had gone down. And if Toby had given a bit more forethought to what he had been doing, he may have been able to live out his days being the only one knowing that he had been behind it all. However, across from where Toby made his exit, the security camera of a bank had picked him up. And he had failed to wear gloves, so his fingerprints covered every inch of his nest, as well as the remnants of the bottles that he threw. Two days later, the arrest warrant for Toby came in.

A battering ram smashed down the door, nearly giving the

eighty-year-old Ms. Henlon a heart attack. SWAT members scoured every inch of the home. In his cave, Toby heard it all happen and attempted to run out the basement door, not knowing that the SWAT team had created a ring around his home, and he ran right into the arms of several officers who wasted no time in tossing him to the ground and throwing cuffs around his wrists.

Even with Toby's arrest, the damage had been done. Chaos had descended on the town of Stanford, the ugliness of it all being laid bare. The investigation into the Stanford Massacre, the impetus for all this grotesqueness, would soon come to its conclusion. When it all came to an end, people around town would breathe a sigh of relief. However, the fear that gripped the town would not relinquish it for quite some time.

While his mother was taking a bullet, Terry had found some alone time and was using it to his advantage. Johnny had been harassing him lately about getting him the addresses for some of the cops around town. With his mother hovering over him as of late, he'd had little opportunity, but now he finally did.

He scoured his mother's room, figuring that somewhere in the midst of all her shit must be something that would get him what he needed. He went to her computer where he began guessing at her password. Terrance, Brian... none of them worked. She changed it so often, that it could be just about anything. Finally, he gave up on that, dubious as to whether he'd find anything there anyway.

Next, he went over to her dresser. He avoided the top drawer, having made that mistake once before looking for cash a few years ago and had only found her underwear instead. He did not need to see that again. The rest of the drawers held only clothes.

Finally, he came to her nightstand where he found an address book sitting inside. *Jesus, Mom. Who still uses an address book? Get with the times*, he thought to himself.

Outside, Brian pulled up to the house. He'd been shopping when he got the call that a bullet had landed Julie in the hospital. He abandoned his cart, and rushed home. He almost joined his wife in the hospital a couple of times by getting into an accident as he tried to navigate around his tears. He stumbled out of his car, leaving the door open as he went to fetch his son.

Upstairs, Terry flipped through the book waiting to see a name that he knew. Enough cops had been around the house over the years that he figured he'd recognize at least a few of them. It just now occurred to him how half-baked this whole plan was. Who knew if he'd be able to find anything? Hell, Johnny still hadn't clued him entirely into what would happen once they did have them. Johnny spoke a big game about how they'd send a message to "the pigs in this town," and how they'd catch the eye of the SSPA. In all that time, he never gave a hint of just what any of that really meant. He knew how Johnny's mind worked, and it could be just about anything. His pulse quickened as it all swam through his head. After getting called in to give a hair sample, Terry once again told Johnny that they needed to slow things down, but Johnny wouldn't hear of it. Having had those pigs touch him only spurred him on even more. Terry grabbed a pen and pad of paper and started writing down some names and addresses.

Brian opened the door, grabbing on to the frame, keeping himself steady, afraid he might pass out. He ascended the stairs which looked like Everest at the moment. "Terry!" he belted out.

Terry perked his head up at the sound of his dad's voice. He hurriedly scribbled down a few more names and stuffed everything away as he heard his father's footsteps get further and further up the stairs. Tripping over his own feet, he crawled out of the room. He opened the door to come face to face with his father, ready to get a lengthy interrogation about why he had been in there. Instead, he simply saw his father trying to compose himself behind a visage of tears.

"We need to go to the hospital. Your mother's been shot. Come on," Brian said, struggling to make his voice sound normal.

Terry didn't so much as flinch. He almost expected his father to tell him it was all a joke. Damn thing seemed impossible, so it couldn't be true, could it? As he had scrambled out of the room, Terry had shoved the paper with addresses into his back pocket. It hung heavy in there now, feeling like a slap in the face of his mother. His mother who could very well be inches from death for all he knew. What would she think if she knew that her own son conspired against the police like this? Conspired against her? He found himself stomping down the steps, feeling the whole time like he needed to shower.

Julie was transported to the emergency room and went directly into surgery. The bullet got fished out of her chest. She ended up lucky in that she would be getting out of there with nothing more than a couple cracked ribs. Thankfully, the bullet managed to miss her lungs. Two hours after surgery, she woke up in recovery. The overhead lights scorched her pupils, but she could still make out her husband and son standing over her. Her throat felt like a desert. She tried to swallow, but felt like she'd start to bleed if she did. She grinned at her family and tried to greet them, but only the start of the words could be produced.

"It's okay, honey. Don't strain yourself," Brian told her as he rubbed her shoulder. "We're so glad you're okay." Julie looked over to Terry and saw him standing there, remnants of tears in his eyes. She reached up towards him. Terry shot out his hand and took hers, squeezing like one of them might fly away. Julie could almost feel her heart shatter at this, not able to remember the last time that Terry had ever held her hand. The whole time, he stared off into space.

28

———

Because of the attacks over the weekend, school had been called off once again, along with a number of businesses. Kara and Brody still had work to do, and the results of the hair analysis had come back, ruling out Johnny, Terrance, and Larry but saying it could be a match for Dennis or William. Given what had been found in his locker, Dennis shot to the top of the list, and Kara and Brody got the warrant to search his home. And thank God it did because after this weekend, they both knew that without something tangible, they would have both been shoved aside in favor of the FBI. They could only hope that they neared the finish line because they feared how much longer the town would survive.

The two drove to his house in silence, a few black and whites close behind. The entire time Kara looked as though she had a gun pointed at her head forcing her to go through with this. They pulled up in front of Dennis's home and walked to the front door. A couple knocks brought Dennis's mother to answer it. She pulled a robe tight around her body and sipped a cup of coffee. Her eyelids only opened about halfway.

"Hello?" she said, blinking against the sunlight that streamed inside.

"Ms. Clements. We're Detectives Smalls and Morgan. Is your son at home?" Kara asked.

"What is this about? Why would you need to see Denny? He's already spoken to you twice. What else could you possibly need from him?"

"We have a warrant to search your home and his car."

"What? No, you can't do that. My son didn't do anything. Please leave."

"Sorry, ma'am. But like I said, we have a warrant. You'll need to let us in." Dennis's mother slid back as though on a conveyor belt. Kara, Brody, and the accompanying officers headed inside.

Just as they did, Dennis came pounding down the stairs. "Mom, who's at the door?" he asked. He came to a stop and almost slipped down the remaining stairs when he saw who had come into his house.

"Hi, Dennis," Brody said. "Remember us?"

"What's going on?" Dennis asked with a shaky voice.

"We'd like to look around a bit."

"I don't understand."

"Can we get the keys to your car, please? And show us to your room?"

In that moment Dennis seemed to emulate a small child. And much like a small child he looked over at his mother hoping she would tell him what to do. That she would make everything all right. But all she had to offer him was a small nod. Dennis shriveled up like a shamed puppy and led them upstairs. Kara and Brody followed him into his room. The walls were lined with drawn pictures featuring an array of characters from pop culture of which Kara and Brody only had a passing knowledge.

"Did you draw these, Dennis?" Kara asked. All she got in

response was an embarrassed nod. Beside his bed there sat a pile of books. Up against a window which looked out on the backyard was a desk covered with a laptop and a few different journals. A couple of the officers went looking through it all. Dennis just went into the corner and sulked against the wall.

"Your keys, son?" Brody said, extending his hand. Dennis didn't even look up at him. He just walked to his desk, snatched up the keys, and handed them over. Brody passed them off to an officer with instructions to look through the car.

Kara sifted through the mess on the desk and looked through the journals. First one seemed to consist entirely of half-complete drawings. Another had notes from what looked like a history class with doodles in the margin. The third she stopped on. Each page had every line filled with text. At the top of each page was a different date.

"This your journal?" Kara asked. Dennis simply looked away. Kara began flipping through it. Most of it seemed innocuous enough. Just rambling accounts of a day in the life of a painfully average teenager, but a couple did catch her eye:

Tuesday, September 12, 2017
Shit has started all over again. What was I thinking that everyone was going to mature over the summer? A couple times today as I walked to class, people threw their hands up like I was going to shoot them or something. And if that wasn't enough, when I was leaving school today, the handle to my car door was wet. Someone had peed all over the damn thing. Why do I even fucking bother? Sometimes I wish all those assholes would go away and leave me the hell alone.

Then there was another from the day before the shooting:

Sunday, October 14, 2017
My story has completely fallen apart. Feels like a random series of

scenes at this point. I'm thinking that maybe I'll ask Mr. Sullivan to take a look at it. He should be able to tell me whether it's a rag or not.

They could be something worth looking at. Something she did find interesting was that this seemed to be the last entry. Since the shooting, he hadn't written a word in here. Not a single reflection on what had to have been the biggest thing to happen to him in his short life. She handed it over to Brody indicating that it was worth a look. He took it and began to peruse the pages.

"Detective Smalls. Detective Morgan!" one of the officers called up from downstairs. "You're gonna wanna take a look at this." Dennis's gaze darted all over the room, wondering what they could possibly have found. Kara and Brody both headed downstairs and followed the officer out to the car. On the way they passed Dennis's mother who sat on the couch clawing at her hair. Once they both got to the car they saw one of the officers standing over the open trunk and looking at a rolled-out sheet the size of a poster.

"What do you have?" Kara asked. She turned down to see what looked like a blueprint. It showed three different floors and in the top right corner, it read, "Stanford West High School." It was a floor plan of the school. That would have been bad enough, but the writing all over it cemented it. At the front entrance, the words "Enter here" had been written in black Sharpie. At one of the classrooms, it read "Exit here." The kicker was the words, "Stash guns here," written over one of the bathrooms. Kara looked down at the floor plan willing it to change. She shook her head as though it couldn't be real. Everything in her had insisted that it wasn't Dennis. But it appeared like she had been wrong all over again.

"Jesus," Brody uttered. "This is heavy. Well, you know what we need to do."

"Yeah. I guess." Kara's voice dripped with disappointment. She handed the floor plan back to the officer who slid it into an evidence bag. She walked back towards the house, dragging her feet the entire way. Dennis and his mother sat on the couch together, their hands entwined.

"Please tell me what's going on," his mother pleaded.

"Dennis, will you please stand up," Brody said as he fished out a pair of handcuffs.

"What?" he whined. Inside he could feel his heart wrench. "I don't understand. I didn't do anything."

"Please. We need to do this." Dennis stood up like a puppet having his strings pulled. He then hung there as though the strings had been cut. Brody walked around behind him and slipped the cuffs around his wrists. His mother buried her face in her hands. Dennis wanted to cry but found that he couldn't. He couldn't feel much of anything at the moment, other than the cold steel enclosed around his wrists. Brody led him out the door with Kara close behind.

Dennis's mother sprang from the seat and took off after them, but one of the officers held her back leaving her to do nothing but scream. "Please! Don't take my baby!" Kara turned away from the scene, not able to look for another second.

Dennis got escorted to the car and sank into the back seat without struggle. At this point he couldn't even tell where he was anymore. The entire world had turned into a blur of colors with no semblance of being. Kara just stood against the back of the car staring up at the sky.

"Come on, Smalls," Brody said. "Let's go." Kara merely looked at him, not able to say a thing, but she didn't need to. "I know you didn't want this, but we can't argue with something like that."

"I know," she whispered. "Just wish it had turned out

differently." But why? Did she truly believe it wasn't him, or did she just not want to be proven wrong again?

The entire drive to the station was made in silence. Kara kept expecting Dennis to start crying or something, but he didn't make a peep. She looked back a couple times almost afraid that he'd died of shock or something. Each time all that met her was the dead stare of a terrified young man. Once they got to their destination, they marched Dennis in. As soon as they entered, the entire place fell into a hush. Almost everyone stood up to get a look at the man behind the Stanford Massacre. A couple even looked like they may start to clap, but the look of confused rage on Kara's face made it clear that such a thing would not be welcomed. Dennis got placed in one of the interrogation rooms and had his handcuffs removed. Kara and Brody stood before him.

"Dennis," Kara began. "First of all, can we get you anything? Water, soda?"

Dennis shook his head without even looking up at the two detectives before him.

"Okay. Well first of all, you *are* under arrest at the moment but as of right now you haven't been charged with a crime. Your mother followed us here, and you'll be given a chance to see her. We'll be back in a little bit to talk to you. At that time we'll review with you your rights. Do you have any questions?"

In reality Dennis had all sorts of questions. *Am I going to prison? What did you find? Will I ever get out of here?* But at the moment, all he could manage was a simple shake of his head. Kara and Brody exited the room where they saw Ms. Clements come flying through the doors of the station.

"Where is my son? I want to see him right now!" she cried. She spun in circles, desperate to find someone, anyone who could give her the answers she searched for.

Kara strolled up to her and tried to soothe her. "Ms. Clements, please calm down."

"Calm down?! You just hauled my son away in handcuffs! Is he being charged with something?!"

"No. Not at the moment."

"Then let him go."

"We can hold him for twenty-four hours before charging him."

"But I don't understand. My son didn't do anything!"

"Well, we're going to figure that out. Now you're free to stay here in the meantime, but you'll need to be calm. Now can we get you anything?" Kara could see Ms. Clements begin to deflate, her anger giving way to despair. She then flopped onto a seat and wept. Kara turned and headed back to Brody where he waited over by their desks.

"There is no part of this that I like," Kara told him. She tried to block out the image of the devastated mother behind her.

"I know. But we go where the evidence leads," Brody responded. He then threw a glance at where Ms. Clements sat. The sight brought back images of Christine crying in anguish when they found out about Mandy. He had an urge to just go ahead and release Dennis so as to save his mother the pain, but knew that he couldn't. "Come on. Let's go do this." The two of them gathered the evidence they had collected; a laptop, and the security footage. They both walked back to the interrogation room where they saw Dennis sitting and chewing on his thumb, his eyes wide and unblinking. The tip of his finger had started to bleed.

"Dennis," Kara started as they both took a seat. "We're going to ask you a few questions. You have the right to remain silent. Anything you say, can and will be used against you in a court of law. You have the right to an attorney. If you cannot afford one, one will be appointed to you. Do you understand?"

Dennis gave a sharp nod while still chewing on his finger.

"We need you to say so out loud, if you will," Kara said.

"I understand," Dennis replied in a deflated voice.

"We have some things we'd like to show you, son," Brody said. "All we want you to do is explain them to us to the best of your ability. Can you do that?"

"Sure." Dennis's voice sounded hoarse.

"Great. Okay, now we took some drawings from your home. The nature of some of them is concerning." Brody brought out three of them and laid them out on the table. One showed an armored woman impaling a troll-like creature on a huge sword. Another displayed the character Deadpool holding a gun with smoke billowing out of the barrel. The third had some other masked character they didn't recognize holding a bloody sword. "Now these pictures are rather morbid. Did you draw all of these?"

"Yeah. They're just pictures though," Dennis responded.

"What are they?" Kara asked.

"This one is a Dungeons and Dragons character," Dennis said, pointing to the armored woman. "This is Deadpool. A comic book character. And this one is a superhero that I was trying to come up with."

"Do you understand why these may concern us? They seem to show a fascination with violence."

"I just like the stuff is all. I've never even held a gun or a sword or anything. Hell, I've never even been in a fight."

"Okay. Well, what about this?" Kara proceeded as she pulled out the journal and turned to the entry from September 12 and began reading from it. Dennis had his face buried in his hands as he heard his words read back to him. "Why are these kids afraid of you?"

"I don't know," Dennis sniveled as he relived his

mistreatment. "They just don't like me because I'm different, I guess. I keep to myself."

"Do you have any friends?"

"No. Not really."

"That must be tough," Brody said. "And them urinating on your car. That's really messed up."

"Whatever."

"Is that kind of treatment normal?"

Dennis only nodded.

"What about that last line?" Kara asked. "You wish they'd go away? What does that mean?"

"I don't know. Just not around. I didn't want them dead though. Jesus Christ."

"Would you consider yourself an angry person?" Brody asked. "Given the way the kids treat you, no one would blame you for being a little angry."

"I don't know."

"Your last entry in the journal was from the day before the shooting. Why haven't you written in it since then? I feel like you'd have a lot to express after going through something like that."

"I don't know."

"You need to give us more than 'I don't know.' Or we can't help you," Brody told him.

"I guess I just didn't know what to say about it. Just too much to process."

"You know a few weeks ago, we looked in your locker at school as well," Kara cut in.

"Yeah. So?"

"Well, we found a book in there that caught our attention."

Dennis threw his eyes all over the room as he tried to think of what she could be referring to.

"Have you read a book called *Rage*?"

"Oh God," Dennis said as he ran his hands through his hair, taking a few strands with him.

"So you understand why we're asking you about it?"

"I read that thing like a year ago. I didn't even realize it was still in there. I had forgotten about it." It seemed as if he said this more to himself than to them.

"So why are you reading stuff like that?"

"I don't know. I read all of Stephen King's books."

"How did you find it? That book has been out of print for years."

"When my dad walked out, he left behind a bunch of old books. This was one of them."

"You seem to be into some dark stuff there, Dennis," Brody said.

"A lot of people are into those sorts of things."

"Fair enough."

"But I don't think most kids have something like this in their trunks," Kara offered as she produced the school's floor plan. She set it out in front of Dennis. He looked it over as though it was an ancient text that he needed to decipher.

"What is this?" Dennis asked after a full minute had gone by.

"What does it look like?"

"Looks like West High."

"I'd say you're right."

"Where was this?"

"Trunk of your car."

Dennis's gaze lifted from the sheet in front of him and met the detectives' eyes for the first time. "But that's not possible. I've never seen this before in my life."

"Well then, how did it get there?"

"I don't know."

"Help us understand this, Dennis?" Brody said. "Because I can tell you right now that if you were to go to trial with this kind of evidence, there's no way you don't get convicted. But if you talk to us. If you confess. If you tell us who you were working with, things will go much easier for you. So please, just talk to us."

Dennis remained silent, having lost any sense of himself at the moment.

"Remind us again," Brody said. "Where did you say you were when the lockdown got announced?"

"Bathroom." Dennis sounded like a caveman with his one-word response.

"That's right. But you left during first hour, right?"

Dennis merely nodded.

"So tell us again. Why were you gone so long?"

"I was crying."

"Crying?" Kara chimed in.

"Kid had called me a psycho in class."

"Still a long time to be gone," Brody said.

"Can I see my mom?" he asked, ignoring Brody's last comment. Brody looked over at Kara, the two of them communicating silently, and seemingly coming to an agreement to let the boy talk to his mother.

"Sure, Dennis," Brody told him. "Stay here. We'll got get her." The two of them gathered everything and headed out.

"Can you go get her? I can't see any more crying today," Kara asked of Brody.

He nodded and headed towards where Ms. Clements sat. Right as he stepped up, she lifted her head, her face looking like it had been doused with a hose. "How's Denny?" she moaned.

"He's fine. He'd like to speak with you."

"Really?" A look of relief and hope popped onto her face. She stood and followed Brody back to the interrogation room. As soon as the door opened, she ran in and hugged her son.

Brody slid away and closed the door. In the next room he and Kara would watch their conversation play out.

"Mom. I don't know what's going on," Dennis cried into his mother's shoulder.

"What did they say to you?" she asked while pulling back a bit but still keeping him close.

"They had a couple drawings that I've done that concerned them or something. And they had my journal where I wrote about kids bullying me at school." His mother nodded along the entire time. She had seen a couple of his drawings and never particularly cared for them, but she didn't want to harangue him about it. She had long suspected that he got bullied. He never seemed to talk much about friends at school. But she assumed that if he needed to talk about something, he would come to her. She would not harass him. Her parents had badgered her about things all the time when she had been a kid, and that was part of the reason that they didn't talk much nowadays. She wanted, needed, to have a good relationship with her son. Especially since his dad wasn't in the picture. She was all he had. He was all she had.

"Okay, well if that's all they're going on, then you're fine. There's probably dozens of other kids in the school that all that would apply to," she told him.

With that Dennis took up the face that he would give as a kid when he got caught doing something bad and needed to admit it.

"What is it?" she asked, recognizing this look.

"They found something in my trunk."

"Found what?"

"A... a..." he broke off and cried into her shoulder.

"Come on, honey. Just tell me."

"There was a floor plan to the school. And there was this writing all over it. Something about stashing guns somewhere."

He spat it all out in a flash knowing he'd never be able to say it otherwise. His mother's face was that of someone who had been tasked with solving an impossible riddle.

"But you have to believe me that I had never seen it before. I have no idea where it came from or how it got there. I swear to God that I didn't do this, Mom. Please believe me. Please." His eyes were a waterfall at this point.

"Of course I believe you, sweetheart. There's plenty I don't know, but I know you. And I know you could never do something like that." She said this, and she meant it, and she believed it. But as Dennis looked her in her eyes, he noticed something. Something so small and fleeting that most would never perceive it. But for a young kid facing a prison sentence, a young kid who felt like the world had turned against him, it was all too clear what laid behind those eyes. Doubt.

29
————

Dennis didn't get charged that day, but he still had to spend the night inside a cell. And that proved to be the longest night of his life. He laid on a thin mattress where the steel of the bed frame continually poked into him, threatening to come through at any moment. Dennis tried every possible position but could not find one that allowed for sleep. The one thin blanket they had given did little to protect him from the chilled temperature of the cell. He had expected that he would end up crying all night, but found that his tear ducts had been sucked dry. So instead, he laid awake all night staring at the cold gray of the walls. He imagined the years to come for him. Would this be his life from now on? He could remember a time a year ago when he had slept until 3:00 in the afternoon. He hated himself when he woke up and looked at the clock. He had wasted the entire day. A day that he couldn't get back. That was how he felt about his life now. His life would be a waste. Even if he lived another eighty years, he would have nothing to show for it. All the dreams that he had for his life. Become a famous writer? Become a famous artist? That wasn't meant to be. The only thing people would ever know him for would be as the kid behind the Stanford Massacre.

When the lights switched on, the only thing that changed for him is that he sat up and stopped pretending to sleep. At that point the time was 7:00, meaning that he had another eight hours before being released or charged. He hoped, begged for the former, but knew that the latter awaited.

And getting Stanford's district attorney to agree to charge Dennis was Kara's and Brody's focus for the day. The first step in it was obtaining a warrant so they could collect the contents of Dennis's school locker. That had managed to come through by the end of the day, Monday, and with the school back in session on Tuesday, Kara and Brody made it their first stop.

As Principal Devin led them back to the locker, gazes followed them the entire time. Kids in the hall stopped in their tracks. People crowded around the doors of classrooms to peer at the proceedings. Directions from teachers to get away from the door went unheeded. Kara and Brody collected the drawings and books from the locker and then made their way to Connor's classroom. A knock brought him to the door. He opened it and all of his students looked up from the story they had been reading. Other than a few hushed whispers to each other, none of them said anything, but they all stared.

"Mr. Sullivan, I'm sorry to disturb you, but these detectives have a quick question for you," Devin said.

"Mr. Sullivan, did Dennis Clements give you anything to read? Possibly on the day of the shooting?" Kara asked in a soft voice so as to not tip off the students as to what was happening.

"Something to read? I... I don't know," Connor replied, confused as to why they would even ask such a thing. And then it clicked. He recalled Dennis handing something to him that morning and asking him to take a look at it. With all that occurred, he hadn't thought about it since. "Oh wait, I remember. Yeah, he gave me something. I haven't looked at it though."

"Do you still have it here?"

"Umm... yeah. I guess I do. I haven't touched it since."

"Could we have it, please?"

"Sure," he said with a shrug. He walked back to his desk. The students had become antsier due to all the excitement. "Get back to work," Connor instructed them. On the floor were piles of paper that he had laid there to make room on his desk. He shuffled through them and a little ways down the pile, found Dennis's story. He scooped it up and handed it over to the detectives.

Having what they needed they headed back to the station where they reviewed all the collected evidence against Dennis. Brody got to work on the report for the DA, detailing everything found in regards to the book, journals, drawings, and floor plan. Meanwhile, Kara went through the story they had just collected. And if the floor plan had been the nail in his coffin, this would be the dirt that got shoveled on top of it. For a kid who was bullied in school, the whole thing played out like some kind of revenge fantasy. It told the story of a boy who had been victimized in high school. After gym one day, a group of boys grabbed him naked out of the shower and shoved him outside in the snow. Being stuck out there for more than half an hour resulted in him losing a toe to frostbite. Years later, still filled with rage, he would set out on a path of vengeance. The pages were filled with scenes of graphic torture as one man had his intestines pulled from his stomach and wrapped around his neck. Another had his head blown off with a shotgun after being nailed to the floor. The last man got shoved into an industrial-sized freezer while the killer watched. As he did so there came a line that Kara could imagine the DA reciting at trial to drive home Dennis's guilt to the jury: *He knew what they would say about him. They would call him crazy. They would call him a monster. He would let them because he knew all he had done was rid the world of the real monsters.* The line read like it had come out of a manifesto. Once again Kara had to accept that her finely tuned instincts needed to be re-calibrated.

By noon that day, the report had been finished, and District Attorney Patrick Durant arrived. He met with Kara, Brody, and Captain Barron in the back conference room. He read the report as they presented all the evidence. It took all of ten minutes for him to agree to charge Dennis with twenty-eight counts of first-degree murder and fifteen counts of attempted murder. With that decided, Kara and Brody visited Dennis in his cell. He simply sat on the bed watching his feet swing back and forth.

"Dennis," Brody said as he stepped in. Kara noticed that he took on a fatherly tone each time he spoke to the boy. "We're charging you with the shooting. You'll be transferred to the county jail and remain there until your arraignment. Then the judge will decide whether or not to grant bail and when you'll stand trial. Do you have any questions?"

"No," he replied in a monotone voice. This was what he expected, and now he found it hard to care. The way he saw it, he had died last night. His body just needed to catch up.

PART IV
GUILT AND INNOCENCE

30

That evening, Captain Barron stepped in front of a crowd of reporters. The rumors of an arrest having been made was blood in the water and the sharks had been circling all day.

"I am going to make a brief statement but will not be taking any questions," he began. "Yesterday, our detectives made an arrest in relation to the shooting at Stanford West High School. Today, we met with District Attorney Durant and filed charges against the suspect. The suspect is sixteen-year-old Dennis Clements who is a student at Stanford West High School. I cannot go into detail right now concerning the evidence against him or any possible motive. The case remains open, however, as we must still identify the second shooter. More details will be released once the suspect has been arraigned. Thank you." With that he walked back into the station ignoring the questions that were shouted.

Dennis was scheduled to be transferred to the county prison in the morning. Meanwhile, Kara and Brody had brought him back into interrogation, hoping they could end the investigation all at once. Kara had taken to standing against the wall, watching Brody do his magic.

Brody pulled up the security footage of Jason coming out of the bathroom and played it on a loop. "Come on and talk to me, Dennis. Because here's what I'm thinking when I watch this, and I've seen it a lot. This person who is coming out of that bathroom seems scared. Watch how they jump back at the mere sight of someone. And then they take off running. I see someone who maybe doesn't want to be there. Maybe they got talked into it. Maybe they were even forced. When I see the other guy, he seems to be in charge. And I think he's enjoying what he does. So the one with the hockey mask, I think that one is you. So tell me what happened. Did he threaten you?"

"No. I mean, that's not me. Neither one is. I wasn't in the building. I mean you have me on camera going into a different bathroom. I never went in there."

"Well, you could always have slipped out at passing time and made your way down there. We'd hardly catch you in the midst of that herd."

Dennis said nothing at first. His brain had gone scattershot now, and he could hardly organize his thoughts. "But I would never..." he finally managed.

"Then why did you have floor plans to the school in your trunk?"

"I had never seen those before you showed them to me."

"Then how did they get there?"

"I don't know."

"Does anyone besides you have keys to the car?"

"Just my mom."

"Well then, I don't see how it could have gotten in there. Do you?"

"No. I guess not."

"Then tell us what happened."

"Can I get a lawyer?"

"Of course. We'll get you a phone," Kara said as she turned

to leave the room. Brody didn't move an inch. Kara looked back at him and would have sworn that he grew in size. His breathing grew heavier. "Morgan. Let's go," she said.

"Enough," he breathed more than vocalized. His eyes drilled into Dennis. "I'm sick of all this bullshit."

"Morgan," Kara beckoned, worried as she noticed tremors passing through his body.

"I am so sick of your fucking act. I know what you did. And you're gonna fucking tell me who helped you."

"Brody!" Kara pleaded, dropping all pretense of professionalism. She saw Brody transform into something otherworldly. She watched as he reached out and tossed the table aside as though it were made of plastic. He swooped down on Dennis, getting so close to his face that a piece of paper couldn't be placed between them. In that moment, Brody didn't even see the petrified teenage boy. He saw only the face of the man who had taken his Mandy from him.

"FUCKING TELL ME!" he screeched. Dennis just shrank into himself like a turtle. Kara slid across the room, threw her arms around Brody, and wrestled him back. She knew that she wouldn't have been able to get him to budge, if he decided not to let her, so she was grateful that he relented. She yanked him out of the room and shoved him across the hall into the conference room.

"What the fuck was that?!" Kara screamed.

"That little shit is playing us like we're a couple assholes."

"So your move is to play psychopath cop with a sixteen-year-old kid?"

"You sure as shit weren't doing anything. No, because he may as well be a puppy to you."

"I don't even know who the fuck you are anymore."

"Maybe you never did."

"Sit down and get control of yourself. I'm gonna try to

salvage this." Kara burst out of the room, slamming the door behind her, half expecting the glass to shatter. She went right back to the interrogation room where Dennis had gone fetal. He still hid his eyes. Beneath the chair, a puddle of urine had formed.

"I'm very sorry about that. We are getting you a phone so you can contact a lawyer. Can I get you anything else?" Dennis only shook his head. Kara slipped out of the room and sank into the wall, trying to catch her breath. *What the fuck is going on*, Kara wondered? Lately, this town had begun to feel like *Invasion of the Body Snatchers*. She didn't recognize anyone anymore. Shooting. Public brawls. Hate crimes. Roid rage hitting her partner. And in the center of it all was a kid who pissed himself when someone screamed at him, but was meant to have gunned down a couple dozen people.

Kara made a beeline for Barron's office. She couldn't sit on this any longer. She walked right in without knocking and shut the door behind her.

"What the hell are you doing? I thought you and Morgan were trying to break the kid," Barron said, looking up from his computer.

"He asked for a lawyer."

"Then get him one. Do you need a refresher in how that's done?"

Kara ignored that and kept on through. "No, but I'm not convinced it's him."

"Not convinced? What the hell are you talking about? We have him dead to rights."

"It doesn't feel right. I just don't think it's him. I've looked killers in the eye before and he isn't one."

"Really? That's what you're going on? How it *feels*?"

"My instincts tell me it's wrong."

"I am sick and tired of hearing about your fucking instincts.

You're lucky your instincts haven't cost you your badge. Now, I want you to get out there, find the other piece of shit involved and never say another word about this. Because if the media or his lawyer find out that the arresting officer thinks he's innocent, then we can kiss a conviction goodbye. And I don't think this town could take something like that right now, do you?"

Kara said nothing. She just looked away from his judgmental gaze and stared at the wall.

"Good. Hopefully you do as I say for once. You can go now," he said, looking back to his computer. Kara left the room wondering why she even bothered. There was no chance that could have gone any other way. As she headed back to her desk, Brody walked out of the conference room, the tremors gone, but the rage still on his face.

"Where did you go?" he asked as he sat across from her.

Kara's only response was to look over at Barron's door.

"You didn't," he said, picking up on what happened. "What the hell were you thinking? And why the fuck would you do something like that without talking to me first?"

"You're gonna lecture me after the shit you just pulled? Besides, we have talked about it. You know my feelings on it."

"Yeah, but I thought you were coming around. But Jesus, I don't even care about that. But you go and do something like that without me, I end up looking like an asshole."

"You don't need me to make you look like an asshole," Kara shot back.

For a moment it seemed like Brody wouldn't react at all to her comment. His face sat flat, and then as he rose from his seat he threw out, "And fuck you too."

That night Brody sat on his couch staring down a bottle of Scotch. It dared him to drink it. He dared himself not to. The scene from the interrogation played over and over again in his mind. He could hear how his voice sounded from when he screamed at the Clements kid. That kid huddled up like some infant. His terror-stricken face. The last time that he'd seen a look like that on someone's face was just before Mandy ran away and out of his life (out of this world). This time it was some sick fuck who had gunned down his classmates. Next time, it might be someone important. And then he would have driven away everyone in his life. And him being half in the bag all the time now was only making things worse.

On his lap sat a photo album tracing Mandy from when she had been born to when her life had been cut short. His Mexican standoff with the bottle continued. He knew that with each drink he would drift further from the man who had been Mandy's father. But without her around, maybe it didn't matter anymore.

The showdown cruised towards a climax when a knock came at the door. Brody set the album aside and headed to answer it, revealing Kara. Brody just stood there and stared for a moment, wondering why she would be at his home. He couldn't remember her ever having been over to his place.

"Kara?" he asked, wondering if his eyes had played tricks.

"Hey, Brody," she said. "Can we talk?"

"Uhh sure, I guess," Brody said as he stood aside and allowed her in.

Kara walked in and came to a stop in the kitchen where she just stood and waited.

"What can I do for ya?" Brody asked as he took a seat at his kitchen table and motioned for Kara to do the same.

"I want to talk about what happened today."

"I acted like an ass. I know. I don't really want to talk about it though."

"It's more than just that. Something has been going on with you as of late. I mean, what have you been doing? Taking a shower of vodka every morning?"

"What's that supposed to mean?"

"Past couple weeks you've been coming in hungover or just plain drunk. I can smell it on you. What the fuck is going on?"

Brody sat looking at her for a moment, contemplating if he really wanted to get into this with her. He had always made it a point not to talk about Mandy. Not to anyone. But it started to seem as though he had painted himself into a corner. "Just... this case is..."

"Brody, I've seen you crack jokes while leaning over a dead body. So please don't bullshit me." Kara happened to glance over into the other room where she saw the photo album sitting open. "What is that?" she asked. Kara walked over and upon seeing what it contained, her face twisted into a question mark.

"Umm..." Brody forced out while throwing his hand over his eyes.

Kara picked up the album and flipped through the pages, stopping on one of Brody holding Mandy when she was just a baby. "Who's this girl?"

"My daughter," Brody said, sighing.

"Your what?" Kara blurted while turning her head around to look at him.

"Her name was Mandy."

"Was? Do you mean she...?"

"Yeah. Ten years ago."

"Oh my God. Bu... Wh... Ho... How?" Kara could barely get the words out. She had so many questions. "I'm sorry. You don't have to answer that."

"It's fine. She was seven. Got kidnapped. Killed."

"Oh my God…"

"Yeah." Brody brushed away a tear.

"And… And this other woman," Kara began as she pointed to a picture of Christine. "Is this your…?"

"My wife. Well, ex-wife. We split up after Mandy died."

"But… but you've never said anything."

"I don't like to talk about it. No one knows anything."

"Is this why you've been drinking?"

"Yeah. Just seeing all those kids. If she was still alive, Mandy would have been there. She could've been one of them."

"I see." Kara looked down at her feet, not sure what to say next. They'd been working together for a while now, but they'd never talked like this. She looked over at Brody and saw that it could all come tumbling down for him at any time. Her first instinct said to take a run for it before she had to deal with the grief. Instead, all she did was rock back and forth on the balls of her feet without a word to say.

Brody broke the silence as he approached her, took the photo album back, and said, "Thanks for coming by." Next, Kara found herself outside, once again cut off from her partner.

31

Kara and Brody's presence at the school was all the student body needed to decide that Dennis must have been the shooter. By the end of the day, they had already tried, convicted, and sentenced him to death. Connor ended up having to spend most of his day telling kids to not discuss it. When the final bell rang he found himself sitting at his desk for a while gazing into nothingness, attempting to reconcile the Dennis he had in class with that of a crazed killer. And he couldn't seem to do it. He wondered what they could have against him. The whole thing made him feel sick to his stomach.

After a few more minutes he realized he wasn't going to be able to make sense of the situation. At least not today. He walked towards the exit, passing Mrs. Turner in the hall. She'd taken Kristin's classes for another week. Around school no one seemed to have heard anything about her. In truth, Kristin would be leaving her room for the fourth time that same day.

Diane had attempted to talk her daughter into going to see a doctor to help her, but Kristin made it clear that she wouldn't go anywhere. After some searching, and hours on the phone with her insurance company, she found a doctor who would pay a home visit. On Monday, Doctor Barrington came by the house.

"Thank you so much for coming. I just don't know what to do about her anymore. She won't come out of her room. She won't even talk to me," Diane said in greeting.

"Well, given her circumstances that's not surprising," Barrington replied.

"But it's been a few weeks, and there's no change."

"There's no timeline with this kind of grief. You did the right thing by calling me. Why don't you show me her room?"

Diane pointed him towards the door and knocked. She got no response, so she called in. "Kristin. Sweetie?"

"I'm not hungry. Go away," Kristin called back.

"No, honey. I have someone here to see you."

"Tell them to leave."

Diane's eyes welled up and she looked to Doctor Barrington for guidance.

He responded with a knowing nod and took over. "Kristin. My name is Doctor Barrington. I was hoping to speak with you." When an objection didn't come he pushed open the door and crept in, nodding for Diane to stay behind. The room had been bathed in darkness, the only light being the little that filtered in through the blinds. Doctor Barrington could hardly make out the body that laid on the bed. He grabbed her desk chair, pulled it towards him, and sat down.

"I understand you've been having a tough go of it as of late. You maybe want to talk about it?" he began.

"No," she said flatly. She faced the wall and didn't look back at him.

"You know, Kristin. You're not the first person to go through something like this. And people often react to traumatic situations the same way that you have. But the problem with this is that it only exacerbates the problem."

"And what would you have me do?"

"Well, there's a few things. One thing I would suggest is keeping a journal where you can record your feelings. You might not believe it, but it really goes a long way towards helping us sort it all out. And then you need to find something to occupy your time. Do you have any hobbies?"

"You're wasting your time."

"How so?"

"Nothing is going to change for me. And I don't want it to."

"Don't want it to? What does that mean?"

"Please leave me alone." Kristin curled up and hugged the wall.

"Come on, Kristin. Please talk to me." But she said nothing. Doctor Barrington would sit there for another half hour trying to get her to talk but the only response was light breathing. "Kristin, I can't do anything for you if you don't talk to me. I want to help. If you decide that you do want to talk, then please give me a call." He stood up and set his card on her dresser before leaving.

Out in the living room, Diane sat waiting with a magazine on her lap. She pretended to read but had spent most of the time tearing the corners of the pages. Dozens of little bits of paper littered the floor beneath her feet. Once the door to Kristin's room opened, she jumped to her feet anxious to know how it went. A small shake of Dr. Barrington's head as they met eyes made it clear that little had been accomplished.

"I'm sorry, but she didn't want to talk," he said with regret in his voice.

"Didn't want to talk? Well, what do you do then?" Diane asked.

"If she won't talk to me, there isn't much I can do. I can't make her open up."

"So what do *I* do then?"

"Look for any opportunities to get her out of the house. Create them if you have to. And be available for whenever it is that she does decide to talk. And please call if she does. Or if she should happen to take a turn for the worst."

"A turn for the worst?" Her face became stricken with fear. "Like what?"

"Substance abuse. Self-harming behavior."

"Do you think that's a possibility?"

"I really can't say. Just keep an eye on her. I'm sorry I couldn't do more." He left the house, leaving Diane with one of his cards as well.

The rest of the night she would check in on Kristin every half hour, but she never got more than a couple words out of her. She would fall asleep on the couch at around 10:00 that night. At 7:00 the next morning she got pulled from her slumber. She looked around the room in confusion at first not realizing that she'd fallen asleep there. But even when that passed, something still hung in the air. She couldn't place it, but it felt as though she had maybe just woken from some vivid dream that had stayed with her. She looked around the room as though she might find someone else there watching her, but found nothing. As she scanned her surroundings her eyes settled on the door to Kristin's room. The door screamed out to her, beckoning her forth. As she peered at it she started to feel that familiar ice pick drive into her heart again. She knew what the feeling had been. She ran towards the door, almost barreling through it. Standing in the room she saw Kristin laying on the ground, a razor blade sitting next to her. Diagonal slashes had been made on both arms. Blood flowed from the wounds.

Diane leapt to her daughter's side and clenched Kristin's arms in her hands attempting to stop the flow of blood. A rush of blood seeped through her fingers as she screamed her daughter's name. She just laid there as limp as a sock. And from what Diane could tell, she didn't seem to be breathing. Over on the desk, sat Kristin's phone. Diane clawed for it, and after a quick fumble, she got it under control and called 911.

"911. What is your emergency?" the operator said.

"My daughter has slit her wrists! She's bleeding everywhere!" Diane screamed into the phone.

"I understand. What's your address?"

"1438 Wintergreen Avenue."

"Okay. Emergency services have been dispatched to your location. In the meantime, you want to try to slow down the flow of bleeding. Grab some towels and wrap them around her wrists as tight as you can."

Diane scrambled to the bathroom, knocking into walls the entire time. She snatched up a couple of towels and was back at her daughter's side in less than a minute. She wrapped a towel around each wrist and tied both ends together.

"Okay, the towels are around her wrists! What do I do now," Diane asked as she picked the phone back up.

"You want to check to see if she has a pulse. Can you do that?"

Diane reached out and tried to feel Kristin's neck, but her fingers shook and slid all around from the blood that soaked her fingers. "I don't know! I can't tell!" she cried.

"Okay, that's fine. Paramedics should be there shortly. I'll stay on the phone with you until then." Two minutes later, two paramedics came through the door and took over. They loaded her into the back of the ambulance, and Diane climbed in with her. She looked down at her daughter's face which had gone pale. The towels had gone beet red and been traded out for bandages. Her breathing became labored and she started to hyperventilate, feeling like she may pass out. What had she done? What hadn't she done? Would this be the last she saw of her daughter? The short drive to the hospital seemed interminable.

32

Wednesday morning, Connor sat in the teacher's lounge knocking back his third cup of coffee already. He had taken to walking into school the moment that the doors were unlocked. His house had become one long uncomfortable silence since his and Brandy's latest spat, so if he could spend his time elsewhere he took the chance. Last night the silence ended, however.

The two of them ate dinner, the only sound being the scraping of silverware and the sipping of their water. Connor avoided looking over at his wife for the most part, but he could feel her gaze the whole time. From the corner of his eye he could see her open her mouth every few minutes as though she were trying to work up the nerve to speak. Then right as Connor finished up eating, she broke the silence.

"So did you know the student that got arrested?" she asked.

Connor looked over at her, taking a final drink of water. "Yeah I did," he told her.

"Wow. What was he like?"

"Quiet. But a good kid."

"Well I guess he wasn't that good of a kid."

Connor got ready to respond before thinking better of it.

"What is it?" Brandy asked, noticing his hesitation.

"Nothing. It's just..."

"Just what?"

"I have a hard time believing he's the one behind that whole thing."

"Why do you say that?"

"He just always seemed like such a nice kid. Just a fragile thing."

"Sometimes you never know."

"It doesn't feel right. I feel like they must have made a mistake."

"Well if you feel that strongly about it, why don't you say something?"

"Say something? To who?"

"The police. Let them know they could have the wrong guy."

"I don't really think they care what I have to say."

"You don't know unless you actually say something."

"Whatever."

"I'm just saying that imagine if he really is innocent. He's probably waiting on someone to help."

Connor opted to say nothing else. He told himself that he just needed to accept that Dennis hadn't been who he thought. But the next morning the same nagging feeling scratched at the back of his brain. It didn't go away as he got ready for work or as he sat and drank his coffee. He tried to refocus his attention, but it would always snap back. It so occupied him that he didn't notice as Lance Milton dragged his feet, coming to sit across from Connor.

"Hey," he forced out as he eased himself down onto the chair. The subdued nature of it all managed to shift Connor's focus. Typically, Lance would slide into a room announcing his presence as though he were in a sitcom. Right now, he seemed to have swung to the other extreme.

"Hi, Lance," Connor said. "You okay?"

"Did you not hear?"

"About Dennis Clements? Of course I did."

"No. About Benson."

"Kristin? What about her?"

"She's in the hospital. She tried killing herself yesterday."

"She what?!"

"Yeah."

"Holy shit. Is she going to be okay?"

"I don't know. I just read something about it in the paper this morning."

"Oh my God. I knew she wasn't coming to work, but I didn't imagine she'd end up like this."

"Had you seen her since the shooting?"

"Just right afterwards. She was in the back of an ambulance. Looked to be in shock or something."

"Guess it stands to reason after what happened to her. I can't say I'm surprised. I don't know how I would've reacted if I had been in that situation."

So why the hell am I surprised? Connor thought to himself. That look in her eye when she sat in the ambulance had been one of death. And what had he done? Nothing. For the rest of the day thoughts of Kristin and thoughts of Dennis wrestled each other for control of his mind.

They continued to fight as he made his way home. Images of Dennis lying in a jail cell. Of Kristin lying in a hospital. They bored their way into his skull, a constant reminder of what he had and hadn't done. Two people that he felt responsible for. Two people left to fate. Maybe there was nothing he could do for Dennis, but Kristin was just a short distance away. Off to the right he saw the hospital rising up into the sky. At the next intersection, he hung a right and headed towards it.

Once there, he got Kristin's room number and headed up. He chose to take the stairs, needing the time to sort out what he would say.

Why am I even bothering? What the hell am I going to say to her? She doesn't want to see me. With every step he had to fight the urge to take off running. *Just stay the hell out of it and try to return to a normal life.* What amounted to normal for him anyway.

As he walked the hall to her room he felt as though everyone stared. His assurances to himself that no one knew him did little to assuage his fear. He knocked unevenly at the door, his fist shaking the whole time. Diane answered, her whole body hanging there like a partially deflated balloon.

"Yes?" she said with a heavy breath.

"Are you Kristin's mother?" Connor asked.

"Who are you?"

"My name is Connor Sullivan. I work with Kristin at school."

Diane squinted and tilted her head in recognition. "Mr. Sullivan? Her mentor?"

"Yeah. I heard about what happened, and I thought I might check in on her."

"That's very sweet of you, but I don't think she wants to see anyone."

"Mom," Kristin called from inside the room. "It's fine. Let him in."

Diane offered Connor what constituted a smile for her these days (but was really nothing more than a slight lengthening of her lips), and stepped aside so he could enter.

"Hi, Mr. Sullivan," Kristin called from her bed. Her skin lay loose and thin on her face.

"Please. Call me Connor," he replied taking a seat beside her.

"Mom, will you step outside?" Kristin asked.

"No way. I'm not leaving your side ever again," Diane insisted.

"Please. I'll be fine." Their eyes met and said all that needed saying.

Diane turned and left the room.

Silence persisted in there for two minutes as each thought of what to say. Connor looked over at Kristin's wrists, eyeing the two cuts that had been closed up with stitches.

"They weren't deep enough," Kristin said.

Connor lifted his head to look at her. Her eyes were fixed on the cuts, a sense of regret in them. He wondered if it was regret for what she'd done or for what she failed to do.

"Why'd you do this?" Connor asked.

"It was easier."

"Easier? Than what?"

"Having to wake up every day. Having to face a town that hates me."

"What are you talking about? Kristin, you didn't do anything wrong."

"Tell that to the person who sent me a death threat."

"A what?"

"Yeah."

"Who?"

"I have no idea. I just got it in the mail one day. A bunch of letters clipped out of magazines and glued to the paper like a ransom note. 'Fuck you, bitch. You let our kids die. And now you're gonna die too.'"

"Oh my God. Did you call the cops?"

"No."

"What did your mom say?"

"I didn't show her either."

"Why not. Someone needs to know about that."

"Please. If it had been more than a threat they would have saved me the trouble."

"Kristin, why are you blaming yourself for this?"

"I literally walked them into the line of fire."

"There was no way for you to know..."

"Don't. Don't tell me that. You're the hero of Stanford. You don't know what it's like to get your students killed."

Connor cursed himself for even coming here. He had traveled way beyond his comfort zone. And he had to admit that she was right. He didn't have the first clue of how she felt. He began to rise out of the seat, ready to leave without another word said... And then he remembered Bradley Neuman. With that he eased back into his chair. Kristin looked over wondering why he had stayed.

"Kristin... you know that plaque that's in the hallway downstairs at school?" he asked.

"Yeah."

"I knew that kid. Name was Brad. I had him in class my second year there. Seemed like a nice kid. Slipped under the radar though. He was just so damn quiet. And as it turns out that's because he was depressed. At the end of the year, he killed himself. And it wasn't until then that I recognized the warning signs. Not only that, but he asked to speak to me just days before he did it, but I had been too busy to talk. Not a day goes by that I don't wonder what he wanted to say. Wondering if I had stuck around that it could have made a difference. But I can't know because I didn't do anything."

Kristin said nothing. She just rubbed her scars while a single tear fell to her chest.

Connor sighed and then continued. "With this job, you'll always have those students whom you wonder if you could've done more. When we take this job, we think we're going to save the world. But pretty soon we figure out that we won't, that we can't. So you know what you do? You stay on the lookout for someone, anyone that you can save. And when all's said and done, if you can say that you saved anyone, then you did more than most. You couldn't have known what was going to happen. And the fact of the matter is that you don't know what would have if you stayed in the room. What you do know is that twenty-three kids got out of that school safely because you took action."

Tears fell from her eyes. Her chest heaved up and down.

"I hope you come back to school, Kristin. You're pretty damn good at your job and those kids are better off with you there." Connor stood and reached out his hand, about to hold Kristin's, but then thought better of it and withdrew. "I hope to see you around. Bye." He turned and walked out of the room. As soon as he opened the door, Diane stood in his way, having been there the whole time. He offered a polite nod, a smile, and then walked by her. He hoped he'd done right by Kristin. That he'd done right by anyone.

On another floor, Julie inched her way out of the bed, wincing every time a muscle moved in her body. Each time it made her feel like her chest had been set ablaze. Brian stood alongside, ready to catch her the moment she slipped. She'd just been cleared to go home, and she was desperate to be rid of this hospital. But with as much pain as she experienced at the moment, she still felt a pang of relief that it had happened. Whatever else went down before this shitstorm came to an end, she would be able to sit on the sidelines. Because the physical pain she felt was nothing compared to the emotional exhaustion that had been inflicted on her. Unless, of course, that it ended with Terry behind bars. But she couldn't think about that. Wouldn't allow herself to.

Terry himself wasn't at the hospital to accompany his mother home as Brian had sent him ahead to make sure that the house looked good for her. Terry went around the house, trash bag in hand, picking up random crap on the ground. He came to his room where he stopped in his tracks and looked on at his dresser, thinking of what lay inside. From downstairs, Terry heard the door open and footsteps on the floor.

"Lipton," a voice called from downstairs. Terry turned at the sound and trudged down, recognizing the voice as belonging to Johnny.

"What's up, man?" Terry said as he came to the top of the stairs and looked down at his friend. "Come on upstairs."

Johnny bounded up the stairs and followed Terry into his room. "I'm sorry about your mom, man. That's some fucked up shit."

"Yeah. It is," Terry replied, his voice monotone. He picked some trash up from the floor before going over to his dresser and removing the SSPA flyer and tossing that in the bag too.

"What the hell are you doing, man?" Johnny asked.

"I don't want any part of them anymore."

"What do you mean? What about our plans, man?"

"What plans? You told me to get these addresses, and that we'd show up all the cops in town. Except you never bothered telling me how we would do that." With that he withdrew the list of addresses from his pocket and ripped it to shreds, staring Johnny down the entire time.

"Fuck you. I've got plans."

"Yeah... what are they?"

Johnny stood there, for once not having the words.

"That's what I thought. For all I know, you were going to get a bunch of pizzas delivered to them. You're all fucking talk."

"What changed?"

"My mom getting shot. That's what."

"Hey, some racist asshole shot her. Not us."

"Yeah, but one inch is all that separated her from a hole in the ground. And I don't want any part of something that could finish the job." Terry turned away, having nothing else to say on the subject. "I got to keep cleaning. I'll see ya later, man."With an aura of protest, Johnny turned and left. The moment he did, Terry didn't give him another thought. An hour later, when Julie arrived home, inching her way into the house, Terry stood there waiting. Brian came in after her, pleased to see that his son had exceeded his expectations about cleaning the house. From floor to ceiling, the place looked spotless. For a moment, he would have even sworn that it sparkled like out of a cartoon. His eyes were soon drawn away from the house as he saw what sat in Terry's arms. Terry held a vase of flowers. Brian hadn't expected this from his son, and looked on at Julie's reaction.

Julie could hardly process all that she took in. Ever since the shooting, Julie kept expecting to wake up from the most horrible, and most vivid of nightmares. The scene that she saw in front of her now brought everything snapping back to reality in the most wondrous of ways. Her face turned up into the biggest smile before her eyes collapsed into tears. Brian and Terry were at her side to make sure she hadn't hurt herself.

"I'm fine. I'm fine," she assured them. "This is all just so amazing. Thank you, both."

"Let's go get you laid down," Terry said as he led his mother over to the couch which he had turned into a makeshift bed for her. They got her settled, and Terry set the flowers on the side table.

"No. Put them on the coffee table. I want to look at them," she said. She watched her son as he did so, and looking up at him she saw what had been missing from him for so long now.

In his eyes, she could see the little boy that she had raised. The child that would run after her if she left the room. And with that, she found the relief that she'd been looking for. She knew at that moment that Terry couldn't have done those awful things at the school. And maybe, just maybe, she hadn't failed as a parent after all.

33

————

Dennis had just spent his first night in the county jail. The bed and pillow they offered provided a bit more comfort than what he had gotten at the Stanford Police Department, but not much. The slop that got piled on his tray for breakfast made him long for the school lunches. With every step that he took, his head would wobble around as he noted where everyone was. He felt convinced that someone would jump him at any moment. In his mind, there existed little difference between here and an actual prison. After that he sat around in his cell willing himself to think about anything but what awaited him. It proved fruitless as he had been told that he'd end up in front of a judge any day.

He had been in there for about an hour when a guard came around to say that he had a visitor. The guard led him to the visitors' room. The walls had been painted a dull white and were lined with tables and chairs up and down the length of the room. At a table towards the back of the room he saw his mother sitting. Despite her best efforts, she still looked haggard. She had pulled her frizzy hair back in a ponytail. She wore a nice blouse, but the wrinkles made it clear that it hadn't been ironed.

Her lipstick was smeared around the edges. When she saw her son, a bittersweet smile came onto her face. A man in a suit sat next to her. A loosened tie hung around his neck. A briefcase sat on the table in front of him where he shuffled papers around.

As he approached the table, his mother stood and opened her arms for a hug, but a shake of the head from a guard dissuaded her of the notion. She lowered them, looked down in embarrassment, and went back to her seat. Dennis slumped down, the chair hard and rigid. He attempted to readjust a couple times before deciding comfort wouldn't come.

"Hi, honey," his mother said with a tone of uncertainty. "How are you?"

"I don't know," Dennis answered.

"This is Mr. Dillon," she said, pointing to the man in the suit. "He's going to be your lawyer." He didn't look up at all. He still moved around papers, his briefcase filled with about a dozen different files.

"How are you paying for him?" Dennis asked.

"He's a public defender." Dennis's heart sank at the sound of that. How much good could this man actually do for him? He could almost see the signature on his death certificate now.

"Hi, Dennis," Mr. Dillon said, finally closing his briefcase, having apparently found the correct file. "Okay, so I just got the file on you from the police this morning. I haven't been able to go through it all, but I did do a quick review of the evidence they've compiled. The good news is that most of the evidence against you is circumstantial at best. The drawings, the story, the book. It doesn't do much for them. Your journal, they'll use to try to establish motive but thankfully there's nothing too damning in there."

"Uh-huh," Dennis said, trying to follow along. Mr. Dillon rattled all of this off, making it hard to hear every word.

"Bad news is that this floor plan they found in your trunk is quite damning. So unless you have a credible explanation for how and why it was there, there isn't much we can do with this."

"How can they pin that on me? None of what's written is even in my handwriting."

"Doesn't matter. They'll just say the other shooter wrote it and then gave it to you."

"So what do we do?" Dennis asked.

Mr. Dillon sighed, looked at Ms. Clements and then back to Dennis. "Our best course of action is to try to cut a deal with the district attorney."

"Cut a deal? What does that mean?" Ms. Clements asked.

"Well, first thing you need to do is tell the police who the other shooter was. That will go a long way towards earning you some goodwill with the DA."

"I can't tell them something I don't know! I didn't do anything!" Dennis protested. His mother buried her head in her arms and cried.

Mr. Dillon was afraid of this. The ones that insisted upon their innocence made for the worst clients. "I'm going to be frank with you here, Dennis. If we actually went to trial with this, I don't see a situation where we win. And with twenty-eight people dead... thank God you're still a minor or else they'd be asking for the death penalty."

Ms. Clements shot her head up at that, a look of utter terror on her face. "The what?" she said, praying that she had misheard him.

Mr. Dillon ignored her questions and continued talking to Dennis. "If you cooperate with them, I can work with them. Get you favorable conditions. And if it is a case of you being forced into something, maybe... MAYBE... you see the outside world again someday. But that is the absolute best we can hope for. Otherwise you are looking at a deep, dark hole for the rest of your life. Do you understand?"

Ms. Clements sprang from her seat and took off towards the bathroom with her hand clamped around her mouth. Dennis sat there looking at Mr. Dillon, studying his eyes. The hint of doubt he'd seen in his mother's eyes had been bad enough, but these eyes didn't even have that. Dillon thought he had done it, and Dennis wouldn't be able to persuade him otherwise.

"I didn't do anything," Dennis told him.

"Well, then we have an uphill battle ahead for us. So we are going to have to dig up something pretty damn convincing. Because I honestly don't know how we win this."

34

————

Connor sat at his desk with a pile of student journals sitting beside him. School ended an hour ago, but here he sat nonetheless. He had fallen way behind in grading these and was now paying the price. He had just gotten to the writing prompt that he'd asked the students to do the morning of the shooting, and some of what he read made him wish for a lobotomy.

I don't no how id define evil. I guess it could be the absence of empahty. I dont think the vigils are evil though. They kinda pussies.

As he read, Connor could feel a headache coming on, but he powered through, marking each one and throwing it in a separate pile. He eyed what he still had left and could have sworn that it had gotten even bigger than when he started. He continued this way, eventually stumbling upon Dennis's. He held it in his hand not even sure what to do with it. He had managed to get through most of the day without thinking about him, but now it all came rushing back.

Not much point in grading this, Connor thought to himself, feeling inclined to just throw the thing in the trash. He couldn't help but think about what might have been in here. Dennis would have written this right before the shooting went down. The thought was chilling, but Connor's sense of morbid curiosity insisted that he take a look. He flipped through the pages. He shuddered about what he might find. If Dennis really had done what they were saying, maybe he'd gone on and on about his plans, and once again Connor would be left thinking of all that he missed. Instead, he saw something much different when he got to the one from that morning and began to read:

I agree that the Vigils are evil. At first glance, it would seem incongruous to compare the manipulation of a chocolate sale with evil acts such as murder, but it is those smaller transgressions that often lead to the larger ones later in life.

I have never really given much thought to how I would define evil. It's such a foreign concept that I suppose I've thought that it defied definition. The absence of empathy seems to be a perfect definition for it though. A hallmark of any psychopath is that they lack empathy, so equating that to evil seems rather fitting. After all, our ability to feel compassion and to feel the pain of others is what separates us from the animals. A sad fact of life is that there seem to be many people who lack empathy in certain situations. Certain people's refusal to care about the death of Noah Spaulding is a recent example. Out in the larger world, when we refuse help to people in times of need, we lack empathy. People often don't realize the kind of pain they are causing if they don't see the victims of it first-hand. We all need to work on building empathy within ourselves and our society. If we did, perhaps we could put a stop to the endless cycle of violence that the world has found itself stuck in.

Dennis's writing proved to be at a much higher level than that of his classmates, but that was of little interest to him at the moment. Ever since he heard about Dennis's arrest he hadn't been able to shake the feeling that a mistake had been made. He kept trying to quell these thoughts with the assumption that if the police had reason enough to arrest him, then he must have been the one. But what he read here... they were not the words of a killer. They were not the words of someone who an hour later would take out a gun and start shooting people. At that moment he felt assured that Dennis was innocent. And so he knew that Brandy had been right. He needed to say something to someone. If a chance existed that he could keep Dennis from rotting away in a prison cell, then he had no other choice. That, of course, raised the question of where to go from there. Would the police give a damn what he had to say? Could he possibly affect the outcome of something this big?

The next day Connor made it a point to get out of school as soon as he could and drove straight to the police department. As he walked from the doors to the front desk he kept waiting to realize this as a fool's errand. A schmuck English teacher was going to convince the police that someone was innocent with nothing more than a journal in hand? Still, he found himself at the desk asking to speak with the detective in charge of the Stanford shooting. After a brief wait, Kara arrived at the desk to welcome him back.

"Hi. I'm Detective Smalls. Mr. Sullivan?" she asked.

"Yes, that's me."

"Please follow me back." Connor obeyed. He held the journal close to his chest like a scared high-school girl clutching her books as she walked through the halls. His eyes darted left and right, his mere presence here making him uncomfortable. Kara led him to an interrogation room and asked him to take a seat. The room managed to seem smaller from the last time he was here. Connor could immediately understand why these rooms tended to be so drab. Its whole architecture set him on edge. He felt ready to confess to something he hadn't even done.

"Please forgive the setting. With sensitive information pertaining to cases, we like to keep it as private as possible."

"Oh no problem," Connor said with a nervous laugh.

"So I understand that you have some information pertaining to the Stanford shooting?" she asked as she pulled out a notepad.

"Yes. That's right."

"Now, we spoke to you before, correct?"

"Yes."

"You were the one that fought the shooter off?"

"Yes," Connor said, his voice filled with embarrassment. He didn't want to talk about that aspect of it.

"So did you recall anything that you couldn't remember at the time?"

"No. It's about Dennis Clements."

Kara tilted her head at him, wondering what he could offer in this regard if it wasn't related to the confrontation he had. "What about him?"

"Well... I feel like a mistake must have been made when he was arrested."

"How so?" She attempted to suppress the tinge of hope that began to rise. She had been attempting to disregard whatever doubts she had about Dennis.

"Well, it's just that I know the kid, and I can't picture him doing those things. He doesn't have a mean bone in his body. He certainly isn't a killer."

Kara pinched her sinuses as she listened to all of this. If she didn't know better, she could have thought she was listening to herself. "Mr. Sullivan, while I can appreciate your point of view, I'm afraid that doesn't do much in the way of evidence."

"I know. I get that, and that's what I was telling myself for a while. But then I came across this," he told her as he handed across the journal.

"What is this?" Kara asked as she took it from him.

"It's a writing journal that Dennis keeps for my class. I give them writing prompts and they respond in these. I was going through them yesterday, and I came across something that he wrote the very morning of the shooting. Like not even an hour beforehand."

Kara flipped through it coming to an end at the page where Connor instructed. She took a moment and read through it.

"Do you see what I mean? There is no way that someone would write something like that when they were about to kill a bunch of people."

Kara could see his point, but she told herself to stay focused. "Well I understand, but this doesn't really prove anything."

"Well, what kind of evidence do you have against him anyway?"

"I can't discuss that. Now is this all you have?"

"Yeah but..."

"Then thank you for coming in. If you should happen to come across anything else that you think may be helpful, then please do share it with us."

"Please. This kid is innocent. He wouldn't hurt anyone. I know it in my bones. I've been teaching for five years now, and I've come across a lot of different kids. Some of them I have been genuinely afraid of. Jesus Christ, I had a kid who got caught dissecting a cat out in the parking lot one day. I know a bad kid when I see one, and Dennis Clements isn't one of them."

"Well, do you have any idea of who may have committed the shooting?"

Connor hung his head. "No. I'm afraid not."

"Then without that or something solid pointing away from the Clements boy, there is very little you can do."

"But this doesn't make any sense."

"Sometimes it doesn't. I'm sorry."

Connor ambled his way through the station and out to his car. He had felt good this morning when he woke up, for what seemed like the first time in years. He woke up with a sense of purpose and direction. Feeling like he could do something worthwhile, but it became clear that he was destined to live a life of quiet desperation.

That night he went to bed, wondering what else he could do, if anything. For the first time since it happened, he actually replayed the shooting in his mind. He relived it, feeling that same sense of fear, dread, and uncertainty that he had that morning. The assuredness that he would end up on the receiving end of a bullet. He went through the face of every student that he knew, wondering which one of them hid a killer inside. But of the long line of students, no one stepped to the front.

35

The morning of Dennis's arraignment had come. Brody and Kara wormed through the crowd. Despite walking side by side, there might as well have been an ocean between the two of them, neither of them having said a word to each other all morning. In fact, they hadn't spoken since that night at Brody's house. Kara had noted that Brody finally showed up not reeking of booze. His standoff with the bottle still happened every night, but so far Brody had been winning.

Brody had been to the courthouse plenty of times over the years. Been there to testify. Been there to see people get convicted after he put them away. Been there to see Mandy's killer get the axe. In all the times he had been there, it had never been like this. Place was packed wall to wall, flashes from cameras making Brody feel like he was staring at the sun. Typically, Brody could shoulder his way through a crowd, but this time it felt like wading through wet cement. Even the waving of his badge wouldn't make room for him. There was no room to be made.

Once the courtroom doors swung open, the crowd cascaded in, and the two detectives moved with the rush. Once inside, their badges did manage to get them a spot up front. They sank into their seats and waited for it all to begin.

The endless babble of the room came to a halt as Dennis shambled into the courtroom. Orange jumpsuit, hands and leg cuffs. His hair shielded his eyes a bit, but the vacant stare still came through. Kid didn't even seem to know where he was. He sat in his chair right next to his lawyer who scribbled so furiously at a legal pad that he couldn't even spare his client a glance. Dennis flinched with every flash of a camera and every hurled insult or question that came his way. Brody looked on, wondering what could possibly be going through the kid's mind. What did go through the mind of someone who could kill a couple dozen people?

"All rise for the Honorable Judge Manion!" the bailiff called out. Everyone stood, Dennis a step behind them, seeming unsure of what to do. The prosecutor looked over at him like a tiger ready to pounce. The judge entered, an older man with a gut bulging beneath his robe and a horseshoe of gray hair atop his head. He eased into his seat and slipped on a pair of glasses. Everyone took their seat.

"Good morning, everyone. We have here case number 16-MR-5472. The People vs. Dennis Clements." Not a murmur was uttered as he went through his spiel. "Mr. Clements, you have been charged with twenty-eight counts of first-degree murder and fifteen counts of attempted murder. How do you plead?"

Dennis just looked on, not focusing on a thing, and saying nothing. His lawyer jabbed him in the side, bringing his attention back. He stood from his seat and looked around the room like a toddler getting his bearings on his surroundings.

"Mr. Clements, how do you plead to the charges?" Judge Manion repeated.

"Not guilty," Dennis said, his voice flat. Brody expected a series of murmurs to pop up, but none did. Manion looked on at

Dennis for another couple beats, almost as if he wanted to give the kid a second chance.

"Mr. Durant?" Manion said as he turned towards the prosecutor. Patrick Durant stood with an air of grace, commanding the attention of all in the room. A strong jaw protruded from his face. Flecks of gray peppered his black hair which he seemed to own with pride.

"We've reached out to Mr. Dillon offering a reduced sentence in exchange for a guilty plea and the identity of his accomplice. But all offers have been refused," Durant replied, emphasizing every syllable.

"Mr. Dillon?" Manion said, turning towards the defense.

Dennis's lawyer stood, wiping away the sweat that seeped out of him. He'd never been in such a situation and was constantly playing catch-up. "Your Honor. My client is innocent and can't very well reveal information that he doesn't have. We plan on fighting all charges."

"Very well. The trial shall commence on April 16 of next year. Anything else, counsel?"

"Your Honor," Dillon continued, quivering. "We would request that Mr. Clements be released under the supervision of his mother. At age sixteen, he is still a minor, has never been in any prior trouble, and hardly has the means to leave town. And with the widespread publicity of this case, there is no where he could go."

"Your Honor," Durant shouted as he stood. "Given the severe nature of this crime, not to mention the extreme unrest in the community, it would be irresponsible to release him."

"Bail is denied," Judge Manion declared without even a moment's hesitation. "Is that all?"

"One other thing, Your Honor," Dillon said with a wince, like he worried that he'd be reprimanded. "Given the intense public opinion about this case and the amount of press that the case has already gotten, we would like to request a change of venue. It would be impossible for my client to get a fair trial from an impartial jury here."

"Your Honor," Durant began the moment Dillon stopped talking. His typical poise had abandoned him. "This town has been victimized and has a right to take part in this case. And to suggest that the people of this town cannot hear the evidence and come to a just conclusion is, quite frankly, insulting."

"Hearing on change of venue will be held two weeks from today. We're adjourned," Manion declared with a swift bang of his gavel. The man had long had a reputation of keeping his courts running without a moment's interruption, and he earned that reputation today. All stood as he exited. Once he did, the crowd began to file out.

After a few quick words with Dillon, Dennis sagged down into his chair and hung his head. All energy had been zapped from him, and his feet couldn't sustain him for more than seconds at a time it seemed. Seated right behind him, his mother wiped away at her tears, not able to catch more than a few at a time. Brody looked over at her, every bit of life drained from her. Looking like every bit of happiness in the world had been burned away. Like she would be happier in the grave than her current situation. And as much contempt as he felt for that kid, he couldn't help but feel a twinge of sorrow for the boy and his mother. Both prayed for some relief that escaped them.

Meanwhile, Kara focused in on Dennis, looking in his eyes. The fear, confusion, and pleading that resided there. Kara had looked many cold-blooded killers right in the eyes, and almost every time, she saw nothing there. Within them, there existed a deep black hole. But not with this kid. She'd tried her best to ignore the creeping doubt that sifted through her during this case. Assuming that she'd gotten it wrong once again, she'd resigned herself to let it go. After all, if she managed to screw things up on a case like this... well, she could kiss her career goodbye. But what if she had been right? Then some poor kid could kiss his life goodbye. She could deal with being a pariah within the department, but she couldn't deal with the other thing. She was going to have to roll those dice.

36

Christmas fast approached, but in Stanford it came without the requisite holiday cheer. Businesses and occasional houses had been adorned with decorations, but far fewer than years previous. And the holiday greetings all sounded forced, made more out of a sense of tradition and obligation than anything else. Around town, fearful stares were made to any stranger. No one could go more than a couple blocks without a cop standing watch. When night came, most retreated inside, not to be seen again until the sun was.

This sense of unease had permeated West High as well. The administration made the decision to not hold the annual Christmas pageant. The staff Christmas party had been canceled as well. The idea of festivities seemed inappropriate.

In class, everyone went through the motions. Connor found it difficult to muster any enthusiasm for what he taught. His mind swirled with thoughts of Dennis, wondering where the truth lay. And it didn't help matters that Dennis's upcoming trial was all that students wanted to discuss. So many of them bragging of their insight to the human soul. After all, they all knew that Dennis had been bad news. Two weeks separated them from Christmas break, and Connor began the day with having to put the kibosh on one such exchange.

"I'm telling you, I wish I could whip that bastard's ass. I always knew he was a freak," Jamie said as Connor began passing out papers at the start of class.

"Jamie, let's not go down that road today. Okay?" Connor told him.

"Sure," Jamie responded noncommittally. Connor proceeded with class from there and introduced the story for the day, *The Lottery*. It told the story of a town that met to stone someone as a sacrifice. Class progressed uneventfully enough until they got to the actual stoning. At that point, Jamie spoke up again. "I'd like for Clements to be on the receiving end of that." A few snickers went around the room along with a couple looks of disgust.

"Jamie. I told you that I didn't want to hear any more of that," Connor said, setting his gaze firmly on him.

"Come on, Mr. Sullivan, you got shot at. You wouldn't want to crack him upside the head?"

"Jamie, I'm telling you for the last time." Connor attempted to control his voice, but the rise in tone was unmistakable, his temper at its breaking point.

"Whatever. I'm just saying prison is too good for the freak."

With that, Connor's temper snapped. His fist came down on the empty student desk beside him, waking the students who slept. "Dammit, Jamie! Get out of here!" Everyone looked around, wondering if this had just happened. Students all knew Mr. Sullivan to be laid back and low key.

"Wha...?" Jamie asked, as perplexed as anyone else.

"Leave. Go. I don't want you in my classroom." His voice had returned to normal, but no one would have mistaken him for calm. Jamie slunk out of his chair and walked out, eyes on him the entire time. Everyone looked around, wondering if one of them might be next. "Please finish on your own. Complete the worksheet and turn it in. No talking," Connor instructed his class. They all got to work, the class never having been quieter. Connor retreated back to his desk. He sat down and looked out on the students, his eyes falling on the lone seat at the back where Dennis should have sat.

Six hours later, Connor remained behind his desk, watching his final hour shuffle out, ready to meet the outside world. Typically, Connor would have been close behind them, but lately he had been staying longer and longer after school. While here, he could fill the time. He could distract from the creeping doubt and guilt that encroached during the unstructured hours of the night. Doubt over whether his student had really been a wolf in sheep's clothing. Guilt over whether there was anything more he could do about it. He enjoyed the monotony of the work he completed. Here there were certainties that he could rely upon.

An hour had passed since West's parking lot had been cleared of cars and buses. Kara parked there looking on at the school, not entirely sure why she was there. They had come to a standstill on the case. Clements refused to speak to them and prepared himself for trial, adamant that he was innocent. Meanwhile, they seemed to have exhausted every piece of evidence they could find.

She stared at the building where so many had died, willing it to tell her who had been behind the mask. Any answers to be found would have to be in there. No matter how cunning someone thought they were, something would get left behind. Always. In her lap sat photos from the security footage. She looked at one of Dennis heading inside the bathroom. The same one he claimed to have climbed out of. Beneath that she looked at a list of victims. She paid particular attention to those who were the last to meet their end.

Kara looked up again at the building to see it produce the body of Connor Sullivan as he descended the outside stairs. Kara recognized him and remembered that he had raised similar concerns about Clements's guilt. It seemed validating to know that someone else shared the same uncertainty. And while she may have been quick to dismiss him before, she couldn't now.

Kara jumped from her car and sailed across the parking lot, hoping to intercept him. "Mr. Sullivan!" she cried out to him.

Connor stopped mid-stride. At first glance, he didn't recognize her. He worried that it was a reporter or someone else who wanted to express their admiration. As she approached, he realized it to be the detective, and now he simply wondered what this could be about. He certainly didn't have anything else to share. And the last time he did, she didn't seem all that interested.

"Yes?" he asked as she strode up to him.

"Do you remember me?" Kara asked.

"Of course."

"I was wondering if we might have a word."

"I don't know what else you could need from me. I've shared all that I know."

Kara looked around them, paranoid that someone may be nearby and able to hear every word. "Well..." she began, choosing her words carefully. "There's a few things that I needed to check out inside, and I was hoping that you might be able to take me through."

Connor looked down at his watch, knowing that the time for him to arrive home had come and gone a while back. Still, he felt obliged to go along with her.

"I suppose I could for a moment," he answered.

"Thank you so much," Kara replied as she followed him back to the doors where his fob granted them access. Right away, Kara could feel a chill as she remembered the last time she'd been through these halls. She could see where the bodies had been laid. She could remember the smears of blood along the walls. Their footsteps echoed through the dark hallways seemingly mocking their loneliness. "So, I need to see the boys' bathroom on the first floor, if you'd take me there."

"What's in there?" Connor asked, hoping to coax something out of the detective.

"Can't get into that." The two walked on in silence, the darkness following them with every step they took. "So how have things been since you returned?"

"Strange. Doesn't feel the same."

"Suppose that stands to reason."

"Every time someone passes by my classroom, I start to think that it's happening all over again. Just this time I won't be so lucky."

"I don't think luck had much to do with it for you. You were damn brave."

"Fat load of good it did. Plenty of others didn't make it out of here."

"Well, you did what you could."

Connor didn't respond, beginning to regret having walked back in here. The two made it to the bathroom and headed inside. The vague scent of urine and feces wafted up to them. As stomach turning as the smell was, Connor knew it would be much worse tomorrow after the students had had their way with it. And the clear tiles would be sopping wet with puddles and littered with paper towels. At least that could be cleaned up though. More permanent were the messages carved into the stalls. Such witticisms as "Principle Devin Suks a Fat One." More than anything Connor felt disappointed that he hadn't at least taught his students proper spelling.

Kara didn't say a word. She simply walked back to the urinals and hoisted herself up towards the window above it.

"Get down from..." Connor started before cutting himself off. His reflex was to chastise such behavior. Thankfully, she just ignored him, so his embarrassment was short-lived. He watched as she twisted the lock and pushed the window open. She pulled herself further up and slid the upper part of her body through, enough that Connor thought she might be making a run for it.

Getting out up to her waist, Kara felt assured that Dennis could have conceivably slipped out through this window as he had claimed. So just maybe he could have been telling the truth. Still, this was hardly enough to absolve the kid. She hopped down and walked out of the bathroom without a word of explanation. Connor just whipped his head back and forth, wondering if he had just hallucinated the bizarre scene. Satisfied that he hadn't, he slipped back into the hall and caught up with Kara.

"Where to next?" Connor asked.

"I want to see Room 117," Kara answered. Connor knew which one she meant. The Slaughter Room as students had come to call it. The one where Ms. Twillman and her ten students all met their end. The one where the shooters made their exit. Since they had come back, that room had been closed off, no one daring to step foot in there. As horrendous as other parts of the school had been, this one had been unspeakable. The two of them walked upstairs and stopped in front of the classroom. Kara looked over at Connor, waiting for him to go ahead and unlock, but all he did was stand there. He wondered if he dared open the door, worried that it would be like opening the Ark of the Covenant. Even though he knew it couldn't possibly, he imagined the room to still be covered wall to wall in hot, sticky blood.

"Mr. Sullivan, would you please?" Kara requested.

With a small frown, Connor withdrew his key and slipped it into the lock. The click of the tumblers sounded like a sledgehammer to him. The door creaked open with a crying screech. The room didn't still contain pools of blood, but the copious amounts had soaked in, giving the whole room a pink hue. Kara stepped inside while Connor stood still, worried that the blood might seep into him as well. Kara flipped through her files and produced a sheet with the list of students on it.

"There were only ten kids in here. That's not a normal class size, is it?" she asked without even looking out into the hall at Connor.

"This was a class for gifted students. Those are always pretty small."

"Take a look at this," Kara said, passing the sheet to him. "Did you know any of the kids?" Connor leaned in, not daring to step a toe into the room and grabbed the sheet with the tips of his fingers. He looked it over, studying the names and the corresponding pictures. His eyes stopped for a moment at a picture of Natalie Leonard. Brown hair, round face. She did seem familiar, but he couldn't quite place her.

"I'm sorry. Can't help you there," he said as he handed the sheet of paper back. Kara headed further into the room, taking all of it in. They had chosen this room. They went out of their way to come here. And they made sure that not a single person had been left standing before they fled. Did one of them know something? Did one of them see something? Connor simply watched her circle the room, wondering what she saw there that he couldn't.

The two of them locked up the room and headed back outside. With nothing but perfunctory goodbyes, they each headed to their cars and left the school behind. That night Connor sat awake in bed. He watched the steady rise and fall of Brandy's chest accompanied by her calm breathing. Most nights she would snore like she had a lawnmower up her nose. If she happened to fall asleep before him, he would need to head out to the couch just to get some rest. Thankfully, tonight it wasn't like that and the rhythmic nature of her inhales and exhales actually soothed him, helping him reflect on his little tour of the school with Detective Smalls.

For some reason, he couldn't get the image of Natalie Leonard out of his head. Her picture hung in front of his mind's eye, swinging back and forth so he couldn't get focused on it. He yelled at himself to knock it off. He had to wake up in three hours, and the last thing he needed was to agonize over some student he had probably never even spoken a word to. Connor forced his head deep into his pillow, ready to let sleep wash over him, but right as he closed his eyes, Natalie's image stopped swinging and it all came into focus. That was Richard's girlfriend. He had seen her talking to him the morning of the shooting. Richard had said that she'd died in the shooting. So as it turned out, she was one of the last people to meet their end that morning. And that detective seemed convinced that someone in that room held the key to figuring the rest of this out. And if he really was innocent, they held the key to absolving Dennis.

37

A s Connor's class worked away at their assignment for the day, Connor typed away at his computer. He went on the district's online database and looked up Natalie Leonard. Chances are that this wouldn't lead anywhere, but taking a quick look would be no skin off his ass. Besides, if he was actually going to do this, he had to start somewhere.

Looking over her grades, he saw that they went up and down like a yo-yo. Mid-first quarter, she had almost all F's. Then they had all swung up to A's by the time she died. Looking at the past years, this roller coaster seemed to have been a trend with her. From there, he looked at her discipline records, not expecting to see anything. Kids in the gifted program rarely ended up in the discipline office. But looking her over, it seemed that she usually had a couple every year. This year she'd gotten busted for vandalism back in August. He read the record over:

Natalie, along with several other students, was witnessed dumping trash and spray-painting the walls of the gymnasium. Natalie will serve ten days of out of school suspension and be required to compensate for damage to the school.

He remembered this happening. Going over the parent

contact records only made the story stranger for her. Around the same time that her grades would plummet, teachers would email her parents saying how she'd come into class, put her head down, and do nothing. Even a few things about her snapping at them. Then as time went on, teachers did nothing but provide glowing praise. What went on with this girl? Depending on the time of the year, she seemed to be an angel or a devil.

Connor recalled that morning when she beckoned to Richard. He remembered that she looked like she may crack if you bumped into her. Looked like she may cry, but was too afraid to. So what did she talk to Richard about? Could she have seen something? Had she known something? Could she be the reason that her class ended up in the killing fields?

Later in the day, Connor stood in the hall, watching the students march up and down on their way to class. Richard appeared in the corner of his eye. The usually clean-shaven boy had become grizzled, a full beard on his face. And one that he seemed to have little interest in maintaining. His hair, which usually didn't have a strand out of place, now flopped all over the place. Looking in his eyes, the kid barely seemed to know where he was.

"Richard," Connor heard himself calling out. Richard's head jerked over. He stared at Connor as though he had never seen him before.

"Hey," he uttered. It almost sounded like a question coming out of his mouth.

"Can you come talk to me for a minute?" Connor asked.

Richard just shambled past Connor into the room.

"Are you feeling okay?" Connor asked.

"I'm fine," Richard replied, sounding as though he'd just smoked an entire carton of cigarettes.

"It doesn't look like it."

"What do you need, Mr. Sullivan?"

"I wanted to ask you about Natalie."

"What about her?"

"What can you tell me about her?"

"Why so interested?" Richard's dazed look changed into one of curiosity.

"Well, I was looking into her a bit, and it seemed like she had a bit of trouble."

Richard's indifference vanished, and his eyes widened in anger. "What's that supposed to mean?"

Connor didn't flinch, knowing that Richard was liable to break his hand if he ever tried to throw a punch. "Well, she got suspended earlier this year, and she seemed to struggle with her grades sometimes."

Richard's rage subsided, and with a gentle shrug of his shoulders, he answered, "She came down with a virus earlier this year. Missed a bunch of school is all. Couldn't keep up with the work."

"What about the suspension?"

"That was a misunderstanding. She happened to be in the gym when everyone got caught. But she didn't do anything."

"I see," Connor said, Richard's explanation not making much sense. None of that explained the familiar pattern she seemed to follow every year. "What about the morning of the... you know? How was she that morning?" Connor continued.

"I don't know. What kind of question is that?"

"So she didn't say anything to you or...?"

"I don't remember. All I remember of that day is her not getting out of here alive. Now, is there a point to all this?"

"I'm sorry," Connor said, knowing that he'd crossed a line. "Forget it."

"I gotta get to class. I'll see ya around." Connor watched him go, feeling more confused now than he had been.

38

_____

Connor looked on at the small house, curtains drawn and not an ounce of light slipping through. The white siding of the house standing out from the dull gray of the sky. The sun hadn't ventured out from behind the clouds for over a week now. A few different bouquets of flowers sat at the front door, the petals wilted and falling off. The grass of the front lawn had died as the temperatures dropped, but the fact that it stood at a foot tall made it clear that no one had bothered to cut it in quite some time.

What the hell am I doing here? Connor thought to himself. Natalie Leonard had occupied his mind for the past couple days. She was one of more than two dozen people killed that day. But he had dared to peek into the rabbit hole, and now he couldn't shake the feeling that Wonderland awaited. Richard hadn't told him the truth about her. Nothing about what he had seen of her record suggested that she had been sick, and a quick chat with Dr. Leland made it clear that she had hardly been some innocent bystander when it came to her referral. He told him that he had caught her with the spray paint can in hand. *Why would he lie?* Connor kept wondering to himself. *He was probably just trying to protect her image*, a part of him would insist. After all, what would it benefit to dredge up some of her lesser qualities? And to bring them up to her parents, it seemed to him like the work of a sociopath. But nonetheless, he was here. He tried to disregard it, but even while dead, Natalie called to him like a siren.

He emerged from his car and hauled himself towards the quiet house. Every couple steps he would stop and yell at himself to head back to the car. *What the hell am I going to say? I want to ask why your dead daughter seemed to be a bit of a screw-up.* He felt like an asshole even thinking about it. He kept telling himself that he wouldn't actually go through with this, but the house only got closer to him. He could begin to see the small imperfections in the vinyl siding. Bits of dirt staining the pure white. Small cracks running along, twisting like a valley. He had become so enveloped in it that he almost ran into the front door. A disembodied hand appeared in front of him and began knocking. He felt like he was back in high school and was about to pick up his prom date, he sweated so much.

The door swung open a couple inches at a time revealing a dark cave behind it with a woman with wiry hair tied back in a ponytail and shrouded in a robe at the entrance. The daze in her eyes suggested that the knock at the door may have woken her up.

"Can I help you?" she said, attempting to sound friendly and inviting, but seemingly choking on the words.

"Are you Ms. Leonard?" Connor asked, as inside he insisted that he make a run for it.

"Yes. What can I do for you?" she asked.

"My name is Connor Sullivan. I teach at West." Connor didn't know what he would say from one word to the next.

Ms. Leonard's eyes snapped shut at this with the realization that this strange man had come to discuss her daughter. A small nod and a step aside welcomed him in. He didn't move a muscle. Like a vampire he felt as though he needed to be invited.

"Please come in," she said.

Connor tiptoed in. Off to the right was a small sitting room with a couch facing two chairs that flanked a window. He walked to the couch and began to sit, hesitating every step of the way as though he was convinced it wouldn't be there to catch him. Ms. Leonard came and took a seat in one of the chairs.

"So what would you like to discuss?" she said with a sense of familiarity. She'd obviously been through a number of conversations about Natalie.

"Well, Ms. Leonard," Connor said, hoping the words would come.

"Brenda," she said.

"I'm sorry?"

"Call me Brenda, please."

"Of course. Well, I just wanted to ask you a few questions about Natalie if you wouldn't mind."

"Were you one of her teachers? I don't recognize you."

"No. Unfortunately, I never had the pleasure of having her in class myself."

"So what is this concerning exactly?"

"I just hoped to get a better sense of who she was."

"What would you like to know?"

"Well, pardon me for saying this, but it seems as though she may have had some trouble earlier this year."

Brenda stared off into nothingness, simply nodding her head, knowing what Connor referred to. "Natalie was diagnosed as manic depressive. She went through phases where she wouldn't do a thing. Took everything in our power to even get her out of bed. Her grades would always suffer then. But then they'd pick up. And later on they'd slip again. Such a shame too. She was so smart. Genius level IQ, believe it or not."

"Yes. I saw some of the classes she was in. Impressive."

"She could have done great things."

"May I ask about the trouble she had with the vandalism?" With the end of each question, Connor half expected to get screamed out of the house.

"That wasn't like her. She just... With her moods, Natalie had such a hard time fitting in. So when someone welcomed her in, they could talk her into just about anything. Just so desperate to be included. Feel loved."

"What about Richard?"

"Who?"

"Richard Lowe. Her boyfriend."

Brenda's eyes narrowed and looked inward. "I'm sorry, but I don't know who that is."

"He's a student at West. He said they had been going out. From what he says, I assumed it was pretty serious."

"Well, I've never met any Richard. But then again, Natalie did keep an awful lot from us."

"I see. Well, I don't want to..." Connor began, ready to make his exit.

"Would you like to see her room?" Brenda interjected.

"I'm sorry?"

"Would you like to see her room? Hasn't been touched since. My husband and I haven't been able to bring ourselves to step foot in there."

"Sure," Connor found himself saying, and immediately regretting it. He wanted out of here. And then he wanted a CAT scan for having ever come in the first place, but still he stood and followed Brenda up the stairs. The walls along the stairs had been adorned with various family photographs, allowing Connor to chart Natalie's growth through the years. One picture showed a puffy coat, with dark hair spilling out, playing in the snow. Another showed a gap-toothed girl with a grin like the

Cheshire Cat holding her backpack tight. As the girl got older the grin seemed to get smaller and smaller until at last he got to one where an upturned corner of the mouth was all that constituted a smile.

At the top of the stairs a closed door awaited them. Brenda reached for the knob, but as soon as she touched it, her hand jumped back quicker than if it had been a hot iron. Somewhere in the back of her head she imagined that Natalie could be on the other side, alive. As long as the door remained closed she could continue believing it. But the moment the door opened and all that greeted her was an empty room, then Natalie truly would be gone. Brenda would have lost her daughter all over again. Still, she knew she couldn't keep the room, or herself, shut off to the world. She reached forward and opened it up.

Connor looked into the room finding that Natalie seemed to have embraced minimalism. Not a single picture, poster, or painting adorned the wall. There was nothing but white. All that occupied the space was a bed, dresser, and desk, not a single thing out of place.

"She was never much of one for decorating," Brenda said. "Please go in."

Connor stepped in, the room feeling like an entirely different world than the rest of the house. He craned his neck as he walked around. He went to the desk where a few textbooks and notebooks were all stacked. Inching open the drawers revealed nothing but some pens and Post-its.

"She'd often spend hours in here, without us ever seeing her. Wouldn't hear a thing from her," Brenda said, standing only just inside the threshold.

Connor headed over to the closet and peeked inside. "Can I ask... did she seem out of sorts at all leading up to the..." Connor stopped, reticent to actually say the word, *shooting*.

"Why?" Brenda quipped. Her typically genial tone suddenly had bite in it.

"I..." Connor could think of nothing to justify such a ludicrous question. He eyed the window and door, wondering which one would allow for a cleaner exit. Connor went to shut the door, when Brenda reached out and kept it from closing. Her eyes were trained on the top shelf. She reached up and pulled a small leather case down, bringing a notebook tumbling down with it. She unzipped the case the tiniest bit and that proved to be enough. Brenda clutched it to her chest and shut her eyes, desperate to hold back her tears, but still they came.

"Is it... what's...?" Connor didn't know what to say. His eyes darted to every corner of the room, not knowing where to look.

"We thought she had stopped," she cried out, her voice shattering.

"What's that?"

"These are bandages and razor blades. Natalie used to cut herself. But she had stopped that!"

"I see."

"God. I can still see her arms. Rough cuts up and down. Oh God!" With that Brenda took off out of the room, dropping the case back to the ground. Connor watched her go, wondering if he should go after her. What was the social protocol for this kind of situation? What an asinine question. There were no situations like this. Connor bent down and picked up the case and notebook, figuring it would be best if they were out of sight when Brenda returned. As he picked up the notebook, it slung open to the first page. Connor glanced down at the page to see a couple lines written down in black, swooping letters: *With all beings there must be much fortuitous destruction.* His eyebrows raised at this, the line seeming cryptic and banal at the same time. With nothing else written, it meant nothing.

Connor stacked the case and notebook back in the closet

and then headed out of the room. At the bottom of the stairs, Brenda sat, her face submerged in her hands. Not a sound came from her.

"Ms. Leonard," Connor offered with some trepidation. "I'm so sorry. I didn't want to cause you any more pain."

No response came.

"If there's anything I can do..."

"Just please go," came the muffled sound of her voice.

"Of course. Please forgive me." Connor crept past her and headed towards the door. He gave her one last look. Those twenty-eight people may have been the ones who stopped breathing that day, but they certainly weren't the only ones that died.

He trotted to his car, the image of Natalie's mother sobbing searing itself into his mind. Even as he climbed behind the wheel, the cries and sharp breaths still rang in his ears. He got ready to start up the engine when something else began to ring in his ears as well: *I can still see her arms. Rough cuts up and down.* And with that a memory crashed back to him like a truck hitting him head-on. He hadn't thought of it since, not even when recounting everything to the police, but now it had become so clear. He could practically feel it underneath his fingertips. Whoever it had been in that mask that tried getting into his room had had rough patches up and down his arm. Or maybe it had been *her* arm.

39

Kara sat awake at 2:00 in the morning, the glow from her computer screen the only light in her bedroom. She had watched through the entirety of the security footage about half a dozen times. Her bed was littered with notes from the case. Every time she went through the footage, she scoured her notes, making sure she had marked off every single person who passed through the frame. Each time she went through it, something felt off to her, and she needed to know what it was.

The clock read 2:30 and the timestamp read 8:15 when something finally jumped out to her. Out of the stairwell, a figure shrouded in a hood ducked into a classroom. A quick perusal of her notes made it clear that they hadn't identified this person. Somehow, they had slipped through the cracks. Kara fast-forwarded the tape to when the first responders cleared the building. When they came to that room, they opened it up, but no one emerged. Where had they gone? She supposed they could have climbed outside, but where had they come from to begin with? Kara rewound the tape to find the figure's point of origin. The same hood didn't show up anywhere else on the tape until 8:10. She noticed the same person come forth from a room, the hoodie being pulled over his head right as he exited. Making sure his face didn't appear at all. Going to a different clip she saw the room number. Room 10. They had no record of anyone exiting that room.

~

By the time the alarm started to sing, Kara had been asleep for all of one and a half hours. Still she didn't feel any exhaustion. She had been waiting for some kind of breakthrough and last night had finally given it to her. She hurriedly threw on some clothes. Typically, she prided herself on her professionalism, but today a pair of jeans and a pullover was all she felt she had time for. She needed to follow through on this, and had no time to waste.

She ended up getting plenty of strange looks when she headed into the main office of West. Every person stopped what they were doing, some even stood as if they mistook her for president. Eyes shifted left and right as everyone wondered who would be the first to speak. Undeterred, Kara marched to the front desk and didn't wait for anyone to greet her.

"I'd like to see Principal Devin," she said as though she were ordering a cup of coffee. The secretary directly in front of her opened her mouth to reply but froze, as though she couldn't comprehend the request. And then to save her, Devin walked out of his office, perhaps troubled by the sudden drop in noise.

"Detective Smalls. How can I help you?" he asked, staggering to a stop and almost tripping over his own feet.

"May we have a word?" Kara said.

Devin looked around at his staff almost as if he wanted their permission. When it became clear that no one would grant it, he just nodded and motioned for Kara to follow him. Once inside the office, Kara immediately took a seat.

"So what can I do for you? We weren't expecting you to be by again any time soon," he said, taking a seat. *We were hoping to never see you again*, his tone indicated.

"I've discovered some new evidence that may be essential to the case," Kara said, fishing out her laptop which still held the security footage.

Devin's face dropped in disappointment. Disappointment that comes from not being able to take any more. "What evidence is that?" he forced out, almost choking on the words. Part of him didn't want to know what it was. The school had finally begun to return to a sense of normalcy, but one that could fall apart at any moment. Her presence had probably already spread through half the building. And it threatened to be that extra bit of weight that brought everything crashing down.

"Please look at this footage," Kara said, paying no attention to Devin's hesitation. She pulled up the clip of the hooded figure entering the empty classroom.

"What am I looking at?" Devin asked.

"That student heads into that classroom, but doesn't come back out."

"And?"

"And if you go back with the tape," which she began to do, "you can see him coming out of Room 10, putting on that hoodie."

"I still don't understand."

"We didn't have any record of anyone having left Room 10. But here we have someone doing just that, and we never see them again after the shooting."

"So you think that that must be the second shooter?" Devin asked.

Kara nodded with a hint of unwillingness. After all, she wasn't convinced that they had caught the first one.

"So what would you like from me?"

"First, can you tell me which room it is that he heads into?"

"What is that? Room 15? That's a computer lab."

"Would it have been empty at that time?"

"Well, I would need to check the sign-up sheet, but most days it is empty." Devin scanned her eyes, hoping he was giving her what she needed. "Is that all?"

"Well, if this individual left Room 10, then I'll need to speak with that teacher."

"Of course. That would be... That would be Mr. Milton's classroom. I'll go get him."

"Great," Kara said, standing up.

"Actually," Devin started while shrinking away a little. "I think it would be best if you remained here. It's just that..."

Kara had been on the force long enough to know the look of anxious fear at the presence of a cop, and everyone in this building had had it since she walked in. "Of course. I'll wait," she told him.

Five minutes later, Devin returned with Lance Milton in tow. His gut, which had before just spilled over his belt, had extended a couple of inches over the past couple months. His eyes hung half closed. As he sat, he took off his glasses and massaged the bridge of his nose.

"Mr. Milton," Kara said, standing and extending her hand. "Detective Smalls. Thank you for coming to see me. I hope I'm not taking you away from anything too important."

"No problem. A TA is covering my class right now. What can I do for you?" Milton had to take a deep breath after every sentence.

Kara went back to her computer and brought up the image of the student leaving Milton's classroom. "Mr. Milton, we've noticed this student leaving your classroom shortly before the shooting began."

Milton said nothing. He just looked on.

"Now we see this person enter a classroom, but he doesn't come out again. And we have no record of anyone having left your classroom at that time."

Milton crossed his arms, wrapping himself in a deep hug. His bottom lip quivered as he tried to find the words. "I... I don't always have students fill in the sign-out sheet." Devin looked down on him, biting his lip and suppressing a grimace.

"Why not?" Kara asked, leaving the judgment to Devin.

"Just seems like a waste of time. Didn't find it necessary," Milton replied, his eyes transfixed on his shoes.

"What would you say is necessary, Mr. Milton?" Devin growled at him. But a quick look from Kara forced him to shut up again.

"Well, can you tell me if you know who this student is?" Kara asked, pushing the laptop towards Milton. He leaned in, peering through his thick lenses.

"Sorry. I couldn't tell you. Not that good of an image."

"Do you remember anyone leaving your class that day?"

"I don't remember much from that day. It's all kind of cloudy in my head. I couldn't even tell you what I had taught that period."

"Well, what did you do when the lockdown came?"

"We're right near an exit, so we took off and headed towards the rally point."

"And you really don't remember someone leaving?"

"I'm sorry. I don't."

"Anyone in that class behaving strangely that day?"

"Again, I..."

"I understand."

"Anyone in that class that you could imagine being..."

"Jesus no. That's a Pre-Advanced Placement class. Kids are

great. I barely even need to write any of them up for that matter."

"Well, I'd like to see a class list all the same."

"We'll get you that," Devin said, staring down the barrel at Milton the whole time.

"Thank you. That's all I need."

With that, Milton looked between Kara and Devin, with a visage of guilt, wondering if he had done something to aid the shooter.

"Thank you, Mr. Milton," Devin said, his voice laced with disdain. Milton's only response was a half-smile, as he slithered out of the chair and then the room. "So..." Devin said, looking over at Kara, shifting around on his feet. He looked like he had to pee, but actually he was just hoping that Kara would vacate the premises.

"I'll take that class list," Kara said, settling into her chair.

While Kara made her line of inquiry upstairs, Connor circled his class as they worked in groups. All the while his mind lay elsewhere, thinking over what he had found at Natalie's home. He couldn't get the feeling of those rough marks on the shooter's arms out his head, wondering if they had belonged to Natalie. But how the hell could it? She was dead for God's sake. Of course, she wouldn't be the first shooter who saved themself as the final victim. And that would explain why that classroom was the last one. She blended in with the victims and everyone was none the wiser.

A voice from the back of his head said that he should call the cops, tell them what he'd found. But what would he tell them? *One of the girls who died, well it turns out that she was prone to cutting herself. And I vaguely remember that one of the shooters had something on their arm which may or may not have been cut marks.* He felt like an idiot even thinking it, so he could only imagine what the police would think if he actually dared to say it.

The bell rang, signaling the end of the class. Like dogs, the kids all jumped from their seats and were out the door in less than a minute. Connor went about making the class look semi-presentable as the next group ushered in. The process repeated along with his obsessive string of thoughts. They would continue all day, only to be interrupted when Milton dragged his feet into the classroom after the final bell, looking like he'd just had the shit kicked out of him.

"What the hell happened to you?" Connor said, looking up from his computer.

"I got called into the principal's office today," Milton replied, trying to make a joke, but his cracking voice giving away the true nature of his feelings.

"What happened?"

"That uh... that cop came by."

Connor perked up at this. "What's going on?"

"They have video of someone leaving my room at the end of first period the day of the shooting. Apparently this guy ducked into one of the computer labs and was never seen again."

"And..." Connor egged him on, thinking he knew where this was headed.

"I don't know. I guess they think he was the other shooter."

"Well, who was it?"

"Don't know. They put on a hoodie right as he left the room. And I didn't have him sign out, so..."

"Do you remember who it was?"

"I wish I did."

"Jesus Christ."

"Uh-huh... So Devin's probably going to be serving me my

papers pretty soon. But, Jesus, I don't even care about that anymore. Did I let this whole thing happen somehow?"

Connor watched a tormented look come onto Milton's face. It wasn't too different from the one that Connor had when he first heard about Bradley Neuman. If it turned out that one of the shooters did come out of his class, then that look may never leave Milton's face. Connor's heart broke as the once jovial teacher seemed on the precipice of becoming a blubbering mess. "You can't know that," Connor said, hoping to offer some small bit of comfort.

"Well, we might know pretty soon."

"Whoever it was, they would've found a way somehow. You having them sign a sheet was not going to stand in their way."

"Yeah. Maybe you're right," Milton said. But it was clear to everyone that he didn't really believe it. Possibly he never would. "See you later, Sully," Milton offered, wanting little to do with this conversation anymore. Connor watched yet another victim of the shooting skulk away.

For the next fifteen minutes, Connor looked down at his stack of ungraded papers, attempting to will himself into actually grading them, but his doubts and worries haunted him. He walked himself back through Natalie's house, wondering if he may have missed something. He looked back at her spartan room. The desk that was much cleaner than his could ever hope to be. The little leather case that tumbled from her closet. The notebook that came with it... And with that something else wiggled itself to the front of Connor's mind. Inside that notebook had been a small message. What had it been? He could picture the curving letters. The pitch-black ink. What did it say? From the fog of his memory, two words came forward: "fortuitous destruction." What did that mean? Anything?

Turning away from his papers, Connor clicked away at his computer and googled the term. He scrolled down the first page hoping to see anything that sparked something. The last result on the page did the trick as he saw the words, "with all beings there must be much fortuitous destruction." That was it. He could see the whole message written in the notebook now. What did it mean? A quick click on the link showed him that it came from *The Origin of Species.*

Connor turned and looked down at the floor of his room. Tucked up by the bookcase that sat behind his desk was a copy of that book itself. He fished it up and began flipping through it, wondering if he might find where the statement was. Maybe it could shine a little light on what that meant. *Why the hell do I have this here, anyway?* Connor wondered as he flipped through the book. *That's right,* he thought as the answer came to him. *Richard had borrowed it from me.* The flipping of the pages slowed down as that last thought cemented itself. Richard had borrowed it. Natalie's boyfriend.

"Milton!" Connor cried as he burst up from his seat. He practically tripped over his feet as he clambered out of his room and down the hall. Milton poked his head out of his room having heard the cry.

"Yeah?" he asked. His once boisterous voice was now just above a whisper.

Connor slowed his run, came to a halt, and looked around awkwardly, realizing that he'd come off far too urgent. "I... I was just wondering if I could see your class list."

"Get in line. Cop took a look at it too. Why do you want it? You gonna try to solve this thing yourself?" It was Milton's attempt at his usual kind of joke, but it sounded forced coming from him now.

Connor chuckled in embarrassment, for the first time realizing that that's just what he had been doing. He had never really given any thought to all that he had done. Just kind of hoping he'd stumble on something to clear Dennis. But doing that would most likely mean finding who really had done it. "Just curious, I guess," he told Milton.

"Whatever," Milton replied as he beckoned Connor to follow him. He went to his computer and pulled up the roster. "Take a look," he said as he turned the computer around. Connor scanned the screen, his eyes coming to a stop at the name, "Richard Lowe."

Connor stepped back a bit, his stomach turning over. Natalie. A quote from Darwin. Video of someone coming out of his class. All the strings led right back to Richard Lowe. But no, it couldn't be. Richard was a lot of things. A little pompous. Stick up his ass. But he couldn't have been a killer. Guy didn't let a speck of mud hit his shoes much less a splatter of blood. After all, these could be coincidences. But how many were too many?

40

Brody drove over to the cemetery to visit Mandy. He hadn't been by in more than a year. He kept telling himself he would. Even gotten in the car a few times, but could never actually start it. Each time he imagined looking on at the tombstone and seeing the epitaph having changed to "It's all your fault." The image of that was enough to send him fleeing back into his house. Now he knew it to be the time.

As he walked amongst the tombstones snow began to fall and dust the ground below him. He felt it appropriate. Mandy never felt happier than when it snowed. If she saw even a flake she would beg to go outside. She'd run around with her face in the air, sticking her tongue out, catching as much as she could. Brody could recall once when the snow had grown high enough that it towered over her. He watched her through the window as she fell and sank into it. He rushed out to her, convinced she'd be in tears, but as he looked down at the hole she had made, he just saw her giggling.

Brody reached the headstone. He had wanted to get her something ornate, but the most he and Christine had been able to afford was a flat slab. Brody looked down on it: *Mandy Morgan:*

Her smile never wavered. He took a seat on the ground. The cold had frozen it solid. He imagined the gravediggers breaking their shovels as they went to work. The winter air pricked at his skin like pins stabbing his cheeks.

Brody would sit there for a whole hour, simply looking on at the headstone the entire time. He kept trying to think of something to say, but nothing came. And he couldn't imagine the point. When all was said and done she would still be there, and he would still be to blame.

From his pocket, he felt his phone. Taking it out and glancing at the screen he saw that Kara was calling. He silenced it and shoved it away. He couldn't speak to her right now. Not yet. Not until he had gotten his head back on straight.

41

The clock neared 7:30, and Connor hadn't left his classroom. He was content to stay there until the janitors forced him to. An hour after school had let out, Brandy had called, inquiring into what he was up to. He simply told her he had a lot of grading to do, knowing she wouldn't like the idea of him playing Sherlock Holmes. Every couple minutes he would stop and wonder to himself what the hell he was doing. He told himself to put all of this down. Wherever this road led, it ended with one of his students being a killer. And once again, he would wonder if he should have known.

He pored over his copy of *The Origin of Species* trying to find out where that quote from Natalie's notebook had originated. Beside him, on a piece of paper, he'd written the quote out in his chicken scratch. Everything he had stumbled across whirled around in his head, and it all formed one picture: Richard. One part of him screamed to call the police. Another part screamed that he couldn't send Richard down the river without knowing for sure. But he had to admit that he was in over his head. Dennis would be starting his second life sentence before Connor found something concrete. He took his wallet out and withdrew Kara's card back from when he'd first spoken to her. He punched in the number on his cell phone and listened to the ring on the other end.

"Detective Smalls," Kara's voice answered.

"Yes. This is..." Connor didn't know where to start. This wasn't exactly the kind of phone call he generally made.

"Yes," Kara said, prompting him to continue.

"This is Connor Sullivan. From West High."

A brief pause came as Kara felt taken aback by the random call. "What can I do for you?" she asked incredulously.

"I believe that I found something."

"Found what?"

"I think it could lead you to the shooter."

"What is it?" Kara's voice perked up at this, hoping the puzzle pieces had slid into place.

"I... Is there a way you could come by and see it? It's not something I can really explain."

"Well, why don't you bring it to the station? I'm still here."

"This isn't something I want getting around. I could be wrong, and I don't want to throw anyone under the bus."

"Very well. Your address?"

"I'm at the school. Call when you get here, and I'll let you in."

"I'll be there in fifteen minutes." She didn't bother saying goodbye.

Connor hung up and looked back down at the mess before him. The words on the page began to blur together from scanning the book for the last hour. He leaned back and rubbed his eyes to the point where colorful shapes popped up in front of him. He could also feel the walls of his bladder start to expand. Figuring he deserved a small break, he came from behind his desk and headed out towards the bathroom. Along the way he texted Brandy, letting her know that he'd be home soon, not even knowing if it were true.

The halls were as dark as he'd ever seen them. Without the mob of students, the halls echoed like a cave.

From the stairwell, Richard poked his head out watching Connor head down the hall. At the end bell he had ducked into an upstairs bathroom and stayed there until he knew that the school had cleared out. Ever since Connor had inquired about Natalie, Richard's instincts kicked in, wondering why Connor would ever be so curious. And then he followed as Connor paid a visit to Natalie's house. He didn't care for Connor's persistence in the matter, knowing that it could lead nowhere good. Richard crept along the hall to Connor's room, knowing that he had the school to himself now. The lone janitor had been knocked unconscious and stashed away in a supply closet. Richard stopped short of killing him, not wanting to unless necessary.

Walking up to Connor's desk, he saw Darwin's book lying open. Laying down next to it was a scrap of paper with a quote on it that Richard found all too familiar. The same quote that he had passed along to Natalie as he prepped her. A list of Milton's class as well, Richard's name circled. So he had not been mistaken to sense Connor's misgivings. He had gone this far, and would not let some second-rate teacher bring it crumbling down. Richard left the room and followed Connor's trail, but not without first taking Connor's keys and locking the door behind him. He came to a stop outside the bathroom as he heard muffled babbling coming from inside.

After his message, Brandy had called Connor desperate for more than some throwaway text.

"What are you still doing there?" she asked.

"I... I got work to do," he told her, having nothing else to say.

"Something is going on with you. You're more distant than usual."

Connor said nothing. He couldn't very well argue. She was right.

"Well?"

"Nothing."

"Please come home. You're scaring me." He expected her to start yelling, but he could tell that the fear was real.

"Okay, I'll be there soon." He had nothing else he could say. He only hoped he wouldn't have to wait on Detective Smalls for long. He hung up the phone, hating himself for what he was doing to his own wife.

As he went to exit the bathroom, the door swung open and Richard appeared before him as if he had commanded the door to allow him in. Connor jumped back, at first not even realizing who it was. As it all became clear, he looked the young man up and down, perplexed by the image in front of him. Richard still carried the bedraggled look from when Connor had last spoke to him. The same scruffy beard. Same loose, ratty shirt. But now it all seemed unnatural on him, and he wore it with disdain.

"Richard? What the hell are you doing here?" Connor asked. All of this was so sudden that all thoughts of Brandy now left him.

"Why have you been asking about her?" Richard replied, his eyes never blinking.

"What are you talking about?"

"Natalie. Why have you been asking about her?"

"I..." Connor stopped mid-sentence, not sure how to answer.

"You asked around about her. You went to her house. And we both know where you saw that quote you have jotted down in your room."

Connor felt himself become light-headed at what he just heard. The room began to tilt and tumble before him as the picture grew clear for him. There had been one too many coincidences. "Richard? What's going on?" he choked out as his eyes wandered down and saw that Richard's hand rested in his pocket. And had been ever since he stepped into the bathroom.

"What did you find out?"

"It was you, wasn't it, Richard?" Their eyes fixed on each other, Richard's gaze not breaking for a second, not even as he withdrew the gun from his pocket.

"Did I not serve Clements up on a platter for everyone?"

Connor wavered from side to side not knowing whether he would faint or throw up. He couldn't even separate Richard's words from the clamor inside his head.

"Why?" he said, his own voice sounding like a foreign language to him.

"Don't give me that, Connor," Richard spat. It was the first time he'd used his teacher's first name, and he said it with such contempt. "Don't act like you suddenly care about the swine that go here. We both know how much you hated them. They dragged you down. You should thank me for thinning the herd."

"Thinning the herd? Who the hell do you think you are?"

"I'm fortuitous destruction."

"You're insane."

"Who have you talked to?" Richard demanded as he started to raise the gun.

"What?"

"You've been running around like Columbo. I want to know who you've talked to."

"No one."

"Bullshit!" Richard screamed, pointing the gun straight out.

"Put the gun down," Connor pleaded.

"Don't waste your breath. We both know how this is going to play out."

"Don't do anything stupid."

"Please. So do you have anything to tell me?"

Connor's silence answered the question.

"Fine. I really didn't want you to end up like the rest of them, but so be it." Richard's arm extended a bit more, making his intentions clear. In that instance, Connor took action. Not until it had all ended could he even say how it happened. The sight of Richard's finger fluttering over the trigger pushed him into gear. Connor leapt forward, covering the couple feet between him and Richard. The whole scene caught Richard off guard, not giving him time to react. Connor angled his shoulder and threw it into the young man's chest. The two of them drove against the wall. Richard collapsed to the floor. On shaking legs, Connor reached for the bathroom door and yanked it open. He rushed into the hall, his feet sliding the entire way. Grabbing onto the wall, Connor regained balance and took off running. He whipped out his phone and attempted to dial 911, but his fingers tripped over all the buttons.

Reaching the staircase, he flew up them as a couple shots rang off behind him, one even landing right at his feet. At the top of the stairs, Connor sprinted towards the front doors, but when he reached them, it was like running into a brick wall. He tried it twice more, but the truth became clear. The doors had been locked. And about a full hour before it should have been. That's because for all of Richard's faults, the kid was a planner. After having eliminated the janitor from the equation he had taken the keys and locked up the building. It hadn't taken long. All but a few exits had already been taken care of. That left Connor trapped and at Richard's mercy.

Connor could hear his student coming up the stairs. He took off the other way and dashed back the way he came. As Connor reached the hallway intersection, Richard came to the top. Connor swerved left and sped the other way. A couple more shots rang out behind him, but he knew better than to look back.

"Oh fuck you. Where do you think you're gonna go?!"

Richard's voice chased after him. Connor thought that over himself, wondering if he had anywhere to go, anything to do. At this moment he wasn't even sure of where he was headed other than away. Ahead of him lay another stairwell. Connor reached them and bound down a few steps at a time. As he reached the first landing his feet twisted over themselves and sent him tumbling. He didn't waste a second springing up and going the rest of the way. Down the hall he could see his classroom off to the side. He could get in there and barricade himself once again. But once he reached there that door proved to be a dead end as well. A search of his pockets produced nothing. Another exit had been blocked.

Panic threatened to set it in, but Connor didn't let it. He sprinted away, again on the lookout for anywhere he could stash himself. Doing a full circle, Connor came back to the main stairwell, but tucked himself underneath them this time and rolled a trash can in front of him. He knew it was a sorry excuse for a hiding spot, but Detective Smalls had to be here soon. He didn't dare actually call the police. He needed to remain quiet so as not to clue Richard in on his location. So all he could do was wait and hope.

Kara pulled up to the school, her phone glued to her ear. "Brody, you need to pick up your goddamn phone," she said in an exasperated sigh. She had tried him five different times since getting Connor's call, but kept winding up at voicemail. "I got a call from one of the teachers we interviewed. I might be onto something. Meet me at the school," she said, leaving him a message. She hung up as she swerved the car into a spot.

Richard had stopped his fast pursuit and now took his time as he hunted through the halls. "I don't know what you think you're doing," he called out. "It's just you and me. Please don't make this worse. I'm gonna find you. There's only so many places you could be."

Connor still huddled away. From the halls, Richard's footsteps rang clearly. It sounded as though he walked directly over him. Connor would hold his breath until he could feel his lungs burn. Every few minutes a shadow would fall across his little alcove as Richard made another pass.

As much as Richard enjoyed the chase, his patience quickly wore thin. And then he recalled the memorial service at the park, where Connor had been considerate enough to offer his phone number to a grieving child. A number that still resided inside Richard's phone. He took it out and sent the call. From where he was, Connor's thoughts finally returned to Brandy. What would her last memories of him be? As someone who would barely talk to her? And why? What did he hope for? That given time everything would just work itself out? That eventually she would let go of everything she wanted out of their marriage, out of life? All the years he had spent on the sidelines, never thinking about how he had put her there too.

Then his pocket lit up as his phone started to sing, acting like a homing beacon. He scrambled, shoving his hand in his pocket to silence it, but at that point, it had served its purpose. Darkness fell over Connor's hole as Richard approached.

"Thank God. This was getting annoying," Richard said with a chuckle as he closed the distance. Connor felt like trapped prey as he saw Richard's head come into view. Knowing he had few options left to him, he grabbed a hold of the trash can and charged out with it straight into Richard. It did little to deter him, but bought Connor enough time to spring onto him, grabbing for the gun. Connor pinned Richard against a wall and attempted to point the gun anywhere that he wasn't. It discharged, a spit of fire and plume of smoke coming out of the barrel. Connor felt like his head had been plunged underwater, all sound being drowned out.

A quick knee to the groin caused Connor to double over and gave complete control back to Richard as he wrenched Connor by the hair and threw his head back, bringing the gun right to his forehead.

"Just couldn't leave well enough alone. No one was gonna miss Clements. And you saw what a mess Natalie's mother is. You gonna drag her dead daughter's name through the mud? You're no hero, Connor. Just another hapless fuck."

"What do you think is gonna happen now?" Connor squeaked, his voice sounding as though he had a muzzle on. "You can kill me, but eventually it'll catch up with you. If some hapless fuck like me sniffed out your bullshit, someone much smarter will too."

"Then I'll kill them too."

"You already lost. You trying to prove that you were better than everyone else? But I found you out, so maybe you're not so fucking superior after all."

"Why don't we let history decide that?"

As Richard and Connor wrestled, Kara walked up to the school, calling Connor's phone. It simply rang and rang as it had recently slid into a corner where Connor and Richard couldn't hear it over their scuffle. Kara went to leave a message when a sound like a firecracker went off, ringing through the halls and making its way out the doors and to her ears. She had heard enough gunshots to know it even when muffled like that. Snapping into action, she began rattling the doors in a fruitless attempt to force them open, but each one was solid. Not wanting to waste another second, Kara withdrew her sidearm and leveled it at the glass of the door. A couple quick shots brought the glass shattering down. She jumped inside, her gun clearing away the next door that stood in her path. As she hustled down the hallway she pulled her phone out and called the situation in, all the while praying that Brody had gotten her messages and was already on his way.

Brody stood over his sink, a bottle of Scotch right beside him. The standoff had finally come to an end, Brody coming out on top. His time at Mandy's grave was what he had needed. A reminder of who he could be when he was at his best.

Next to him, his phone chirped, letting him know that he had gotten yet another message. Kara had gotten something up her ass today and wouldn't leave him alone.

With the last of the liquor having snaked its way down the drain, Brody headed away, desperate to get some rest. Desperate to drift off where perhaps he wouldn't be haunted by all of this. As he turned, his phone began to buzz once more. Out of habit, he looked down at it, ready to ignore Kara's call. Looking at the screen, however, he saw that this call came from the station. This, he couldn't just send to voicemail.

"Morgan," he whispered into the phone.

"Morgan," Barron barked out. "Just got a call in from Smalls. She's at West High School. Shots have been fired. Get your ass out there now!"

Brody froze in place. He had ignored Kara all day. If she ended up leaving that place in a body bag that would be two people that he'd left to die. It seemed that that's what he did. He drove people away... Mandy, Christine, Kara... and then they paid the price.

"Did you hear me?!" Barron growled.

"Yes, sir." Brody rushed. Gathering up his gun, badge, and keys, Brody sprinted to his car, moving faster than he thought his body would allow. He only had about a five-minute drive to the school. He prayed that it wouldn't be too long.

Connor braced himself and Richard hovered over him. The gun stood a couple inches above, but Connor would swear that he could feel the barrel pressed right against his head. The hot steel searing his skin. The smoke wafting up his nose. He clenched his eyes shut, wondering if he would actually see his life pass before his eyes. Each moment from first memory to last playing out like some kind of home movie. He would have a chance now to relive each and every one of his failures, his biggest one happening right now. But he saw none of that. All he saw was Brandy. Sitting alone at home right now, wondering when her husband would bother to walk in the door. Wondering when he would start acting like a husband again. Once the bullet shattered his skull, would she know? Would she feel it?

The explosion of a bullet sounded out, but it came from much further than if Richard had fired it. Another came right after it. A few seconds later, one more came. Connor opened his eyes, only daring to do it about a millimeter at a time. Once he had pried them open enough for images to actually dribble in, he saw that Richard still stood above him. The gun no longer leveled straight at him, now sagging a bit from its original height. Richard looked around like a dog wondering where the barking had come from. In doing so he had taken his eyes from his victim below. Connor took his brief stay of execution and wrapped his arms around Richard's legs and wrenched them as hard as he could. The young man went tumbling, Connor rolling over on top of him, his elbow driving right into Richard's eye.

One floor above, Kara heard the scuffle and took off towards it. In two leaps, Kara cleared one flight of stairs, rounded the corner and began down the other, coming upon the two men wrestling on the ground, Connor beating Richard's hand against the floor, praying that he would finally lose his grip on the gun.

Kara didn't waste a second, pointing her gun forward, opening her mouth, and screaming, "Police! Freeze!" The two men stopped in a second, looking like someone had paused a movie.

"Mr. Sullivan, move away," Kara ordered, her voice dropping only a single octave. "You," she continued, aiming her gun at Richard. "Let go of your gun." Richard's palm opened, and the gun slid out onto the floor. Connor relinquished his grip and began to inch away, worried that if he moved too fast something would go wrong. He stood and hustled his way over behind Kara, trying not to cry from relief. Once he reached her, Kara made the rest of the way down the stairs, her gun never once losing its mark.

"On your knees," she ordered. "Slowly." Richard obeyed as he hoisted himself into position. Connor looked on, watching every move Richard made, noting that before putting his arms up, his hand seemed to have spent a few seconds too long at his ankle. As Kara approached, he soon found out why. Once she came within striking distance, Richard shot out his hand with a switchblade, jamming it right into her arm. Globs of blood flung out as she screamed in pain. Richard jumped to his feet, seized hold of the detective and with one hard shove, drove her into the wall, her head colliding with it, sending her sinking to the ground.

Connor looked on, forgetting how to move, forgetting how to breathe. That is until he saw Richard retrieve his and Kara's gun, and take control yet again. Kara's gun slid into his waistline, as his finger flirted with the trigger of his own. The sight of that gave Connor authority of his faculties again, and he spun himself around and made his retreat. Knowing that the detective could wait, Richard gave chase.

The two of them zoomed down the main hall. Up ahead, Connor could see the shattered glass from Kara's entrance, his exit. He gathered the last bit of speed he had and charged his way there. Richard came so close he could almost feel breath on the back of his neck. Glass popped beneath his feet as he reached the first set of broken doors. Once he stepped into the foyer, the breath on his neck became a full body on his back. Richard had caught up and with a leap brought both of them to the ground. Connor scrambled forward, desperate to see the outside, convinced that he would then be safe. Shards of glass stung his hands like thousands of bees.

From the safety of the outdoors, the black of night lit up with the flash of sirens. The silence being broken by their beeps and whistles. As a team of officers sprang into action, Brody led the way having gotten there just as the rest had arrived. All caution had been thrown to the wind as he raced to save his partner. Connor increased his rate of crawl, feeling like he may actually have a chance now. A blow to the side of his head from Richard's gun quickly expelled such ridiculous notions. Connor collapsed, his head feeling as though it had been gripped in a vice. Richard forced his face even further into the glass-strewn floor. Small cuts began to pop up all over Connor's cheek, joining the blood that now trickled out from his temple.

Richard hung the gun lazily, all strength having been taken from him. Before he could finally give Connor the bullet that had been waiting for him all night, Brody approached, lifting his

311

sidearm at the sight of the mess that lay before him. Richard didn't waste a second, moving his gun from Connor's head to Brody and letting off a quick shot, the bullet landing on the right side of Brody's chest and forcing him to the ground.

Connor looked as the cop tumbled. At his hand laid a shard of glass. He realized that he had used up all of his lives tonight, and that he wouldn't get another chance. Gripping the shard, drawing more blood from his hand, Connor rocked his body around while driving the glass right into Richard's gut. The stabbing stole Richard's voice, only allowing him to open his mouth in shock as he reached for his wound, finally surrendering the gun. He fell back on his heels, allowing Connor the freedom to clamber away. Connor sank into a corner, blood covering his hands and one side of his face. The rest of the cavalry had arrived now. Half descended on Richard, working away at his bleeding gut and calling for paramedics. Others headed into the building looking to see what else lay in store for them. A few others came upon Connor, beginning to treat him. The entire time, his eyes never left Richard as he writhed around on the ground. This student that he had watch grow. Connor kept waiting for the nightmare to end.

42

Stanford's emergency room received five patients all at the same time that evening, the seriousness of their injuries varying greatly. The first had been a janitor who had awoken to the sound of the police sweeping the building. A quick evaluation showed nothing more than a mild concussion.

Kara had been adamant that she didn't even need to see the doctor, but Barron insisted once he got to the scene. A quick exam of her arm revealed that no veins or arteries had been cut. The whole time that stitches were put in, Barron stood over her shoulder, making her recount the story from beginning to end no less than three times.

"Why the hell did this teacher call you?" Barron asked, trying to sniff out some bullshit.

"We've spoken to each other a couple times concerning the case," Kara answered, choosing to follow the thread and needle through her skin rather than her boss's stares.

"What does that mean? If you shared any evidence with him..."

"Don't be ridiculous. Of course I didn't. I interviewed him

during our first round. Then he took me around the school while I scouted a few things out."

"Was Morgan with you when you did this?"

"No."

"Why not?"

"I was..." Kara hesitated, unsure how this next part would come across.

"What?"

"I was trying to chase down anything to show that Clements could be innocent. Mr. Sullivan happened to be at the school at the time. That is all."

"Jesus. Still chasing down that fantasy of yours."

"Fantasy? I was right."

"For Christ's sake. This Lowe kid being guilty doesn't prove Clements is innocent."

"He told Sullivan as much."

"Well, until we get the full story, Clements stays right where he is, as far as I'm concerned. Anyway, your penchant for chasing down hunches almost got two cops and a civilian killed tonight. Good going." Having had the final word, he left the room.

Kara listened to his exit, watching as the last of the stitches were put in place and a bandage got wrapped around her arm. She didn't like the son of a bitch, but she had to admit that he was right. She wanted this win and wanted it bad. The Llewellyn case had rocked her, and she needed to be right. Not only that, she needed everyone else to be wrong. She wondered, did she really believe that whole time that Clements hadn't done it, or did she just need to show up Barron and the rest of the department? Maybe she would've rebelled against any suspect they brought in. Either way, Brody lay with a bullet in his chest now because she needed to play super cop.

Connor was relieved to hear that his injuries weren't as bad as he had assumed. But he still despised every moment he had to spend in the hospital. Dozens of small cuts had opened on the right side of his face, prompting the doctor to tell him he looked like Two-Face. Typically, Connor would appreciate such a reference, but he could just barely get a sense of where he was at the moment, the whole thing in the school feeling more like a movie he had just watched play out. He kept waiting to be presented with his Oscar.

The deeper cuts came on his hand from where he'd palmed the shard of glass. The doctor assured him he'd end up with one hell of a scar after it had healed, saying it as though it was something to wear with pride. Connor gave that a polite chuckle with no life behind it.

As the stitches sewed up the gash in Connor's hand, Kara walked into the room and took a seat, rubbing the spot where her own stitches resided. For a moment, only silence existed between the two of them.

"Is this a bad time?" Kara finally asked.

"Guess not," Connor answered.

"So, can you tell me what happened tonight?"

Connor relayed the story back to her from his and Kara's tour of the school to Connor being left a bleeding mess.

"Why would you do all that?" Kara asked, desperate to keep any judgment out of her tone, knowing she was in little position to judge.

"I don't know. I was stupid. And now look at us," Connor said, motioning to his hand and Kara's arm. "And what's going on with the other cop. The one who got shot?"

"Don't know yet."

"I made everything worse, didn't I?"

"Hardly."

"How did I not?"

"Well for one, if everything you said pans out, then a sixteen-year-old kid gets to go home. That's not nothing."

"I just couldn't believe it was him. I needed it to not be him. I needed to know that I knew my students."

"I know how you feel."

"But..."

"But what?"

"No matter how you look at it, I got it wrong. Again..."

Kara looked on quizzically, unsure what the "again" was in reference to. "How so?" she asked.

"Maybe it wasn't Dennis, but if it was Richard... Well, then either way I was wrong about somebody. No matter how you slice it, I didn't see it."

Kara shook her head. Suddenly she found herself speaking, unsure if she was directing her words at Connor or herself. "As much as we want to think that we know how the world works, you can never really be sure. You can never really know. Sometimes until it's too late. So while in the midst of it, you just have to do the best with what you're given. And I'd say you did that tonight. Hold your head high."

Connor wanted to believe her and only hoped that one day he would. In that moment, Brandy stepped into the room. The sight of her finally broke Connor. Broke him of all of it. The shooting. The hero worship. Dennis being arrested. And now almost getting killed. The forlorn look that she'd been giving him for the last couple months (last couple years actually). They all collided and a squall emerged from Connor, bringing him down to his knees. The doctor jumped back and Brandy bolted to Connor's side, cradling his head in her arms. He laid like that until he didn't have a drop of water left in his body to cry. Kara watched the whole thing unfold and then extricated herself from the situation.

Once he had regained control, Connor laid back and allowed the doctor to finish cleaning him up, a bandage the size of a winter glove going around his hand. Once the doctor left the room, he recounted the entire story to Brandy. She looked on as though he spoke an alien language. After all, this kind of thing didn't happen to people like them. She couldn't even find the words to respond when he had finished his tale.

The two sat like that for a full five minutes before Connor finally said, "I'm sorry."

"Don't be sorry. You did what you had to. And you're gonna be okay, so..."

"I don't just mean tonight," Connor continued.

"What do you mean then?"

"For a while now..."

"Connor, with what happened at the school..."

"But even before that," he cut her off again. The two seemed engaged in different conversations. "I don't know where I've been lately. What I've been doing. It's just..."

"Just what?"

"I've never really felt like I was good enough for you."

"Why would you say that?"

"I don't know. Just how I've always felt. Felt about most things really. And maybe I set out to prove myself right about that all these years. This time though... this time I wanted to be proven wrong."

"Connor, look at me," Brandy said, cushioning his cheeks in her hands. "You are a good man. The best I've known. And you never need to prove anything to me."

"I could name a thousand times when I wasn't."

"So could anyone if they took the time to think about it. But I know what's in your heart. And that's always good enough for me." After that, nothing else was said between them for the rest of the night. Nothing else needed to be said. After getting released, the two went home and immediately went off to bed where they slept without interruption for the next twelve hours.

Not a second had been wasted getting Brody to the ER. Once in surgery, the doctors discovered that he suffered some internal bleeding and had a collapsed lung. Right away, they went about trying to make sure that Richard Lowe didn't get another victim added to his tally.

Kara paced the waiting room, not daring to sit down, knowing she'd be asleep in moments. She'd already drank the place dry of coffee, so this was the only option left to her. She kept her eyes on the door, waiting for news on her partner. Out of the corner of her eye, she saw someone come in from the outside, looking bewildered. Kara looked over to see a face that she vaguely recognized. Knowing how creepy she must seem, she tried not to stare, but couldn't help it. Eventually it clicked. She was looking at Brody's wife that she had seen in the photo album.

Tentatively, she edged over to the woman, and spoke. "Excuse me. Are you here for Brody Morgan?" she asked.

The woman looked over, bags hanging low and heavy under her eyes. She'd obviously been pulled from her bed to come here. "Yes," she spoke in a soft voice. "I'm Christine. His wife or ex-wife, rather," she responded.

"I'm Kara Smalls. Brody's partner," Kara said, offering her hand, receiving a limp shake in response.

"What happened?" Christine asked.

"He got shot. He's in surgery now."

"Is he going to be okay?"

"I don't know. I haven't heard anything, yet. Brody is strong though. I'm sure he'll be okay."

"Son of a bitch is too stubborn to die." Kara chuckled a bit at this, the laugh sounding strange, given recent events. The two women took a seat and waited. Two hours passed without a word spoken between them. Then a doctor came through the doors.

I would like nothing more than to tell you that Brody pulled through, and went on to live happily ever after, but very rarely does life tie things off with a bow like that. Two hours into his surgery, Brody went into cardiac arrest and passed away. Upon hearing it, Kara half expected time to slow down, or even come to a halt, but it went by just as it always does. Kara could see Christine slump down in her chair, not crying, but simply looking on. Kara looked around, everything seeming to take on a sepia tone. Part of her boiled up, wanting to find Lowe and make sure that he didn't make it through the night. But she couldn't do that. Richard may have pulled the trigger, but she had aimed the gun. *You had to be the hero, didn't you, Kara?* she thought to herself. Sure, she had saved some kid from prison, but she'd gotten Brody killed in the process. For the briefest of moments (but long enough, that it would haunt her for years to come) she wondered if it was worth it.

From beside her, she could hear Christine's soft weeping. As a matter of habit, she began to move away. After all, what could she possibly offer to this stranger? But right as she began to lift herself from the chair, Christine's hand sprung out and grabbed a hold of hers, wanting to be with anyone. Someone who could understand what she felt. Kara froze, unsure of what to do, where to go. Instinct told her to dash, but as a single tear seeped from her eye and down onto her chest, she realized that she needed to be with someone as well. She settled back into her seat and gripped Christine's hand tighter.

The two of them sat there for the next half hour, not saying a thing.

After a while, they were allowed back to see Brody's body and pay their respects. They stood on opposite sides of the bed, staring down. Kara felt like Brody must have shrunken, his frame not quite as imposing as before. *I guess dying will do that to you*, she thought. She felt a tinge of guilt at the gallows humor, but put it away knowing that Brody would appreciate it.

"How was he towards the end?" Christine asked, her red eyes looking down onto her ex-husband.

"Well..." Kara hesitated, not wanting to taint his name with some less than savory stories about Brody's final days.

"He called me while drunk not too long ago. I thought he'd given that up."

Kara said nothing, not wanting to drag Brody through the mud more than she already had.

"Did you know that we lost our daughter?"

"Yes."

"He always blamed himself. I guess I did at first too. I just wish I'd told him what a good father he had been."

"There's some things I wish I'd told him too." Wished she'd told him that she could never have done this job without him. That he'd been a voice of sanity for her. "I like to think he knew though," she continued. She told herself that he must have, hoping that it was true. This was one thing she wouldn't allow herself to doubt.

The last patient was Richard Lowe himself. He had passed out on his way to the hospital and had also been hurried into surgery. In the course of it, the young man lost a section of his small intestine. Despite this, and to the disappointment of some, the doctor announced he'd make a full recovery. Kara didn't feel that disappointment as she stalked around outside Richard's room, walking past the armed guards. She savored every ounce of anticipation, waiting anxiously for her chance to talk to the bastard. To finally get her answers.

43

Two days passed before the doctors cleared the police to interrogate Richard. Kara came in and took a seat on the side of his bed where a pair of handcuffs held him in place. Richard watched the video camera being set up with a look of boredom at having to go through with these proceedings. Once all had been arranged, the room was cleared save for Richard, Kara, and Barron who sat towards the back, allowing Kara to take charge. Richard had waived his right to a lawyer at that time.

"Name and age," Kara demanded. Despite her best effort to remain professional, she couldn't help but hide the loathing she felt for the young man before her. The young man who had taken her partner away from her.

"Richard Lowe. Eighteen," he responded, picking away at the hem of the bed sheet that lay over him.

"Are you a student at Stanford West High School?"

"Well, I have to imagine that I've been expelled by now."

"Answer the question," Barron barked from the corner. It would prove to be his only input during the interrogation.

"Yes, I am," Richard responded, throwing some side eye towards the captain.

"Did you plan and carry out the shooting at Stanford West High School on October 15th of this year?" Kara asked, continuing with the interview.

Richard didn't answer at first. He simply looked over at her, taking in every inch of her face, seeing if it would break. She gave him nothing. "Yes, I did," he finally answered.

"Did Natalie Leonard assist in you carrying out the shooting?"

"Yes."

"Did Dennis Clements take any part in the planning or carrying out of the shooting?"

"No."

Kara offered Barron some side eye of her own, managing to catch a begrudging nod. "Why did you commit this crime?" she continued.

Richard paused again. He looked up at the ceiling as if the answer had been written there. After a beat he reached over for his cup of ice chips. He threw a few back and chewed away at them, a hint of a grin on his face. Kara and Barron waited the entire time. Richard placed the cup down and stared off once more. Without looking at either of the detectives, he finally answered, "Because I could." For the next hour, Richard walked Kara through it all. From when the plan first blossomed within his mind to him lying in the hospital bed.

Richard had walked the halls of the school countless times, marking down every security camera. He studied Zach Levinson as he checked people in day after day, noting which button granted access. He mapped out the entire school and planned out his path. Two towns over, Richard visited a gun range where he perfected his shot. When it came to getting the guns, he didn't want anything that could be traced back to him.

Thankfully, anyone with a pulse knew Jeremy Farrah fancied himself as Tony Stark with the shit he kept stockpiled. And since the house was 180 degrees from Ft. Knox, he had been able to slip in and out one night with all the hardware he needed.

In the midst, he did run into problems. One, this shit happened all the time now. What would make this one special? He needed to be sure to up the body count as much as he could. And for that, he couldn't be alone. He kept his eye out for whom he might deem worthy enough to join him. Natalie proved to be the answer. He had known her by face and name for years, but had hardly spoken two words to her in all that time. Each day, she would hunch herself and slink the hallways, petrified of all who crossed her path. With that look of fright also came a look of longing that Richard noted. At lunch she would sit herself in the corner and watch all the cliques come together. Tears would form in her eyes as she dreamed of joining them. Towards the start of their senior year, Richard remembered seeing her loom over a table of kids for several minutes before finally forcing herself onto them. Not long after, he witnessed her coming out of the principal's office having been caught vandalizing the gym. Her expression shifted from shame to joy on a dime. Shame for what she'd done. Joy that she had been included.

Richard approached her soon after and went into telling her how beautiful he found her. How he had longed to tell her for years and didn't want to leave high school without having said something. In just a couple weeks, she had pledged her undying love for him. And with that, he told her what he wanted her to do.

"Richie, stop joking around," was her initial response.

"I'm not joking," Richard told her.

"We can't do that."

"Why not?"

"Be... because..." She couldn't believe she had to answer such a question.

"I thought you loved me," Richard said, feigning hurt. He even produced a few tears.

Over the years he had learned how to mimic many emotions, despite his lack of them.

"I do," she insisted.

"Then why won't you do this? Because I don't think I can be with someone who would question me like this. You need to trust me. Or else this will never work."

The mere mention of that shook Natalie. It still took some more prodding, but at that moment, Richard knew that he had her locked in place.

The second problem: Could he possibly get it all done and still be gone by the time the police arrived? Thankfully, fate played its part here and served up the shooting of Noah Spaulding and the resulting protests. The news of the force being all the way across town gave Richard the perfect time for his masterpiece to be played out.

When the day came, he found that the thing played out like a beautiful symphony that he was conducting. No one got in his way, and even though she proved sloppy, Natalie served her purpose. When it came to their escape he had earmarked her class as being their exit, and made it clear that all had to die so they couldn't reveal that she hadn't been in class. He explained that she would stay in the classroom and play out like the sole survivor. Of course, when the time came, he made her number twenty-eight on the kill sheet. With her death, no one could trace this back to him. Since Mr. Milton was stupid and lazy enough that he didn't make the kids sign out, there would be no record of him ditching class. He knew that attendance was always a little late getting entered for his second hour, so no one even knew of him not showing up for that class either. And after a climb out the window, he dumped all the supplies and slipped back in with everyone else outside. In the chaos, he proved nothing more than just another face in the crowd.

And as much as he enjoyed carrying out his plan, he found the fallout to be so much more enjoyable. He laid on the tears, playing the role of victim, eliciting sympathy that he didn't deserve. Even let himself go a bit, so all would buy it. He attended memorials, watching as people perished from grief. He had to suppress a snicker every time. And when all fingers pointed at Dennis Clements, Richard knew how to lay on the finishing touch. With Mr. Sullivan within earshot, he acted his part of the enraged boyfriend, loving the image of Dennis flailing in the wind. And once he saw which car belonged to Dennis, all he needed to do was slip in his mapped-out plan into the trunk. From there, the police did the rest.

But then Connor Sullivan happened. From the moment he'd asked Richard about Natalie he could tell that something was rotten in Denmark. Why ask if the son of a bitch wasn't onto something. So he watched and listened. Watched as he poked around asking everyone about her. Watched as he visited Natalie's mother. All of it leading to the other evening.

As Richard told his tale, he had a look of self-awe on his face. When he finished, Barron turned off the camera and exited. Kara gathered her things, thinking of nothing but the shower she would need after being in a room with the insect before her. She headed towards the door, ready to never say another word to him when he stopped her.

"What happened to that cop?" Richard asked. "The one I shot."

Kara just turned around, bearing daggers down onto him. Her look said it all.

"Huh," he said, seemingly indifferent at the whole thing. "You know him?"

"He was my partner," Kara said flatly.

"Damn. You must really hate me. You probably want to kill me right now." He almost laughed at that.

Kara leaned back against the door, thinking it over for a moment. That had been her compulsion when she first heard about Brody. And since that time, getting answers from this bastard dominated her thoughts more than any act of revenge. Looking at him now, she could make peace with how things had ended for Richard.

"No," she said.

"Really," Richard said, fascinated by the answer. "Why not?"

"Because look how it turned out for you. After all your planning and scheming you end up here, with a hole in your gut. And nothing gets better for you from here on out. Whatever you were trying to do, you failed."

"Did I?" Richard sniggered.

Kara said nothing. She simply looked in the boy's eyes seeing that nothing laid behind them.

"Look at what happened to this town," Richard continued. "It almost fell apart. Pushed a little further, it could have burned to the ground. I managed to pull that off with nothing more than a mask and a couple guns," he said, clearly proud of himself.

Kara looked down at the ground before simply responding, "I hope that's of some comfort when you're burning in hell." She turned and walked out of the room, never to speak to Richard Lowe again.

44

Six months after being charged, Richard Lowe stood trial. Despite his confession, he still insisted on pleading not guilty by reason of insanity. Throughout the trial his mother continually fell into hysterics and had to be escorted from the courtroom several times. Richard's father, on the other hand, refused to attend. In fact, their initial visit after the arrest would prove to be the last time he'd ever speak to his son.

It took the jury less than an hour to convict. Many called for him to be given the death penalty, but Richard had been fortunate enough to have his sentence handed down by a judge who had become known for never giving such an order. Instead, he received twenty-eight consecutive life sentences, one for each victim, along with another 150 years, ten years for each instance of attempted murder. In the end, Richard only served five years, finding himself on the receiving end of a shiv in the prison showers one morning. Only his parents attended the funeral.

With the perpetrator of the Stanford Massacre behind bars, many in town felt a sense of relief and ease. They all wished life would go back to normal for the town, but of course, that is not the way the world works. Once something has been broken, no matter how well it has been put back together, the cracks will still be there. And the cracks in Stanford ran deep, and for many they found that they would never truly recover from the trauma they had been a victim to.

With the wave of goodwill they received for having solved the shooting, the police department chose that time to quietly announce that no disciplinary action would be taken against the two police officers involved in the shooting of Noah Spaulding. The news met with little protest, the town far too exhausted to encourage any more civil unrest. Noah's parents would take the department to court and settle for a paltry $500,000. In the end, Noah's name became another used in rallying cries the next time people had to take to the streets to protest police brutality.

David Llewellyn's case against the department and Kara got unceremoniously dropped, his lawyers realizing that all leverage in the case had been lost.

Julie Lipton would work for the Stanford Police Department for another twenty years before retiring. After having been shot, she found that her home life actually managed to calm down, Terry's hostility having drained away. She felt such immense elation that her son had returned to her. However, she would never forget about the time when she suspected that her son may have been a killer. She would live for another fifty years, and this fact still visited her from time to time. Most days she went on living her life, never once thinking of it. However, sometimes when she would look upon her son, or as she lay awake at night, she would mull it over, not knowing what to make of it. She often toyed with the idea of letting Brian in on this secret, but ultimately, left it to be her own to bear. Thankfully, as she succumbed to cancer, and Terry and her grandchildren gathered around her, this was the furthest thing from her mind and she passed on in peace.

Kristin Benson entered psychiatric care for a month after her suicide attempt. At that time they deemed her to no longer be a danger to herself and was released. She never did return to Stanford West High School, officially resigning the day that she got out of the hospital. Her mother had to go and retrieve her belongings from the classroom, most of which Kristin would burn. Come the summer, Kristin and her mother moved from Stanford and never returned. Despite her mother's insistence, Kristin had decided long before that her teaching career was over. Driving by a school often made her sick to her stomach, so she knew she would never be able to work within one. Instead, she found a job as an editor at a small publishing company and lived out her days in relative calm and peace. For years to come, she had to deal with the looks and whispers of people who recognized her, but in time that ceased. As did the calls from reporters begging to hear her story. After having been five years removed from Stanford, Kristin got married, thankful that she hadn't completely scared off everyone else in the world. On a mental level, she finally accepted that she couldn't take on the guilt of her students' deaths. However, she would continue to struggle with it until the end of her days, never truly forgiving herself, often finding herself waking in the night as she heard the shots go off inside her head.

Dennis Clements was released and cleared of any connection with the shooting after Richard's confession. This did little to shake the stink of jail from him. So many still assumed that he must have played some part. And if not, then he must have done something else that warranted their scorn. Dennis finished off the year being home schooled before his mother moved them a couple states over. This proved far enough to outrun the looks they received, but in the end Dennis still opted for changing his name once his eighteenth birthday hit. With this he reluctantly gave up his dream of becoming a writer, opting for a quiet life. He'd had more than enough excitement for several lifetimes.

Kara received a special commendation for solving the Stanford Massacre. It was with great reluctance that she actually took it. She wanted to be done with this case. And she felt like a fraud having a gold star hanging on the wall. You shouldn't get an award for getting your partner killed.

She stood at the front of an endless crowd that came out for his funeral. She received a plethora of condolences along with pats on the back for nailing Lowe. All of it went right by her. After everyone passed by, she stood alone at his grave, where he shared a plot with his daughter. The sun beat down on her, ordering her to go inside a nice air-conditioned home. But she didn't move. She stood there wishing there was a little bell that Brody could ring from below the earth.

Before leaving, she withdrew her commendation from her jacket and laid it on his grave.

Connor and Brandy Sullivan left Stanford at the conclusion of the school year, Connor finding a job teaching in St. Louis. They entered marriage counseling as they worked through all that had been left unsaid for years. One year after moving away, they welcomed their first daughter. They would have two more together.

On the day he left, he walked the halls one last time saying his farewells to the rest of the staff. While many were sad to see him go, none were surprised. Connor's last stop on his way out the door was the plaque dedicated to Bradley Neuman. This time Connor didn't hide his eyes like he had done so many times before. He faced it head-on and looked at the picture of the smiling teenager before him. An inch of a frown formed on Connor's face as he silently nodded and walked out of the building one last time.

Fifteen years later, a man named Ben Timmons knocked on Connor's door. Connor, a paunch having established its place on him and his hair now mostly gray, answered it to see someone whom he vaguely recognized.

"Mr. Sullivan?" Ben Timmons said in greeting.

"Yes. Do I know you?" Connor asked.

"It's Dennis Clements. From back at Stanford."

Connor fell back a step, never expecting that part of his life to come knocking at his door. He peered at the man in front of him. Dark hair lying flat on his head. A few wrinkles tearing across his face. Eyes set back behind a pair of glasses. And it was in those eyes that Connor saw the kid he once knew.

"If this isn't a good time..." Dennis said.

"No. It is. Please, come in." The two men went in the house, taking a seat on the couch.

"So... Dennis, what..." Connor said, trying to find the words.

"It's Ben now actually."

"What's that?"

"I changed my name some years back."

"I see. So what have you been up to all these years?"

"I'm sorry, Mr. Sullivan. I don't want to take up much of your time. I just wanted to come by and say thank you."

"Thank you? For what?"

"When I was in jail, you were the only one who believed that I didn't do it. And not only that, but you proved it."

"No, please. You don't have to do that."

"No, I do. It's long past due."

"But I really didn't do much. Most of it was dumb luck on my part."

"The fact that you did anything, is just..." Dennis hung his head, not knowing what else to say.

"I'm just glad that it worked out."

"Well, I just want you to know that it meant a lot. And I won't forget it."

Connor looked over at Dennis, and while it may have been a thirty-one-year-old man sitting on his couch, all he saw was a sixteen-year-old kid, scared and confused.

"You're welcome," Connor finally said. The two talked for another few minutes before Dennis excused himself. They parted with a handshake. Though they'd never see each other again, they would often think of one another.

In Stanford, life went on as it does. Over time the phrase Stanford Massacre took on a mythical quality, causing some vague sense of déjà vu whenever one said it. After enough time, no one was left that could recount to you what those couple months in the fall and winter of 2017 were like. The doubt and suspicion that hung over the town like a heavy miasma. The fear that it may all come crumbling down at any second. Still, much like the people who lived it, the town never truly forgot. Bullet holes were covered over. But still they laid there, scars beneath the surface.

THE END

ACKNOWLEDGEMENTS

This book would not have been possible without the many who helped me along the way. First, I must thank my wife and my parents who have encouraged and enabled my writing even at times when I was ready to throw in the towel.

Further thanks is owed to those who helped me in developing this idea and giving feedback throughout the writing process: my wife Nicole and my friends Tammy Denton and Alex Dabney.

Of course, a huge thanks is due to everyone at Bloodhound Books for helping to make my dream of being a published author come true and for help in getting this book ready, particularly Ian and Tara for the help in editing. I am eternally grateful.

This book is influenced a great deal by my time in the classroom, both as a student and as a teacher. Therefore, a special thanks is owed to all those that have shared that time with me. Those I've learned from, those I've learned with, those I've taught, and those I've taught with.

And finally to my daughter Taryn, whom I'm thankful for every day.

A NOTE FROM THE PUBLISHER

Thank you for reading this book. If you enjoyed it please do consider leaving a review on Amazon to help others find it too.

We hate typos. All of our books have been rigorously edited and proofread, but sometimes mistakes do slip through. If you have spotted a typo, please do let us know and we can get it amended within hours.

info@bloodhoundbooks.com

Made in the USA
Monee, IL
09 August 2021